## TITLES BY KAY HOOPER

### BISHOP / SPECIAL CRIMES UNIT NOVELS

*Haven*

*Hostage*

*Haunted*

*Fear the Dark*

*Wait for Dark*

*Hold Back the Dark*

### THE BISHOP FILES

*The First Prophet*

*A Deadly Web*

*Final Shadows*

# FINAL SHADOWS

KAY HOOPER

JOVE
New York

A JOVE BOOK
Published by Berkley
An imprint of Penguin Random House LLC
1745 Broadway, New York, NY 10019

ISBN: 9780515153354

First Edition: December 2018

Printed in the United States of America
1 3 5 7 9 10 8 6 4 2

Cover photo © Mark Owen / Trevillion Images
Cover design by Rita Frangie
Book design by Laura K. Corless

# FINAL SHADOWS

*The Bishop Files*

***Final Report***

***August 31***

*To Whom It May Concern:*

*I hardly know how to begin this report. There are many reasons, not the least among them being that I myself got much more deeply involved in the situation than I had any idea of becoming when I first became aware of what was happening in the then loosely organized, almost entirely underground psychic "community" I was only peripherally aware of at that time.*

*I believed that not only could I remain on that periphery, observant and seeking to understand without interfering with what was happening, I believed it would be best for me to do so. Best for their struggle. Best for my own growing teams of psychic agents and investigators, the SCU and Haven. Best for these "civilian" psychics, living their desperate, secret lives alone for so long by necessity even as external events and a growing threat pushed them to reach out, to form connections between themselves and others like them in a response that was, I believe, entirely organic rather than in any way planned.*

*At least in the beginning.*

*I have come to understand that in ways I never understood before, I myself am a part of that psychic community, connected to it, linked in a way I had not believed was possible. It is something apart from the connections I feel for my teams within the SCU, a different sort of bond formed for a very, very different reason. But another organic, naturally evolving link that quite literally became necessary for the continued existence of psychics and even, perhaps, of our human species.*

*And the more specific links, links between myself and Miranda, between John Brodie and Tasha Solomon, between Sarah and Tucker Mackenzie, between a ten-year-old orphan child named Annabel and her unusual constant companion, and last but not by any means least the link all of us have with a remarkable woman named Murphy—those connections and others began to assemble, finally, the puzzle of what was really happening here, and why.*

*Even the "bad" actors in all this had their parts to play, and often very highly unexpected and even positive ones. Though I have often found a clear line of demarcation between good and evil, black and white, it more often seems there are many shades of gray, many complex combinations of both good and, arguably, evil.*

*Evil acts do not necessarily mean that all involved are evil. And seemingly benevolent acts are not always what they seem. Lessons hard-learned.*

*And perhaps it is simply a universal truth that if, between the goal and the reaching of it, too many years pass, too much distance exists, too many events occur, too much "new" history is built and old history lost, then those once obsessive goals begin to be questioned at least by some, previously ruthless methods begin to be questioned, then that, too, is another piece of the puzzle, and a vital one.*

*Understanding that puzzle and what it meant had finally come, but also understanding the part each of us had to play in order to triumph. And we had to triumph. There was so very much at stake in this battle. This war. Far more than most people will ever be aware.*

*Few of us are able to go through our lives feeling certain of why we're here, of what part we're destined to play in our lives, let alone in our world, our history. Few of us are ever granted the certainty of knowing that our actions have true meaning, not only for ourselves but for others, even for the whole of humankind, and perhaps even its destiny.*

*But if any mortal can know the truth, or at least part of the truth, an unexpected and wholly remarkable part of our history and our future, a small group of very special humans knows it now. I know it now. If any mortal can look at his or her world and be certain that their own acts* matter *in the existence of that world, even the continuance of it, that group of people and I know it now. If any mortal can be certain of his or her place, or his or her part, in defending the very existence of our own species . . . it is something of which we are utterly certain now.*

*The story is incredible. Some would never believe it. If I had not been a part of it, I am not sure that even I—with so much knowledge of the capabilities of the human mind, both "normal" and paranormal—would have, could have, believed it. But I was a part of it, I bore witness to what happened and why, and I am very much a believer.*

*I will set down as much of this knowledge and understanding as I feel I can as we agreed, here in these private reports, which may or may not be opened and read one day, depending on your decision and those who come after you. After us both.*

*Perhaps not would be better. But I will leave that call to you or to someone who comes after us to make. There will always, I fear, be the threat of some outside enemy determined to destroy us, and should that happen in the future, then perhaps our world will need to know that we are capable of fighting back. Even quietly, secretly, and without fanfare. Capable of fighting back, and of winning.*

*Despite even my own doubts as to the wisdom of revealing what lies within my report, I only hope that one day the truth can be known.*

*I believe we owe that much to the warriors, to the fallen, to the silent, unnamed, unacknowledged, and largely unknown watchmen on the walls of our civilization who have guarded us, the most vulnerable among us, and even our society, without our awareness. As dangerous as the truth may prove to some, as unbelievable, as frightening, it is a truth all of humanity should know.*

*Respectfully submitted.*
*Noah Bishop, Unit Chief*
*Special Crimes Unit, FBI*

The darkness drops again; but now I know
That twenty centuries of stony sleep
Were vexed to nightmare by a rocking cradle,
And what rough beast, its hour come round at last,
Slouches towards Bethlehem to be born?

—W. B. YEATS

# ONE

*Wake up.*

*You need to wake up.*

*Henry, you have to wake up.*

*They're going to kill you.*

Henry McCord had a lifetime of practice in hiding the fact that he saw dead people. A medium, that's what it was called. He'd been a medium for thirty-six years, more or less. He could actually remember the first time he had seen the dead and understood just what he was seeing. At his grandfather's funeral. The old man had stood on the other side of the casket and winked at him.

Henry had been six.

So, thirty years, really, of learning to cope in whatever way he could. Realizing early on that grown-ups didn't want him to talk about the dead people, that it made them really uncomfortable. Which had puzzled a childish Henry, since it seemed to him they would have liked to know that they didn't just go into the ground in a box and get covered with dirt, that there was something more than that. It had reassured Henry, at least then.

Now . . . he didn't even know if he still believed that. And despite his several conversations with Bishop, he was still unconvinced that he could ever learn to control his abilities well enough to make some kind of better use of them.

He still didn't get how seeing dead people could be put to any real use at all, far less some larger, more important use. Not even in investigating crime, since Bishop had told him somewhat ruefully that the dead, especially the murdered dead, seldom showed up to help in any way at all, far less to tell those investigating the crime who had killed them.

So what was the use in that?

What made that a larger, more important use of his abilities?

Having some sort of control over what he could do had appealed to him, if only when he'd thought he might be able to control it. He had tried. When he was alone. When he could try without fearing somebody would come along with a giant butterfly net and scoop him up and take him away to a mental hospital where his "gift" would be medicated away . . .

*They took you. Not doctors. The others.*

Others. The others. The others?

What the hell?

Henry had thought he was asleep and dreaming, but . . . it didn't feel like it was a dream, that voice in his head. It didn't feel like his soft bed beneath him. It felt like something cold and hard, something not a mattress. Something that was maybe metal.

And . . . he was almost sure he couldn't move. Almost sure his wrists were tied down. His ankles. Something tight around his head holding it still.

*They've got you, Henry.*

*Who's got me?* He wanted to ask it out loud, but something told him he should remain silent. And he wasn't sure he could have said anything out loud anyway. His mouth felt like it was full of cotton and his entire face felt like he'd been shot up with Novocaine.

*Them.*

It meant nothing to him, and yet . . . and yet it did. It frightened him on a level so deep it was primal. It meant coldness and darkness and . . . and shadows. It meant shadows moving all around him, implacable and remorseless, bent on doing . . . whatever it was they meant to do to him. It meant something cold and slimy that had slithered into his life, into his mind.

Maybe into his soul.

*Not spirits? Not the dead?* He asked not knowing if there would be someone, anyone, to answer him. Not knowing if the voice inside his head might not be his own.

*No, Henry. The dead aren't curious to know how you're able to see them. The dead don't want to turn you inside out to learn what makes your ability work.*

Henry felt an even deeper, icy jolt of terror.

Unlike what he'd seen in various movies and TV shows about ghosts and hauntings, Henry had never had to face a negative experience because of his ability. No angry or malevolent spirits, no spirits that looked disfigured or deformed or even showed the causes of their deaths. None who had made any attempt at all to frighten him.

Just helpful spirits dressed in period costume who led the way through basements and attics and storage buildings to things that belonged in whatever building he was restoring. That was all.

Henry had never been afraid of them.

He was afraid now.

*They'll use your fear. You have to—*

*Who are you?*

*Henry—*

*Who are you? How do I know you're even on my side?*

*What* is *your side, Henry?*

*It's— I want to live. I want to go back to that house I was restoring near Charleston. I want to go back to my life.*

*Then you need to listen to me.*

*Why?*

*Because I survived what you're about to go through. Because I didn't let them break me. And you can't let them break you.*

*But—*

*Listen to me. You have to answer them when they ask you questions. You have to be helpful. Because if they can't get any answers from asking, then they'll start cutting. And burning. And . . . putting things inside you.*

*Things?*

*Things to . . . examine you. Things to help them get answers. So you have to answer them. You have to try as hard as you can to keep them talking.*

*But I don't know much. About how it works, what I can do.*

*Don't tell them that, Henry. Not until you have no other choice. Because when you tell them that, they'll want to find out if you're lying. They'll hurt you. They'll try to break you.*

*How?*

*Just . . . don't let them do that. Do you hear me, Henry? Cooperate. Answer their questions. Don't make them hurt you.*

*Who are you?* he demanded insistently.

*A friend. Please, Henry, just . . . hang on.*

---

Juno Hicks leaned against the hard wall, trying not to pant out loud because she'd been tired to begin with and the effort had been so great. To reach through walls, over an unknown distance, and touch another mind, a mind not hardwired as hers was to communicate like this.

Not another telepath.

Still leaning back against the wall, she looked around at the tiny cell that had become her world. Eight feet by twelve feet.

She had paced it off.

That was her world, and had been for God only knew how long. A narrow cot. The kind of stainless steel toilet-with-sink arrangement found in prison cells, right out in the open with no privacy. One chair, bolted to the floor.

One chair.

She had never sat in it, avoided it instinctively for some reason she didn't question. And none of *them* had ever sat in it. None of *them* ever came into this room, except to drag her out of it.

She knew they watched her, even though there was no observation window or port or camera she could see. But they watched her.

She knew they watched.

And maybe she'd taken a chance reaching out to Henry, talking to him, when all she'd intended was yet another desperate telepathic exploration of whatever lay beyond these walls, beyond the short hallway and the other . . . The Room . . . that was all she knew of this place, all they'd allowed her to see, at least with her eyes.

So she reached out, hoping to sense something that might help her. If she got the chance. If she could run. Silent, hoping none of the psychics who had sold their souls to *them* were nearby, or if they were that they were unable to detect her efforts.

She was very careful.

But today she had touched Henry's mind. And recognized him as another prisoner, another . . . subject. New, frightened, bewildered. In no shape to answer the questions she had wanted so desperately to ask him.

*Do they know about us?*

*Will anyone come for us?*

*Does anyone care what's happening to us?*

No, Henry could not have answered those questions, not today. Maybe . . . maybe later. She hoped. She hoped so bad. For some kind of news.

For some kind of hope.

But for now he was another victim. Someone she had to try to help, to try to warn. So maybe he would know just enough to escape their punishments.

She held up one hand and stared at it, at the bandage that made her hand a fist because it covered the stumps of what had been her fingers.

"Hold on, Henry," she whispered. "Hold on as long as you can."

---

"Report."

Sebring stood before the group of her superiors, more relaxed than many might have been because she was a highly capable and confident woman.

Some would have said arrogant. Had said, in fact.

Brisk and impersonal, she said, "There have been increasing signs that the resistance movement is gaining strength. Their numbers grow almost daily, and it's clear they have hidden assets providing them with important resources."

"What kind of resources?" the man at the head of the table asked.

"High-tech equipment and access to information, contacts within various branches of law enforcement and the government, fast travel when needed, possibly weapons. Plenty of money."

"How high up in law enforcement?"

"FBI."

He didn't quite flinch. Not quite. "Bishop?"

"I believe he's made contact with them, something we anticipated. He could very well be helping them, providing intel and support. He may actively be searching for missing psychics on his watch list."

Another man said, hoarsely, "We agreed. We agreed to stay as far away from Bishop and his psychics as possible. *Including* those on his watch list."

"Yes, sir. But since he has not exactly published his watch list, nor visibly branded any of the psychics on it, our only means of determining which psychics are in contact with him is observation over a period of time. Sometimes over months. Until he does or does not make contact with them, or we see some other sign that tells us they are not his." Her voice was not at all disrespectful, merely matter-of-fact.

"Our psychics—"

"Risk alerting Bishop if they touch the mind of one of his psychics. I've been given no reasonable explanation as to how he's able to do it, but our scientists are certain that once he has made contact with a psychic, he knows when that psychic is . . . in trouble. When that psychic is taken. He knows, or they are able to call out to him somehow, even if they are not telepaths. So all we can do is watch, and wait, and follow our protocols.

"But we are tracking psychics we're reasonably sure are not on his watch list. Those we can take." She paused briefly. "You ordered me in recent months to increase the number of subjects, to locate and take more of them. You've been concerned with numbers. Higher numbers mean we have to move faster. Haste means a greater possibility of mistakes."

"We can't afford mistakes," a third man said harshly.

"Yes, sir. I am aware. My people know their jobs. I merely point out that the risks increase when we move faster than originally planned."

"And the resistance? Do they know?" the same man demanded, his voice still harsh. "Do they know who we are? What we are?"

"Of course not, sir. And as yet, they have no idea why psychics are so important to us."

"As yet?"

Coolly, she said, "Logically, they will either work it out by putting together disparate pieces of the puzzle they've managed to acquire over the years or else will get on their side a psychic able to tell them what they need to know. It's only a matter of time. It was always only a matter of time. Especially once their technology, primarily in communication and information-gathering, reached a certain critical stage. That stage, I believe, has been achieved."

"We're close," one of the other men at the table muttered. "Too close to allow them to interfere."

"My people won't allow that to happen, sir."

"I trust you're as confident as you sound, Sebring." It wasn't a question.

But she answered it nevertheless.

"Of course, sir. There is no reason not to be confident."

"There is Duran. And there is, still, Tasha Solomon."

"I have factored both into my calculations, sir. Duran is being manipulated, his work interfered with, his progress slowed. And Solomon is wholly occupied with . . . personal concerns. Neither of them present any obstacle or danger to your plans."

"And Bishop?"

"It's still an open question as to how deeply he means to involve himself in this. Even to search for psychics on his watch list he risks at the very least his position and authority within the FBI. He has spent too many years building his unit and Haven to risk both out of concern for a few missing psychics."

"You're sure?"

"Of course, sir." She was honestly surprised that anyone would even question that. Risk everything he'd built only to search for a psychic or two, likely dead by now anyway?

No, of course Bishop wouldn't do that.

She was certain of it.

---

"Should you be so close to Charleston?" Murphy asked.

"Well, it does seem the place to be. For now, at least. Don't worry, I'm shielded by more than my own abilities."

Murphy nodded, confident in that, at least.

She should have been, since she'd helped set up that very careful, multilayered security.

The leader of their resistance sat back in her chair and looked across at the other woman, both of them alert despite the lateness of the hour.

"And we do have a lot to discuss. Especially since we know considerably more now than we did even just days ago. Good work, finding both of their main office buildings. And learning what makes them different."

"I wasn't the only one searching. We have some damned good assets." Waving that aside absently, Murphy added, "I think that gives us an extra reason to push now that we know they don't present the united front we believed they did. Maybe our best bet now, our best strategy, is divide and conquer. Or, at least, divide and confuse like hell."

The other woman smiled faintly, but asked, "Are you sure it's the best time to try this? Already a lot of balls in the air, and we can't afford to drop any of them. For one thing, we have a major rescue operation set for less than a week away, probably the most important one of this war. And unless I'm misreading Bishop badly, he's more than determined to find the missing psychics on his watch list."

"If they're still alive."

"I think he believes they are. That he can still save them. And I don't believe he'll accept our experiences in that as a good enough reason to stop his search."

"Yeah."

"So we have that variable, that . . . wild card, to factor into our plans. The rescue operation is something for which we've been readying our people and other assets for many weeks now. And even that's been adjusted, more people and assets called upon, as Tucker and others find more facilities."

"I know. And I agree it could be and probably is the most important action we've taken in this war so far."

"So is it the right time to push Duran? Is the risk worth the potential benefits of whatever intel he'll part with?"

Murphy was frowning a little, but not with uncertainty as her response clearly showed. "I think a lot depends on what happens between now and then, as far as that rescue operation goes. Even as carefully as we've planned, it could all change in a heartbeat. We don't have a single precog on our side able to see how that operation—or any other—works out for us. Which means all we can do is play the hand we're dealt with the cards we have."

"Agreed."

"As for Bishop . . . I don't doubt he has assets looking for those psychics, that he and Miranda are using their own knowledge and senses, especially now that we all agree Duran knows they're in the game. They don't have to use Miranda's shield all the time to hide themselves, which means that, whatever they do for us, for this war, they also have their own agenda. And I hope they find them, Bishop's missing psychics. God knows we've never been able to, once they're taken."

"If he finds them . . . it's more than likely he'll find where they're taken and held."

"Something else we've never been able to do," Murphy noted.

"Their main offices plus the facilities where they take and hold psychics . . . if we had both, it could be a major turning point. Potentially a huge amount of intel over and above the chance to hurt them and get some of our own back. Knowing the locations of both could, at the very least, give us actual targets to hit, and hit hard."

"You know their security's going to be hell to breach."

"And we both know we have some very, very bright people working on those problems, ongoing." She shook her head slightly, but her eyes were bright. "We all knew Bishop could be a game changer. Maybe this whole thing is finally tipping in our direction."

"Maybe."

"Your relationship with Duran could be another key."

Murphy winced. "Relationship. Gotta be another name for two enemies who trust each other about as far as either one of us could throw a Buick."

"Well, whatever it is, it's been helpful. And now, perhaps . . . a lot more than helpful."

"Well, I am pretty sure I've hit a tipping point with him, boss. If he isn't ready for that one last push now, he never will be."

"And afterward? Making the giant assumption that all this goes our way eventually?"

Murphy didn't need the question explained. "He's taken a lot of chances to help us, even risked his life, I think. Certainly risked his position. I don't believe he would have done that only to see his own people destroyed if we won decisively and could . . . dictate what happens to them. I think it's really about survival with him. Survival of his people. He wouldn't be Duran if he hadn't thought of a time after this war, win or lose."

"But would he remain dangerous?"

"I'd want to keep a close eye on him for a while," Murphy said honestly. "On his operations. Make sure we know what he and his people are doing. My guess would be some kind of business, a company, investigation and security, at least in the beginning. His people are already trained for that kind of work."

"Not military?"

"Not something I think we should ever agree to, at least for the foreseeable future. And I think Duran would know that."

"What about the political aspirations?"

Murphy shook her head. "You know we've found evidence they've managed to place people on the very bottom rungs of that ladder, and worldwide, but I'd be very surprised if that was ever a part of their original plan, before some of them figured out they were stuck here. Surprised if Duran knows *for sure* what his superiors had in mind, have in mind, and pretty damned sure he wasn't happy about the situation. He was . . . almost . . . too willing to get rid of Wolfe. I don't think he approves of the political aspirations."

The boss smiled faintly. "Why not?"

"For one thing, any mistakes are on far too public a stage to suit him. And bad mistakes would be costly."

"And for another thing?"

"It was never about conquest with him. Never about domination, power. Like I said, he's about survival. He genuinely believed, for a very long time, that the mission was to save his people. A positive goal, not a negative one. And I think that's important, a vital distinction, especially now that we know about the other faction. Something we can add to all the times he's had chances to kill, to destroy and didn't. Duran doesn't want to destroy. Maybe that's his mother's influence, whether or not he's consciously aware of it. Or maybe it's just the life he spent growing up here."

"You think he admires us?"

"I think he doesn't believe we're inferior."

"You do realize we're banking a great deal on how this one man will respond to our plans?"

"Of course." Murphy smiled suddenly. "But everything we've found out, especially recently, tells me we can do that."

"With high confidence?"

Murphy's smile widened. "With high confidence."

# TWO

MONDAY, JUNE 3
CHARLOTTE, NORTH CAROLINA

The roar of the flames was ungodly.

Noah Bishop and his wife and partner, Miranda, were no more than half an hour later than planned in reaching the small, innocuous house in its normal Charlotte suburban neighborhood with its *almost* cookie-cutter houses, each with neat, spacious yards and the privacy of hedges and well-pruned trees, and the occasional nice, well-maintained fence.

The sort of fence that both maintained privacy and allowed several of the larger homes to also host quiet home businesses that were tolerated so long as they did not disturb the peace of the neighborhood. Because it was a *nice* neighborhood.

The sort of neighborhood where people were outwardly friendly and waved smilingly across streets and yards and fences but were basically uninterested in neighbors and kept their business to themselves and their noses out of other people's business. Suburb or not, Charlotte was a huge city, with a huge city's impassivity.

And this normal suburban neighborhood in this huge city naturally boasted good electronic security guarding most houses as well as a Neighborhood Watch, and many dogs inside the houses and patrolling fenced yards.

Not a sound came from any of those early warning systems.

The dogs, in particular, were almost eerily silent. Many had been visible as the couple had silently made their way to their destination, dogs standing at gates or on front porches or inside the houses peering through windows, turning their heads to watch the strangers passing, yet all of them otherwise unmoving and silent.

Bishop, who knew dogs, made a troubled mental note.

When the report was filed, everyone questioned, when what was left of the house had been poked and prodded and examined, it might or might not have been something noticed by others, perhaps commented upon, and if so would be listed as one more inexplicable thing in a world filled with them.

No one had noticed anything unusual, that's what they would most likely say, what they'd tell the police and fire marshal. The peaceful house that served as a quiet short-term convalescent home for people recovering from surgeries was always quiet, more secluded than some of the other houses in the neighborhood and with a larger yard than most, its caretakers pleasant, the patients hardly seen at all by neighbors too polite to peer over the tall privacy fence.

Everything had been fine, had been normal, and *why* would anyone want to burn down that lovely house?

But it was burning. And they were late in arriving.

No more than half an hour late.

But it was enough.

The predawn morning was lit with a hellish glow because the roof was already burning savagely with hungry flames, burning too quickly, too intensely, too needfully, to be anything but deliberate. The drought of weeks past had left everything a tinderbox. And still there must have been the need for absolute certainty, the need to destroy utterly, because the house had, clearly, been liberally splashed with an accelerant of some kind, inside and out, just to make certain that the roar of the fire would be swift, hungry and fierce. And not just the roof, but the once-pretty shingle siding and the shrubbery planted near the house, and even where there seemed little to burn, fire blazed, blocking every window and every door.

Burning. Burning, all of it.

Bishop and Miranda could see nothing but flames as they raced toward the house already knowing they were too late. Every possible entrance—and exit—was blocked by the fire. A wall of flames no human could breach. The whole place deliberately turned into a living, writhing, gleeful hell.

They stopped only when they had to, when the wave of heat blasting back at them was searing even twenty yards away, nearly knocking them off their feet as the fire's hungry roar increased. And even then, what stopped them was the inescapable certainty that there was no way in.

And no way out.

Dimly, sirens could be heard, so already a neighbor up early or awakened had noticed and called first responders. Because the house's fire alarms would have been disabled, of course, detectors destroyed and lines to emergency services severed, just so there would be more time for the fire to take hold. More time to destroy . . . everything.

"Shit," Miranda muttered, and went utterly still, her intense gaze fixed on the flaming pyre.

"Goddammit, Miranda, don't—"

"I have to. You know I have to."

And she was already reaching out with every one of her senses, as unable as he was not to use every tool at her disposal when lives were at stake. And she had to do this, her rather than him, because it was the shield she had made that protected them both, something organic to her, and only she could shatter it in a violent instant without harming both of them. The intensely powerful psychic shield created out of desperate need that had been in place for years to hide herself and her younger sister, Bonnie, from the monster that had destroyed their family. And, more recently these last months, to hide Bishop and herself from those who would be interested, if not horrified and panicked, at their involvement in this.

The force of Miranda's emotions blasted through everything, the shield, the fire, the burning walls of the house, the very atoms of what remained inside, an almost visible wave of energy sent out by her to probe desperately inside that house. And the shattered shield or just the burst of energy jarred both of them nearly off their feet.

Neither of them really noticed, then, that walls that should have burned longer collapsed, some inward and some outward, from a new force that did not come from Miranda but from inside the house, a desperate, untaught, wordless terror reaching. That the few unbroken windows shattered in unison, which should not have happened, that the fire itself wailed suddenly as if in agonized protest, an eerily human cry of torment.

Miranda blasted through her shield and through nearly everything else until she knew for certain what they had already known.

Until her normal senses were no longer muffled, and the extra ones came alive all in a rush with all the stunning sensitivity of raw nerves; everything she saw was painfully bright and in painfully bright colors; the noises of the fire, the wail of sirens and the distant cries of neighbors finally awakened, the acrid smell of the fire that made it difficult for her to breathe; until the world around them became crystal clear once again, until she could feel her husband's arm around her, feel the very heartbeat pulse of the earth beneath her feet and feel the swirling energies in the air around them, almost all negative because ash residue was the awful waste product of the evil and horrific crime tragically committed here tonight.

All that rushed at Miranda, stealing her breath for a moment, hurting her eyes, burning her nose. But she was experienced even in handling the deadliest of evil, and it was only seconds that she was vulnerable at all, until the dark energy could find no way into her, until her senses were all back to normal.

Until she was whole, herself. Until nightmare imagination became all too horribly real.

"Ah, Jesus, Noah, they left the girls." Miranda's voice

was hard with the sort of iron control both had learned in unspeakable situations. "Deliberately. Nobody panicked. There was time to get them, save them—but that wasn't the plan. At least three nonpsychics, the caretakers, probably drugged. The moms were all asleep in their beds, also probably drugged or conditioned to sleep through anything till morning. They didn't have a chance." Her voice was still hard, still controlled by an iron fist, because there had been so many horrors along the way, so many events they should have been able to prevent.

Like this one.

But this one struck a personal note for both of them, a deeply personal agony, because they had lost a child unborn not so very long ago, taken from them in violence, and such a loss could never be something about which they could ever again be impersonal.

Miranda's beautiful face was a mask of control, her electric blue eyes unusually dark, as dark as holes in the world.

"All of them?" Bishop demanded hoarsely, his own abilities coming alive just moments more slowly than hers, muffled just a bit more, a bit longer by her powerful shield even after it was shattered. Until his mind and senses adjusted.

"We counted a dozen two days ago. There are a dozen in that house. They were already burning in their beds before we got here. Already beyond help." She looked at her husband with those dark, dark haunted eyes. "The babies too. Three were close to term, very close. They're gone now. They're all gone now. Noah . . . they were psychic. Not latents, not the babies. They were powerfully psychic already, especially the ones close to term. They would have been born with every ability they would ever possess. That's how they knew . . . how they understood . . . what was happening to them. But they didn't have the control, the knowledge, to stop it."

"I know," he said. "I heard . . . the last of their screams."

Bishop took her hand in his, and for an instant they stood with their gazes on the inferno before them, bearing the searing heat that struck them in waves physically as well as the searing heartbreak and rage that struck even stronger blows.

Perhaps if they had been on time . . .

"Did they know we were coming?" Bishop asked her.

"I'm not sure. All I know is that it was deliberate. That someone did this, knowing what they were doing. And that they aren't here now, didn't stick around to—to watch."

There was nothing else they needed to say. Nothing more about what had happened here. Nothing more about their overwhelming pain and grief. No discussion or debate about the decision to fade back into the darkness, and make their way, silent and unseen, past exclaiming and horrified neighbors, and the first responders, and the first of the media, before anyone at all noticed their presence.

There was nothing they could do.

Not here, at least.

And not now.

---

Tasha Solomon woke with a scream locked in her throat, her arms held out as if reaching for something that was now forever beyond her grasp. Her heart was thudding against her ribs, her breath rasping, and in her mind were the heartbreaking echoes of something more than a nightmare.

What she felt had no language in her own mind just then, only pain, the worst pain she had ever felt in her life, tearing, ripping pain, a grief so overwhelming it was an actual physical agony, so much pain she wasn't sure she could bear it.

"Tasha?" Brodie was in the open doorway of her bedroom, wearing only sweatpants, his dark hair a bit ruffled from sleep but wide-awake as he always was in the need of an instant. He rarely slept much except for catnaps, her Guardian, and insisted on remaining on the comfortable couch in her spacious one-bedroom condo where he could be ready for trouble should any come, but there had been no reason to be on guard tonight, no reason not to expect a peaceful night.

It had been weeks. Weeks of calm. No threat.

Now the threat felt overwhelming.

He came into her bedroom, turning the lamp on her nightstand down low, sitting on the edge of the bed, concern and something else in his sharp sentry eyes.

They hadn't quite figured out what was between them, not yet at least, even after weeks spent almost continually in each other's company. Both innately guarded people knew, and accepted however warily, that there was something, a connection that had been forged weeks before, and right now all he was certain of was that she was suffering horribly and shouldn't be alone.

"Tasha." He wasn't even aware that his voice had changed, had deepened and roughened.

She reached out before he did, unable to face this alone, blind and desperate for some kind of comfort, for the healing touch of someone else who understood, and he responded instantly, enfolding her in his arms, holding her tightly. He could feel her tears wet on his throat, feel the shudders racking her body.

"They're gone," she whispered against his skin. "All of them. Oh, God. They screamed. I heard them. John, they screamed. The babies. The babies understood. They knew they were dying. They knew they were burning alive and couldn't save themselves."

John Brodie had gone to great effort these last weeks, since becoming her Guardian, to keep his own mind quiet and still, to project the sort of shield he had been taught to protect his mind and his privacy, a peaceful surface that psychics tended to see as a calm ocean. Not because he feared any touch of Tasha's—she had, in fact, already read him telepathically, and deeply enough that he still felt somewhat shaken by that unexpected intimacy—but because he was not a born psychic, was not sure even now *what* he was. Until he was certain of that he was unwilling to risk either the other senses honed to a deadly knife-edge sharpness necessary as a Guardian or any unconscious use of abilities he did not yet understand, far less control.

Especially when any of that was driven by emotion.

But he opened up just a bit in that moment, relaxing the ever-present guard because she was in such pain and it went against his very nature not to try to understand, to help.

He stopped blocking the new, untested, and distinctly unsettling connection between them for an instant, just an instant, opening the door on his end just far enough. And in that one instant he knew what had happened, and how, and he felt the shattering grief not only of lives lost, of innocent lives and new lives brutally taken, but of vast, untapped power destroyed with the casual cruelty of an uncaring foot crushing beneath it something not even recognized as being alive.

The jolt of pain he felt in her and shared with her was as powerful as a knife to the heart.

Gone. They were gone.

They were gone forever.

"Tasha . . ."

"I felt them . . . I felt them die . . . John . . . I don't ever want to feel anything like that again. Ever."

"I know." He held her, his hands stroking her back, trying to soothe, the heat of his body trying to warm the bone-deep chill of hers.

He wanted to reassure her. Needed to badly. Not because she was his responsibility, his charge as her Guardian, but because she was more. Because these past weeks and a knowledge of each other deeper than words can ever be had made her more to him, so much more.

Because they were linked, connected, bonded. Because even though he had not told her so, she had become more important to him than anything had ever been in his life, more important even than the war to which he had dedicated his life, and the much-loved wife whose murder had been the catalyst for that decision a decade before.

She lifted her head from his shoulder and looked at him in the dim light, her normally pale green eyes darkened, wet, still suffering, and he would have done anything in his power to ease her pain.

So he did.

Without even thinking about it, he opened up the connection between them completely, opened the door he controlled all the way, instinctively sending through all the warmth and comfort stored for so long inside him. He sent caring and gentleness. He sent a strength she could lean on when she had to. He sent the utter certainty of an ultimate triumph even if that seemed far beyond reach right now.

And he sent sorrow, for the soldiers lost along the way, those who had fought at his side. For the psychics lost, stolen from them, taken in dark secret and in open violence. And sorrow for these recent tiny souls lost, for the pitiful, damaged women who had never been granted the chance to bear their special offspring, and for the tiny new souls who had never been granted the chance to breathe and live and be.

He sent to Tasha, shared with her, all that he was.

Tasha wasn't even certain he was completely aware of the gift he was giving her, or whether he would later regret it, but for now she accepted it gladly. The awful pain eased as much as it could. All the dark, cold corners of herself began to lighten, to warm, to feel less empty, and she was so grateful.

She had been alone for so long, alone for most of her life even when her adoptive parents were alive and had loved her very much. Alone because she had always known she was different and yet had to pretend to be like everyone else. Alone and with no one to share the pain and loneliness of being different.

Tasha would never have believed he would be the one, when mere comfort and understanding were not enough, who truly reached out, physically as well as psychically. She was almost afraid to believe it now. But he was holding her in his arms, first only to comfort, she knew that, to share her pain and do his best to ease it.

But, somehow, when he opened fully the connection between them, when he felt and shared the agony she was nearly drowning in, the screams of unborn infants with whom she felt an odd kinship, something changed.

For the first time in his life, John Brodie saw into someone else's soul.

And what he saw moved him unbearably.

Tasha was, dimly, aware of that. Of his surprise. Of the complex tangle of emotions he didn't try to hide from her. But then one of them or both of them took that last step separating them. There was a different kind of reaching, a sudden awareness when the moment of comfort became something else entirely.

She didn't know what changed in that moment.

She didn't care.

From the cold agony of tragedy and loss, Tasha felt more than comfort and understanding begin to fill her being. She felt herself changing. His mouth was on hers, seducing even though it didn't have to, driving away the coldness and the pain.

He was who Tasha needed, what she needed, and everything inside her, every sense, every instinct, told her so. Her mouth was alive beneath his, her body straining to be closer to him. All their senses reached out, their minds, touching and twining and settling into place with an ineffable sense of belonging.

Still, she had to hesitate one last time, had to ask and to ask aloud, uncertain, fearful of more pain.

"John . . . are you sure?" she whispered.

"More sure than I've been of anything in my life."

"We don't know what it'll be, what *we'll* be after this."

"We'll be together. Stronger together. Better together." He drew a deep breath and let it out slowly as though releasing burdens he had not even felt until that moment. "We'll belong together."

"I'm not the woman you lost," she had to say.

"You are the woman I love. There are no ghosts between us, Tasha. No regrets. You are not second best to me. We were meant to be together. And you know that as well as I do."

*I love you, and I couldn't bear it if it was just comfort.*

*It isn't.*

"It's more. It's so much more." His arms tightened around her, and his mouth covered hers again, this time with utter certainty.

Tasha had not known what to expect. Not because no man had kissed her with desire, with longing, but because Brodie had not. It was so much more than she had ever felt in her life. His strength flowed into her being, his gentleness. His ruthlessness and his compassion. His loneliness and the comradeship found here and there along the way. His rage and his sweetness. His pain and his joy. His commitment to his cause . . . and his utter and complete commitment to her.

He was right. It was so much more.

She was barely aware of her sleep shirt removed and flung aside, or his sweatpants following. Barely aware of the bed beneath them, covers pushed away. Of the lamp-lit room that showed them just enough soft light.

Tasha would have said Brodie was the most controlled man she had ever known, just as she would have said she was the most guarded of anyone she had ever known. But that night, in the last of the darkness outside and dawn's promise only beginning to lighten the sky, she discovered how wrong she had been. About both of them.

He was not controlled when he touched her. His mouth burned and his hands shook and his body trembled. His heart hammered in his chest, and his breath came as quickly as her own did, because her guard came crashing down at the first touch of him.

He touched rich curves, his fingertips and his lips exploring silky skin with a hunger answered instantly, without thought, by her own fiery need.

She felt a hard body beneath her probing fingers and lips, firm skin over hard muscle earned in a lifetime of physical work that owed nothing to a gym. A powerful body marked here and there by the scars of battles past, by close calls in deadly encounters. She cried without meaning to, her lips pressed to each scar old and new, as if her love could heal those marks on his flesh and in his soul.

She gave as fully as he did, offering up everything she was to him. The triumphs and tragedies, the good times and the bad ones, the aching loneliness of a life lived apart from others and the joy of finding others who understood.

The utter joy of finding him.

Their connection, not one initially forged in love but in life-or-death need, grew in those moments. Evolved. It became more, stronger, surer, once-gossamer threads uncertainly linking their two minds becoming threads of something stronger than steel, something that could never be broken, weaving a more stable, permanent, immutable bond and anchoring it deeply inside both of them.

And along with all that was something new.

Something neither had planned and both needed.

Something that would change everything.

# THREE

It was still before dawn when Duran made his final patrol around the periphery of the downtown Charleston area they had (over his objections) settled on as their base. For now, at least. There were two locations in the area, one familiar to Murphy and her people because Duran had used it before, and the real base, the new one, well hidden and designed, despite his misgivings, with more permanence in mind.

There was too much complacency, he thought, too much arrogance in their self-certainty, in their belief that they had the right to do this. Any of this. Even with battles lost to Murphy and her people, even with valuable psychics lost, they were still convinced theirs was the superior force, still convinced they were right, more than right.

Entitled.

Duran was no longer sure of that. He had not really been sure of that, he knew, for quite some time now. He had seen too many mistakes made by those on his side, and knew of a great many others before his time. Too many assumptions that turned out to be wrong. Dangerously wrong.

Too many experiments with unwilling subjects and results all the records clinically referred to as "unsuccessful."

Duran thought of them as tragic.

He doubted Sebring thought of the matter at all, except to immediately turn her attention to locating and obtaining more psychics for more experiments. Because that was her job, and because she was dedicated to men who were obsessed with a cause she still believed in.

As for the other side, Murphy's side, they were a people to whom freedom and the right to control their own destinies as well as they could represented a very, very large part of who they were, perhaps even stamped in the very cells of their bodies, embedded in their DNA. Many had died over the years at the hands of his own people rather than submit, concede, and be mastered.

More of them than Duran liked to admit.

Probably many more than he knew of, especially in those very early years.

And, secret or "underground" as they still mostly were, Murphy and her people had either gotten better at recruiting allies, psychic and otherwise, or else more had been triggered, awakened somehow, especially in the last fifteen years or so. They had seen and understood things they were not supposed to, or took notice of patterns, or simply felt the threat and found their way, somehow, into this supposedly secret war, because their numbers were growing.

It was a disturbing realization.

And it was not the only one for Duran.

More than ever, he had the sense of decisions made and connections forged and encounters that had somehow, suddenly and unexpectedly, brought them all to a dangerous precipice. And not only his people, but Murphy and her group as well.

He had, once, stood on the relatively thin edge of a glacier, conscious of the ocean moving beneath him as a tangible sensation; he was feeling something similar now. Things were moving, quietly but unstoppable, unseen, like the powerful ocean under ice. Things set in motion both knowingly and unknowingly, finding their own momentum, becoming in some way he could only feel, a force beyond his or anyone's control.

Even though all his logic told him otherwise, his instincts told him they were coming to the end of this, one way or another. After so many years. After so many of the first generation had died off, most of diseases new to them. Only a few healers, perhaps ironically, surviving that and living still. But the seeds of a second generation had been planted even then, and many had survived to be born here. And the third generation, their numbers small, but increasing slowly, more and more born with the immunity they required to survive. For a long time, for generations, they had been forced to concentrate on that, on increasing their own numbers, building their immunity to disease.

And those intense efforts had proven successful. Generations born here now. Looking less and less different from humans as they adapted, as this world shaped them. Born here and living here, thriving here, calling this place home if only silently.

As he did. He was not sure any other place would be, could be home to him after this.

And he had no idea how to feel about that.

But he had a job to do.

For now, he patrolled because he needed to be moving. Needed some reassurance he doubted he'd find. Some sense of hope that all this had not been worse than fruitless.

Hope. That was not a word in their native tongue, but they had learned it here. At least some of them had.

Perhaps they had learned it from Murphy and her people, so very outnumbered and outgunned, at least in the beginning. Forced to do little except try to save what psychics they could.

But now . . . they weren't *just* trying to locate and protect psychics before Duran and his people could find them, before Sebring and her group could find them, not anymore. They were actively working against him, seeking intel that, on the surface, should have had little value to them. Yet they looked, and in looking, in locating intel, they had found ways to slow him down, distract him, distract even Sebring. To interfere.

Too many were actively involved in this now. People like Tucker Mackenzie not only gathering intel but also alerting the world that psychics like his wife existed, pushing the issue a step or two closer to mainstream belief with his work. And others on their side, Murphy's side, some other geniuses in many professions, also gathering vital information and, even if slowly, changing the way psychics were viewed.

Dangerous information. Dangerous changes.

And honing other skills that might be weapons one day. Perhaps one day soon.

Which was a dangerous thing indeed.

Duran could respect, understand, even do what he could to mitigate damage—to his people and to Murphy's.

But Sebring and her group . . . they were vicious. They did not respect, or understand, or appreciate being outmaneuvered.

To them, the enemy was an inferior race, good only for the . . . science they might provide. The biological information.

Even if they had to tear their subjects apart all the way down to their atoms in order to find what they sought.

---

Robin Brook sat up abruptly in their bed, conscious of a chill deeper than her bones. David Grant, who had shared her life and her bed for more than a year now, sat up as well, almost in the same instant.

It was still dark, and outside their Chicago apartment, in a fairly busy but not hectic part of the city, a *safe* part of the city, the streets were unusually quiet.

Or maybe, Robin thought, that was because of the only now fading screams in her mind.

Quietly, David asked, "What the hell was that?"

"Did you hear them?" She was reasonably sure he had heard, or at least been aware, because their minds had been linked since before they'd moved in together.

"I heard . . . something. Faint cries. But not close." He had always been the calmer of the two, taking things as they came and rarely losing his Zen-like serenity.

"South," she said without even thinking about it.

"South of here. Another state, I think. Far away." Robin tended toward calm herself, helped along by an innate sense of humor that rarely failed her, but there was nothing even remotely funny about this.

"You got more than I did, love," he said, still quiet. "What was it?"

She drew a deep breath and let it out slowly. "Babies, I think. Babies . . . dying."

"How could either of us pick that up? We read each other, yeah, and read some other people up close. But babies . . ."

"I think they were reaching out."

"To us?"

"To anyone who could hear them." She looked at him, his face clear to her even in the dim room because it always was. "David . . . I think they were psychics. A lot of them. And I think somebody killed them. Murdered them. I—I think there was a fire."

"Set deliberately?"

"Yeah. To kill them. To kill the babies."

He knew her too well not to know her response. "You want to do something about it. We talked about this in the beginning. Love, we did everything they told us to do in order to safeguard ourselves and still lead normal lives. We have letters and recorded statements locked up in the safes of two different lawyers *and* in bank safe-deposit boxes, with all the instructions on what to do if we suddenly . . . disappear or seemingly die in some kind of accident. But they told us to still be careful. To not take any chances."

She didn't hesitate. "They gave us a number to call. I want to call. I want to find out if anyone else felt that.

Something bad happened, David. Something . . . horrible. Those babies were targets. And we—we've talked about maybe having a family, right?"

He leaned over and kissed her bare shoulder. "Of course. We both want kids."

"We were both born psychic," she said steadily. "It's more likely than not that at least one of our kids would be too, and probably more than one."

"Something else we've talked about, yeah."

"I want to call, because I think we need to know if the children of psychics are in danger. And I think we need to know if there's anything we can do to help."

He looked at her for a long moment, her face as clear to him as his was to her, darkness or not. He could feel her worry, her fear. And he shared it.

"I'll get the number," he said, throwing back the covers.

---

Katie Swan said, "I can't." She said it, by now, like a litany. Like a plea. *I can't do this anymore. Please stop. Please let me go home. I won't tell anyone. I promise, I'll never tell anyone.*

*Jesus, who would believe me anyway?*

She had no idea what time it was, even what day it was. Time passed in her windowless prison, in the tiny cell where she could rest if they decided to let her rest, eat when they gave her food; time passed with nothing to mark its passage.

But she was so tired.

"Try again." The voice was cold, implacable, remorseless. It might have been a machine, repeating the command again and again with no sign of frustration or impatience. Just as it had the last time she had been brought to this . . . Testing Room. And the time before that, and the time before that, stretching backward into an unknown infinity.

They woke her at irregular times; her own internal clock told her that. She never knew how long she had slept or whether they were drugging her. All she knew was that she always woke exhausted and aching all over. Sometimes the lights went out in her cell when she was still awake, and she nearly screamed at the heavy weight of the darkness settling down on her. They offered food that was tasteless, and when she refused at first had informed her coldly that she would eat or they would get nourishment into her by some other means.

She ate the tasteless food. And tried to sleep when she was returned to her cell.

They tested her. And she tried to please them.

Again and again. Deliberate, relentless. And, at first, they had hardly hurt her at all.

At first.

"I can't," she said again, numb.

"You can. It's what you do. Move it."

Before Katie on the stainless steel table lay a dagger, turned so that it was aimed, roughly, at a man-shaped stuffed target across the room. It was, perhaps, ten feet away from her.

It might as well have been ten miles.

How many times had they tested her like this? A hundred times? Two hundred?

She was so tired.

The room was as familiar as her cell, with its whitewashed cinder-block walls, the small table bolted down, the hard chair on which she sat bolted down, the observation window, the closed door.

The target.

How many times now? Brought to this room and told to move a series of objects. A feather, a pencil, a small rubber ball—easy things at first, even if she had had to concentrate hard to move anything at all.

Because she'd never been able to control it, she tried to tell them that. She was afraid, and fear had never been something that had helped her control it.

Couldn't they understand that?

They had. Because after that, after she'd cried in fear and pleaded with them, they had tried something different the next time.

Pain.

She thought they were using some kind of electric shock, but all she really knew was that it hurt. It hurt bad. They fastened her wrists to the arms of the hard metal chair, and then told her to use her abilities to move whatever lay on the plain table before her.

The feather, the pencil, the small rubber ball.

It should have been easy, but it wasn't. She tried, she really did, but the objects, even the practically weightless feather, rewarded her efforts with no more than a twitch.

She tried her best to move the easy things, because she didn't want the jolts of pain that were punishment for failure. She tried her best, and eventually, at some point beyond her ability to measure time, she moved what was put in front of her because she didn't want them to hurt her anymore.

Then harder things. Heavier things. Larger things.

She had tried for countless minutes or maybe hours to move a cinder block placed on the table. It hadn't budged until something in Katie had snapped, and she had cried out in frustration.

The heavy piece of masonry not only lifted, it literally flew across the room and crashed into the glass protecting her tormenter, safe in her little watcher's booth.

The glass—or whatever it was—had not shown even a scratch. The cinder block was in pieces on the floor. And the face behind the window had never changed expression.

"Again," she had ordered.

Over and over.

Move this. Lift that. Now drop it. Lift it. Move it.

In an endless loop of time and effort and exhaustion.

"I wasn't born with it," she tried to tell them. "It's only been a couple of years since I was thrown from a horse and hit my head. There hasn't been time to learn to control it."

"Try again," the emotionless woman behind the glass ordered now, her voice perfectly clear even though Katie couldn't see a sign of a speaker anywhere in her whitewashed cinder-block box of a room.

"Move the knife. Hit the target with the knife."

A faint warning tingle around her manacled wrists made Katie focus on the target across the room. On the red circle drawn just where a human heart would be located. She stared at the target, then at the dagger on the table. It twitched, perhaps an inch or two.

"Try again."

"I couldn't kill a person," she whispered, suddenly more afraid of that than of anything in her life. "I could never—"

"It's a stuffed target. Try again."

"I need to rest. I'll do better after I've rested."

"Try again."

"Something to eat—"

A stronger shock.

Katie whimpered and tried to focus on the dagger. She had moved the far-heavier cinder block in frustration, other things when her emotions flared. But this time she had been ordered to aim, to be precise. To hit a target.

Something she had never done before, with the single exception of mentally pulling something toward herself and reaching out to catch it in her hand. A pen. A book she'd been reading. The TV remote.

This was so, so different.

Beyond frightened and wary of the shock, she tried to bargain. "If I do it, if I hit the target, then you'll let me rest."

"Of course," her tormenter said with suspicious promptness.

Desperate to rest, to be out of this horrible room if only for an hour or two of blessed unconsciousness, Katie concentrated, and with all the strength and focus she could muster, bolstered by fear, she made the dagger lift—and then shoot across the room and hit the stuffed target.

"You missed the heart. Do it again."

---

Duran continued his patrol, but he couldn't shut out the thoughts and speculation crowding into his mind. It didn't happen often, and when it did it tended to be times like now, in the dark watches of the night when he was alone.

He suspected that Murphy and her people had decided to form a more permanent base in this area of their own. A new tactic for them, since to date they had remained highly mobile, no cell of their organization remaining in any one place long enough to be noticed by the wrong people.

It was the way they were set up, like the French Resistance during World War II, small groups, or "cells," of highly mobile people scattered about, all with the same mission but self-contained, reporting to someone who reported to someone else who reported, eventually, to whoever was running the organization.

Duran had no idea who that was.

But he knew there were more cells now than ever before, knew that their efforts were more organized, more efficient. More effective. And, always before, highly mobile.

So what was the significance of this apparent stable base in Charleston, this newly renovated building of condos where Tucker and Sarah Mackenzie lived? In the pro column, a still target was always easier to hit than one always on the move, and at least he would know where this cell was based.

In the cons column was the simple fact that he had no idea why they had changed tactics.

And what really troubled him, far more than he would have admitted to anyone, was that this building's security, like that of his own new base in the area, had been enhanced beyond the known state of technology, in a very short time for a building of that size, with not only the aid of virtually endless funds, but also with the highly trained expertise of new players brought into the game.

They had tapped resources he'd had no idea were so deep and well funded, and that was troubling. In part because he still could not identify most of those assets, the sources of this new energy and manpower. And in part because those he had been able to identify posed a greater danger to them than ever before.

But he knew now who was living in that ultra-secure building, and that was certainly a worry. The Mackenzies. A mated pair who could not be taken and could not be turned. The certain knowledge of which had not yet reached Duran's superiors—and he trusted it never would, because they would not view the information with indifference.

To them, dangerous psychics they could not take or use were better dead. Always, even if those psychics stood within a bright and unwelcome spotlight of notoriety. And sooner rather than later. It was an absolute in their world.

But this was not their world.

And as long as he was able to prevent it, they would not be allowed to destroy only because they could not control. That, to his mind, was among other things an unpardonable waste.

As long as he was able to prevent it.

Still, it did not mean Duran could ignore the Mackenzies or any of the others who had managed to remain at large and had put themselves out of his reach. Because they weren't just going to ground as had once been the rule for most of them, disappearing, hiding out from both Duran's people and the world itself. Drawing no attention to themselves. Remaining quiet, their abilities kept secret, their lives kept peaceful.

They had been harmless then.

Most of them.

But now . . . now more of them were joining the fight. Now even those who had made a different choice at some earlier point were coming out of hiding despite the threats they knew well, grim and determined and with far better control over their abilities than Duran had bargained for.

New enemies.

He expected losses. Expected some plans to prove . . . unsuccessful. That was just the nature of things. What had always been the nature of things.

So many different plans in different places had been attempted, some of them ambitious. Some costly in resources, but with a potentially worthwhile payoff.

Some too ambitious.

So there would always be adjustments to be made along the way.

But there were more players on the board than ever before, on the board and in motion, like that unstoppable ocean moving silently under ice, and that made Duran uneasy. It made him uneasy that Murphy had uncovered information he'd intended to leave long-buried, and it made him uneasy that players recruited by Murphy and her group, especially recently, had more skills and more resources than ever before.

"Hello, Duran. Fancy meeting you here."

# FOUR

He had been moving, unusually preoccupied by his own thoughts, in the darkness between two buildings, but stopped the instant he heard her voice, consciously aware of a wry lack of surprise that she had found him in the night.

Murphy had the knack of finding and knowing all kinds of things he would have kept from her if he could have.

"Can you see in the dark?" she asked in an idle tone, perhaps honestly curious. Or perhaps not.

When she stepped closer to him, emerging from the darkness not three feet in front of him, he caught the catlike gleam of her sharp green eyes.

"Not one of my abilities," he admitted, holding his voice calm and steady. Keeping his hands in the pockets of his zip-up jacket because it was chilly this early even in June and he hated the cold. And because it was an unthreatening position. Which counted for quite a lot when one was facing Murphy.

"It's one of mine. Does that surprise you?"

"Not really," he said dryly.

A low laugh escaped her. And another half step brought her closer, so that he could see more than her eyes, so he could see that angular, striking, curiously youthful face, her hair pale in the dim light, so likely some shade of blond now.

She changed it often, apparently on a whim. At least once it had been purple.

He could see that her own hands were also in the pockets of the army jacket she often wore.

He didn't have to see the gun she undoubtedly had trained on him inside one of those pockets. This was not a temporary truce, a white-flag meet planned in advance. This was two wary enemies encountering one another in the night.

Enemies met carefully, especially in the dark.

And Murphy was nothing if not very, very careful.

"What are you doing back in Charleston, Duran? You agreed to pull your people out weeks ago."

"Yes. And I did. But—it wasn't an open-ended agreement, Murphy." Something she had once said to him. Something he knew she would remember.

"So many things aren't. In our world, yours and mine. In this world of . . . lies, half-truths, and a kind of understanding born of experience."

He couldn't tell how she felt about that.

"Why are you out patrolling?" she asked suddenly. "This is not something you normally do. In fact, I've never known you to do it before. Ever."

"I've done every job I've asked my people to do," he said evenly, wondering how closely she had been watching him, and for how long. "Even a simple patrol."

"Is that what this is?" Her head tilted slightly, birdlike, and the sharp green eyes caught what light there was and gleamed. "But you're not a simple man, are you, Duran? Nothing about you is simple."

"I imagine that could be said about most people," he responded in a pleasant tone.

"But some more than others. I did notice you took care of our little problem weeks ago. Eliot Wolfe. So no run to be lieutenant governor of the state. Or any other political office. Not for him, at least. Never for him." There was the faintest of emphasis on that last word.

*She knows there are others being readied and placed in positions of power. But does she know who? Where? Does she know why—even though I don't?*

He didn't know how he felt about the possibility of that either.

"Wolfe had become a liability. You were right about that."

"I was also right about Tasha Solomon and Brodie."

Something in her voice made his own attention sharpen. "There was a connection," he said slowly.

"There's more now," she said. "Much more. A complete and total bond. What seems to require an intense emotional as well as physical joining, at least for us. Not that I wanted to intrude on their privacy, you understand, but . . . Well. The psychic thing. It keeps a lot of us more connected than you might think."

It was something Duran had long suspected and about which he was far from happy. But all he said was,

"That's not something you can control. Not something you can deliberately create."

"Not a weapon for our side, you mean?"

"Not a . . . tool, shall we say."

"No, it doesn't appear to be," she responded readily. "So far, at least. Nor can you create that . . . tool . . . deliberately. Or even by accident. Because it isn't happening among your people, is it, Duran?"

He was silent.

Being Murphy, she didn't really care that he was silent. She had things to say, for whatever reasons of her own, and she would say them.

"It's never happened. You don't have a single pair of bonded psychics. Even those born psychics you stole from their normal lives and managed to . . . breed . . . never formed any sort of psychic or emotional bond, did they, Duran?"

He remained silent.

Murphy still didn't seem at all disturbed by his lack of response. "It was something we figured out when we understood that Tasha was among your earliest generations of . . . engineered . . . born psychics. Perhaps even the first truly successful generation, part of the first truly meaningful experiment. Born in one of your little breeding operations, her parents two born psychics captured or co-opted by you into mating to produce offspring. But no bond ever formed between Tasha's biological parents, did it? Even the mother was probably unable to bond with the child she carried and bore, despite the human biological imperative to do just that. It was one reason Tasha was adopted out to nonpsychic *parents*."

"No, they didn't bond," he said finally.

"Did the mothers even recognize their children once they were born?" She sounded mildly curious, but also as if she wanted a theory confirmed.

Duran wondered how far he was putting his head into a noose, but heard himself answering anyway. "The mothers didn't even remember being pregnant or giving birth within hours afterward."

"Uh-huh. What about all those other born psychics you so carefully matched with more born psychics? Did those men and women bond at all?"

"No."

"Didn't you give them time for a little romance before you shoved them into a bed?" she asked mockingly.

"That wasn't—" He cursed himself silently, because he always had trouble guarding his tongue with her, and Murphy was quick. Too quick.

"That wasn't why they didn't bond," she murmured. "Because that wasn't the way you handled the . . . situation. It's something else I've been thinking about these last weeks. Pondering. Why there are clearly damaged mothers carrying psychic babies, but the babies are never kept there long after birth. Not long at all."

A part of Duran wished he could have been surprised by her knowledge. But he wasn't.

"What I think," Murphy said slowly, "is that your people didn't know it was anything more than biology. Only the mating of a male and a female. Should have been just that simple. But there were failures that bothered your medical people and scientists because it was clear *something* was lacking. So the decision was made to go with pure science. In vitro fertilization, for one thing.

Conception in a petri dish without all the messy human complications of bringing two people together and hoping to strike a spark.

"So much simpler. Just abduct a few human females and steal some eggs, abduct a few human males and steal some semen, mix together under the proper laboratory conditions, add in biological material from your people, whatever substance or attributes your scientists developed that was the latest promise of a breakthrough, and let biology take its course. Then all you need is a willing—or mindless—womb in which to plant your creation.

"That would have been the most efficient, especially if you're aiming for your idea of the . . . perfect . . . offspring. And it *was* only biology. So, of course, your people tried with some of your very willing women first, those females of your people with all the traits you wanted passed on to their offspring. Their eggs, I'm guessing, and enhanced. And the sperm of psychic human males, also possibly . . . enhanced. Those were the fertilized eggs implanted in your females in those very early days more than decades ago. Am I warm with that one?"

Duran was silent only a moment. "There was some early laboratory experimentation. Which ultimately failed to produce . . . acceptable results."

"I'm guessing serious birth defects."

"Which produced early miscarriages," he said briefly.

"Did any survive?"

"Not long," he replied in an even briefer answer.

"I guess some wombs are more hostile than others

to . . . the implantation and nurturing of genetically manipulated new life."

"So it appears."

---

Sadie Fletcher knew, as she fought her way out of the nightmare, that Duncan had been right there with her. It was part of their connection: He shared her telepathic communications and she shared his clairvoyance.

Which was, even after several years together, still a bit disconcerting. Especially when it happened during sleep.

She finally woke with a jerk to find her husband's arms around her, and knew instantly that he was already awake.

"It wasn't a nightmare," he murmured.

Sadie could see past his shoulder that it was still dark outside, before dawn. Inside, their bedroom was lit only by the light in the bathroom beyond a half-closed door. She couldn't bear totally dark rooms.

"It wasn't?" She wanted to believe it had been. Surely it had been.

"No. I don't think so. I think . . . a lot of very, very young psychics screamed out for help, even knowing it was too late for anyone to help them."

"There was a fire," Sadie said, her voice shaking. "Someone . . . I think someone did it deliberately. To kill the babies."

Duncan nodded silently.

"Jamie," she whispered. Their two-year-old son, sleeping peacefully just down the hall, was already showing definite signs that he had inherited his mother's telepathic abilities.

"We can't know he's in danger," Duncan said steadily.

"What I got was something that happened far away from here. Not sure where, but . . . We've taken all the precautions they recommended, and then some. We won't let anyone take or hurt our son, Sadie."

She drew a shuddering breath. "I still don't want to—to fight with the others. I know it's selfish of me, but—"

"Shhh." His arms tightened around her. "You were pregnant with Jamie when they found us. *They* said it would be too dangerous for us to join. That we might be able to help later, but not then. They told us how to protect ourselves and Jamie. And we have the number we can call. Any hour, they said, day or night."

"Maybe we should call, Duncan. Those babies . . . So many of them. So many of them murdered horribly. What if the other side is going after babies, after kids? Psychic kids? Born psychic kids?"

"Sadie—"

"We need to know that. We need to know what's happening."

He was silent for a few moments, his hands stroking her back, trying to soothe. But he knew his wife. "You won't rest until we know what's happening, will you?"

"I can't. We have to know if the other side is more of a danger to us now, to Jamie. Something might have changed."

He couldn't deny the possibility of that. They had been warned that too much was still uncertain, that they were still learning about the other side. Their capabilities. Their motivations and goals.

"Call now, Duncan. Please?"

He kissed her gently, then shifted slightly to reach for the lamp on the nightstand. And then for the portable phone of the landline they had kept only for this . . . possibility.

---

Murphy nodded slowly. "I'm guessing you also discovered, when you returned to the old-fashioned way, that the couples you were matching based on DNA or fertility or some other criteria simply had absolutely nothing else in common. In fact, I wouldn't be surprised if you had to routinely give the men little blue pills and the women something similar to force a physical response in order to get any kind of mating accomplished."

He was silent.

"Come on, Duran. You know I'll find out sooner or later. Save us both the headache."

"We were unable to . . . force . . . actual matings between your people without medical intervention," he said finally.

"There's a whole lot of bad in that sentence," she observed without visible emotion.

Duran was silent.

"So . . . he got a little blue pill or something like it. And what did she get? A female response in a human mating is a lot more complex than a male's, especially when she's confronted by a stranger, and even more when the goal is a pregnancy. A lot more has to go on in the female mind and emotions before the body is willing and accepting. Maybe because we're the ones who take all the risks, the ones who carry and bear the offspring. We have a biological imperative to choose our mates carefully."

He was silent.

"Rape?" she said coldly.

"No physical force," he said after several very long beats of frosty silence.

"No *physical* force. But there were a lot of social restraints placed on women back when your people started all this, restraints that too many of them would have been raised to obey. Good girls need a wedding ring first. And it wasn't part of the plan to marry couples, at least not unless and until you knew a mating would be . . . successful . . . for your purposes.

"That being the case, something was surely needed to induce compliance if not willingness, especially in the women. So you did what was necessary. The men were easy. Easy to manipulate, easy to arouse or, if not, certainly easy to drug, and I'm sure you made sure most never knew they'd sired offspring. But the women . . . That took more than a little blue pill. That took something that was more than a temporary fix. Because it wasn't just about sex with the women, a few minutes of mindless physical pleasure. They had to be willing to get pregnant. To carry to term. To give birth."

"Murphy—"

"I'm not really guessing."

"Yes. I know."

"I want confirmation, Duran."

"Why?"

"I want to know how much damage was done."

He was silent.

Murphy nodded. "The women were a lot more trouble. So you fucked up their minds to make them willing for at least nine months," Murphy said. "Some kind of psychological or physical tinkering with their minds, their brains. A flood of synthetic hormones at best. More likely something a lot more drastic. Because whatever you did turned them into happy walking baby factories. Compliant, even perhaps eager. Stepford mamas. You do understand that term?"

"I'm familiar with it. Stepford women: mindless robots intended to replace living women."

"Right. Fictional, or so we'd always believed. And naturally programmed with all those lovely male ideas of . . . perfect womanhood."

"We did not intend to alter their personalities," Duran said.

"Really? But whatever you used, whatever you did, to make them willing, well . . . it did alter their personalities. Maybe erased their personalities. Even more, it lasted longer than you'd bargained for, didn't it, Duran? It lasted indefinitely. Perhaps even permanently."

"There are always unintended consequences," he said evenly. "We've discussed such things before." He got the distinct impression that Murphy was controlling what he knew was a formidable temper.

He was not surprised.

He was very wary.

"Stepford mamas who loved getting pregnant, being pregnant, who followed all the habits and rules to keep themselves healthy, who loved their babies—until they were born. Then the moms forgot the whole experience, as if it had never happened, focused entirely on the next man, the next mating, the next pregnancy. Their own bodies and minds demanded that. You had created in them a biological drive to mate and give birth—but not to love and nurture their young. More unintended consequences?"

He nodded, silent.

"Yeah. But that wasn't all, I think. After those first . . . manufactured . . . psychic babies they bore, after whatever it was you did to make them so happy to breed for you, none of your Stepford mamas were psychic anymore," she said softly.

That did surprise him. And he wasn't sure whether she was guessing—or whether she or one of their other psychics had gotten past the shadows and close enough to know for certain. Or even if they could know for certain.

"No. They weren't. Most read as psychic, but seem . . . unaware. Unable to tap into and use those abilities."

"No matter how strong they were before."

"No matter."

"Things like that happen when you fuck with Mother Nature," Murphy said, her voice almost a growl. "It's all about those unintended consequences."

Duran knew he was standing on very uncertain, potentially deadly ground. He still didn't have to see it to know her gun pointed at him unwaveringly. He could easily imagine her finger on the trigger, curled and tense, waiting. And not for the first time, he wondered if he was out of his mind for having developed this relationship with this woman.

"Still, because of whatever it was you'd done to the women, and perhaps even to the men, the Stepford mamas *were* able to bear psychic babies for you. I mean, the abilities were still in them, just useless to them. Except to pass on to the next generation."

"Yes," Duran said.

"So for any other use, you lose a born psychic female when you turn her into a breeder. That's her only value to you after that." She drew a breath and let it out slowly. "And not only is no bond possible between her and the mate you choose for her, no bond possible between her and the child she bears, but the person she was, the individual she was, no longer exists. And, really, if you're honest you'll admit it was so much easier to live with your little experiment once you saw the permanent changes. I mean, once that happened, you had to see the benefits. They were all yours, and all they wanted was to make babies."

"Murphy—"

"Their lives mattered only in terms of . . . function. Because any offspring they bore was considered more important to your cause. And that was fine with you. No matter what it took to turn them into willing and happy breeders. No matter what it took to disintegrate the original personalities. Because you didn't hesitate to break them, Duran, did you? Even after you knew you were doing it. Didn't hesitate to destroy the people they had been. Not your breeders, your Stepford moms."

---

Sarah Mackenzie came into the huge living space that was the central hub of their condo in more ways than one, finding her husband immediately where he sat at his big desk, the complex technology surrounding him so advanced that top government IT people would have stared in fascination.

Probably drooling.

Not being an IT person of any kind, and quite familiar with Tucker's skills, Sarah said only, "It isn't even dawn."

"Did I wake you, love? I'm sorry."

"No, something else woke me." She was already

dressed in jeans and a pale sweater, and came to sit casually on one of the few uncluttered areas of the desk so she could face her husband. "The same thing that woke you."

"A nightmare," Tucker said.

"I wish it were only that. I really do," she said softly.

He leaned back in his chair and frowned just a little. "All I got were bits and pieces, just enough to know about the fire. More the fact, the knowledge of what happened than anything else. But it doesn't make sense, not what I got. Burning one of the shadow breeding houses once it's closed down I understand; it's a fairly decent way of getting rid of any evidence, especially if they can make it look like an accident, faulty wiring, a gas explosion, something like that. Which I imagine they can do."

Sarah nodded. "And probably have done before now. But . . . that house hadn't been closed down. There were people in that house, Tucker."

"I had a sense, more of a worry, but . . . are you sure?"

"As sure as I can be with knowledge that came out of the blue, not a vision but just . . . knowledge. Nothing I went looking for. I didn't hear anything or feel anything, and I didn't have a dream or a nightmare beyond what you saw and felt. A fire. Flames consuming a house. A shadow breeding house. But I know that house wasn't empty. I know lives were destroyed."

"The crossroads?" he said after a moment, using the term Sarah had coined for what Tucker and others believed was a sort of universal consciousness surrounding the earth, the knowledge and experiences of every soul who had ever lived, alive as energy that could never be destroyed. So no knowledge, no experience, no history was ever lost. Nothing was lost, ever.

Electrical impulses from countless minds, preserved forever, or as near to forever as humans could hope for.

And, even more, a place where past, present, and future existed as well—a fact about which Tucker's genius brain was still busy, on some level, theorizing and considering.

But whatever it was and however it existed, they knew it was real. And to their knowledge, among all the psychics on their side, only Sarah had been able to tap into that virtually at will. And occasionally without trying.

"Were you there?" Tucker asked.

"I think so. I think it was the crossroads. Just that dim dream at first, what I think you dreamed too. A house in flames, a shadow house. It was disturbing, but it faded, and I was still asleep."

"I know. It's why I left you and came out here. You seemed to slip from the nightmare back into peaceful sleep. That was what I felt, at least."

Sarah nodded. "And true. That was what happened. But then something inside told me I needed to know . . . more. I didn't even wake up. I just reached out, the way I have before."

"I didn't sense that," Tucker said.

She smiled in faint apology, knowing he'd understand. "It seems to close the door between us, when I do that. Or nearly. Not something I do deliberately."

Tucker nodded, neither offended nor hurt. They had been bonded, connected, the two of them, long enough now to know that certain realities existed and defined that connection, beyond anything they controlled.

"What did you get at the crossroads?" he asked.

"At first just a clearer image of the fire. It was awful in

my mind then. More real. I knew it wasn't just a nightmare. I could see it, and hear it, and smell it. And I wondered what was being destroyed, because it had to be more than just the house. I wondered. And then I knew."

He leaned forward suddenly and reached for both her hands, holding them gently. "What else?"

She wore a faint, troubled frown. "You know. You guessed without even needing the crossroads. It's why you really came out here. Why you pulled yourself out of that dim and distant nightmare and came out here to search for facts. Psychics were lost in that fire. Powerful ones, I think. I couldn't get a fix on who or even where, exactly, but . . . psychics died."

"You were able to confirm it was a shadow breeding house."

Sarah nodded.

"Psychic babies died?" His voice was steady.

"Yes. All before they ever took a breath."

# FIVE

"*Was* it deliberate? Arson?"

"I want to say no. I really do. But . . . I think the fire was set deliberately. And the best I can say about that is that I got the strongest feeling that it wasn't sanctioned."

"Not sanctioned. One of theirs went rogue?"

"It's happened before."

He nodded slowly. "Yeah. But . . . why do this? The one thing we know absolutely and for certain is that they're after psychics. We may not know why, but we know they want or need psychics badly enough to employ every method we've thought of and a few I don't even want to imagine to get their hands on psychics. To take them, turn them somehow, even create them."

"We know some of those taken are . . . damaged," Sarah said. "Maybe killed. Probably killed."

"Yes . . . but I don't believe the aim is the death of psychics; that doesn't make sense to me. The opposite, if anything. They want more psychics. What we've found so far of their breeding operation goes back decades, and it's a huge, costly operation. Costly in money, in time, in manpower. In resources to produce whatever paperwork is necessary. In bribes so no awkward questions are asked.

"And it's produced psychics, plenty of them, even if some like Tasha escape somehow before they can be controlled and used for whatever the ultimate purpose is. That must have been a problem they had to solve along the way, and early on given our resistance to being . . . enslaved in any way.

"By now, they've probably developed a way to have some sort of psychological hold over the psychics they breed. That would explain the Stepford mom Bishop and Miranda found returned to her home, as well as those we've gotten people close enough to see. Some way of controlling them had to be a goal, and one they've reached in the decades since Tasha and any other of her generation were born. I'm betting they can control all the women now. So why destroy one of their breeding operations, destroy some of the very psychics they're trying so hard to produce?"

"I don't know," Sarah said.

---

"You broke your breeders," Murphy repeated. "But not just their will. Not just their resistance. You took away everything that made them unique. Everything that made them who they were. Their minds, their personalities. You broke them all."

It wasn't a question, but Duran nodded silently. "Unintended consequences. Believe it or not, Murphy, I would have chosen *not* to break them."

"Well, your operation continued long after you must have known about that particular . . . unintended consequence. So I guess it was an acceptable consequence to you. Or your superiors."

"I would have chosen not to break them," he repeated.

"But your superiors didn't give a damn, huh?"

"They wanted results. They didn't particularly care how those results were achieved."

"Or the human cost."

It hadn't been a question, but Duran answered anyway. "Or the human cost."

Murphy nodded slowly. "Because the babies read as stronger than either parent, didn't they, Duran? Maybe stronger than both parents combined. Like Tasha, filled with amazing potential and far more control over their abilities than you'd dared to hope for."

"A high percentage. Not all."

"Uh-huh. I don't think I want to ask what happens to the babies born healthy—but not psychic."

Duran stiffened. "They are adopted by nonpsychic couples who deeply desire children but have been unable to conceive."

"Offended, Duran?"

He decided not to answer that.

"And then there was Tasha. A born psychic, perfectly healthy, raised by adoptive parents to have a . . . normal life. But you still needed to find out—and notice I'm giving you credit for this—whether you could produce psychics the good old-fashioned way. Up to a point, at least. You still had traits you wanted to pass on to the next generation, assuming one could be produced."

When the silence had lengthened, he finally said, "Of course."

"Yeah. So you matched them up, by whatever criteria suited your purposes. And the one certain match we know about was supposed to be Eliot Wolfe, the man who murdered Elizabeth Lyon *Brodie* a decade ago, after he stalked her and terrified her."

"He was clumsy," Duran said.

"That's what you called it?"

"Unforgivably clumsy."

Murphy let out a quiet, humorless laugh. "But not so clumsy that he had to be destroyed when he ruined that part of the plan, when he did worse than just cause her to run, when he chased her down and murdered her. Because other plans had already been made, hadn't they, Duran? Plans for the political future of Eliot Wolfe couldn't be set aside so *easily.* That was a major piece of the Big Picture. Such a major piece, in fact, that even murdering Elizabeth Lyon *Brodie* was not a mistake bad enough to derail those plans, to knock Wolfe off that ladder."

Duran drew a breath and let it out slowly. "The decision concerning Wolfe's future was made at the highest level. But that hardly need concern you now. He's dead. That plan was destroyed."

"Well, that piece of the plan was, anyway." She smiled at him with all her teeth. "But it was still something I had to consider, that part of your plans. Something I had to wonder about. I mean, since Wolfe was allowed to live even after he was so . . . clumsy . . . with the first mate you chose for him.

"He had to be a part of your long-range plans, your Big Picture. Because so much was invested in Wolfe even after he fucked up with Elizabeth. And, clearly, in the Big Picture, Wolfe had to have a mate. So you intended to match him with Tasha Solomon. Tasha Solomon, who had learned all on her own to hide what she could do, to control it so well. That was very impressive. And, to your plans, to the Big Picture, very important. Because Wolfe was all set to live a highly public life. A life in which exposing psychic abilities before you were ready would have been a very bad thing."

Duran said nothing.

But Murphy nodded as if he had. "A very bad thing. So Tasha fit right in with your plans. She was important. And you were going to be more subtle this time. Introduce them casually, see if a spark happened naturally.

"In the meantime, she was always watched. Her whole life, you had people keeping an eye on her. Friends. Maybe family members. Neighbors and teachers. Probably others. All watching over Tasha Solomon, at first simply because she was a rare survivor of your initial breeding program, for her potential, and then later because she was destined to be Wolfe's mate. And you didn't want any more mistakes."

Duran was still not sure how Murphy knew that, whether her people had somehow discovered it or whether Tasha Solomon had turned out to be an even stronger psychic than he had realized.

What if she could read them?

What if she could *see* the truth of what was there?

If she could see, and understand . . . if she had some ability unknown before now that enabled her to recognize his people *and* his tools . . . then Murphy and her people had an ace that made him feel queasy.

His people could be killed, after all. None of them were bulletproof.

If Tasha Solomon—and perhaps others—could see or sense more than the shadows that frightened them, the shadows that triggered an instinctive aversion that kept them at a distance . . . If any in the resistance were able to see the truth, then Duran's people were vulnerable in ways they had never before been vulnerable.

And his superiors, if they knew that . . .

---

Annabel Blake was still adjusting to her new life. Adjusting to having warm clothes that were not hand-me-downs, and hot showers or long baths in her own private bathroom where no one pounded on the door or yelled for her to hurry, and there were soft, clean towels to wrap herself in afterward. She was adjusting to voices that were quiet and not angry, adjusting to the dawning certainty that no one was going to slap her or pinch her or knock her down.

She was adjusting to having more than enough very good things to eat.

Even snacks!

She had a wonderfully comfortable bed, a lovely bedroom filled with pretty things all to herself, like nice clothes that fit and a real comfortable reading chair. She had lots and lots of books on shelves, and a TV if she wanted to watch that. And she'd have her own laptop, Tucker had told her, as soon as he could figure out how to protect one from being shorted-out when she touched it, and he hadn't even gotten mad when that happened, but only laughed and said that Sarah couldn't touch them either.

That was the most amazing thing to Annabel, that now there were adults who treated her with kindness and affection. Adults who never yelled at her.

She wasn't entirely convinced just yet that it was all real, if she was perfectly honest with herself.

And she tried always to be that.

Because it was important to be honest, no one had ever had to tell her that. Just like no one had ever had to tell her to keep her honesty to herself in the succession of miserable foster homes in which she'd lived.

But, now . . . now she could be honest out loud. Sarah had told her so, her eyes gentle and smile kind. Annabel could be honest out loud, and talk about whatever was on her mind, and nobody would laugh at her or call her stupid or hit her or lock her in a closet or make her go without supper or punish her in any way at all.

It seemed more like a dream than reality, or at least the reality she had known for almost all the ten years and seven months of her life so far. Maybe that was why she was still unable to sleep through the night, waking often with a jerk to find herself listening unconsciously for a heavy footstep, or braced for an angry hand to yank her out of bed for some puzzling or imagined offense.

*You know that won't happen anymore.*

*Do I? Can I be sure?*

*Yes. You can. Here. With these people. They have already come to love you.*

Annabel lay in her warm, comfortable bed, the faint but comforting night-light Sarah had helped her pick out allowing just enough gentle light to make her feel . . . safe. Make her feel nothing could creep up on her in darkness and hurt her.

But she was still adjusting to her new life, and she wasn't at all sure she really believed in her luck.

*What if it's all a dream?*

*You know it isn't.*

*They can't love me. Sarah and Tucker. They're kind, so nice and kind, but I'm thin and scrawny and always a lot of trouble. I eat too much, and can't do chores properly, and grow out of my clothes too fast, and I spend too much time with my nose in a book—*

*Not here. None of that is true here. You know they don't believe you are anything but a gift. To them, you are precious. And you always will be.*

*Because I know things? Because I can do things?*

*That is not why you're precious to them. You're precious to them because you have a glowing spirit and an exceptionally kind heart. Because you're good. And because you were intended to do great things one day.*

*Great things?*

*You'll help them. We'll help them.*

Annabel considered that. Warm and comfortable in her bed, where nothing had ever hurt or scared her. She lay there and gently stroked soft black fur, and thought for a while.

*This time, I didn't wake up because I was afraid.*

*I know.*

*I woke because I was sad.*

*Yes.*

*Why did someone want to hurt them like that? The babies?*

*There are bad people in the world, Annabel. You know that better than most.*

*I know. But the babies weren't big enough to cause trou-*

*ble for anybody, were they? They didn't have chores they didn't do right, or talk back, or eat too much. There was no reason even for a mean person to hurt them like that.*

*You don't worry about that now. You need to sleep. You need to rest, Annabel. To grow stronger. To not be cold or hungry or afraid anymore, because you're safe now. Safe with them. And you always will be. That's important. For both of us.*

She trusted him implicitly, because he had saved her. He had brought her here, where she was safe and warm and maybe even loved.

Smiling, Annabel snuggled a bit deeper into her soft bed, and felt Pendragon snuggle with her.

---

Murphy, seemingly unaware of having dealt quite such an unwelcome shock, was going on calmly, "But that plan was derailed too, wasn't it? Only this time it wasn't because Wolfe made a mistake. This time it was us. This time it was Brodie. And it was no mistake. Once Tasha met Brodie, once he pulled her out of that little maze test of yours, a connection formed between them. They began to bond."

They had not really talked much about Duran's "maze test," he and Murphy. All she knew—all he *thought* she knew—was that it was a test, a kind of artificial psychic construct placed temporarily in the mind of a psychic or someone he or she was reading, planted deep below the subconscious. To the psychic, it looked and felt like a maze, a dark and confusing one. The larger the maze, the more "connections" the psychic had made with others through their abilities.

Tasha Solomon's maze had been, according to Astrid, the psychic Duran often used, huge. Which indicated extraordinarily powerful psychic abilities and *possibly* offered some indication of how many minds she had touched with those abilities.

Duran didn't know if Murphy knew that. He believed she knew only that the construct was a fairly benign test to find out if a psychic could be brought willingly over to Duran's side. At least from him that's all she knew. He had no idea what Tasha Solomon might have told her.

"We've already discussed that as well," Duran said mildly.

"Yeah, we have. And we both know that the maze is only one of your little tests. That you and your people are constantly devising new ways of testing the limits of psychic abilities. And trying to match psychics at more than the physical level, so they may be closer to forming a connection to each other. That you're, perhaps, even curious to find out if psychics on your side *can* form a permanent, unbreakable bond with another. *I'm* curious, Duran. Have you tried your little maze test with them? With psychics who've been on your side for a while—willingly or somehow forced to be?"

He didn't allow her scorn to disturb him. Much. "And why would I do that, Murphy?"

"Well, the more highly developed psychics on our side, whether born or triggered, seem to form those deep and permanent bonds with someone else more quickly when they're tested in some way. Faced with unexpected and unusual external—and internal—pressures. This whole war of ours tests them, of course. And some have responded to those external forces by bonding with a partner. But at least with Tasha Solomon and Brodie, it seemed to happen more quickly in that maze of yours."

"That was unusual," he said immediately.

Murphy smiled. "Was it? Yeah, maybe. You dropped her into that maze so quickly after we'd made contact. I told you that. I told you it was too soon to test her when it was still so new to her, when she was spooked and unsettled.

"But maybe I was wrong about that. So hard to find absolutes in this world of ours, isn't it? I mean, Brodie wasn't even psychic. Never read as psychic. Not even a latent. And yet . . . something happened between him and Tasha at their very first meeting. Maybe it wouldn't have without the maze. Maybe. But . . . a connection was made. An unexpected bond formed between two people."

"Yes," he admitted.

"Well, given that, and given the experience Tasha described, your maze seems at least a possible way of deliberately forming a connection between two psychics. What we've been talking about. Those very special bonds that seem to bump those two psychics right off the top of your Most Wanted list."

"I never said that."

"You didn't have to. We've found lots of psychics over the years, especially the last ten or so. Even bonded psychics. We hid them, or told them what to do to protect themselves. And, of course, we've kept in touch, made sure they remained all right. So we have a lot more data.

"And we have some very bright people to really study that data. Like Tucker Mackenzie. Someone who shares that very special bond with his *very* psychic wife. He was curious. And, of course, concerned for her safety. Even though they've taken all possible precautions, just as others who go public have done. You know all about those."

Duran inclined his head slightly.

"But I was wondering something else. I mean, you used Astrid with Tasha. You use her a lot in your maze tests. With male and female psychics. And she hasn't connected with any of them, has she? Never formed a lasting bond. Nothing more permanent than a few scatterings of . . . bread crumbs."

Duran was silent.

Murphy eyed him for a moment, then smiled again. "You've already tested your psychics. All of them, Astrid included. How many times do you send them down into that maze before admitting defeat?"

"You're so sure the attempts fail?"

"Why, yes. I am sure. Because you still have no pair of bonded psychics."

"Perhaps Tasha Solomon and Brodie are simply unique."

"Oh, I believe they are. Though not quite in the same way I think you'd like to believe they are. And I also believe you've left no stone unturned in your quest to create bonded psychics on your side. Recently, at any rate."

"It was not an original goal," Duran said finally. He wondered if she kept circling back to that because it was more important even than he had realized—or because she wanted him to *believe* it was more important.

Either was possible with Murphy.

"Another unintended consequence, I would say. I doubt you had any idea that by tracking down psychics, driving so many out of hiding so they instinctively reached out to others of our kind for help and support, your own plan caused them to often make connections with each other. Connections, bonds, that your psychics simply can't forge. Even in your maze."

For the first time, Duran wondered if it had, indeed, been the fault of his people, the fault of their plan, that at least a handful of psychics, driven out of hiding or otherwise forced to reach out to others, had discovered a seemingly foolproof way to put themselves beyond their reach. And if that were so . . . then the longer this went on, the more psychics on Murphy's side might pair, might bond—and become far stronger together than they could ever have been separately.

If it was even possible that his maze test aided them in that, even some of them, even just Tasha Solomon and Brodie . . .

He made a mental note to tell Astrid and the others to discontinue the maze tests immediately.

Murphy laughed softly. "Unintended consequences. There are more than . . . just a handful . . . of bonded psychics on our side, Duran. Quite a lot more."

Duran knew she couldn't read him. He *knew* that. But, somehow, Murphy found a way to drag his thoughts out of hiding, even while standing in the darkness. And that was a very disconcerting realization.

She was smiling. "The human will to live, to survive, is a remarkable thing, Duran. We don't like feeling trapped. We don't like feeling hunted. It drives us, quite often, to band together. To pool our resources. Marshal our strengths, our defenses. It drives us to achieve things we never would have believed possible."

"It's an admirable characteristic," he said finally.

"But frustrating for you."

"Perhaps."

"Oh, I imagine it is. And more. Our will to fight for our freedom is just as strong. Which is why your torture techniques have met with so little success."

She said it so calmly that for an instant Duran missed the import of just what she had said. *Of course they know we've been taking psychics alive even when bodies are left behind to be falsely identified; they knew that, she knew that, long ago. But if they know what happens to some of them then, if they have even an idea . . .*

Did they know how many had been lost?

Did they know how few of those unwillingly brought over to his side even survived?

# SIX

In the same calm, almost offhand tone, she said, "Have your tamed and traitor psychics told you, Duran? Have they told you that the ones you take and torture, the terrified ones, cry out to us? When they're being examined? When they're being hurt in ways no living being should ever be hurt? That they're able to reach us, reach our strongest psychics and sometimes even our weaker ones for quite some time? That we hear their screams? That some of us even feel their pain?"

He waited, silent.

"I imagine not. I imagine your tamed and traitor psychics, like Astrid, would really prefer that you not know how your captured and tortured psychics cry out for our help. How so many of them have even reached beyond those of us who knew about them to touch other minds and beg them for help as well. To draw even more allies to our cause. And in calling out, to us and to others, how much information they've managed to send us."

"You would have moved against us," he said, almost automatically.

"Duran. We *have* been moving against you. It may have taken us a few years to recognize the threat, to play catch-up, but once we know what we're up against, we make our plans. And execute them. We get busy protecting our people, and our freedoms. Forge new alliances. Gather all our resources and find new assets. And we make our own long-range plans. We step back and take a good, long look at the Big Picture."

"And what do you see?" He had to ask.

"What's there. Why do you think I agreed to this little pseudo-truce with you?"

"Because we have a common enemy," he said.

"Do we? Well, once upon a time, I thought you might be right about that common enemy. That was reason enough, I believed, to work under a flag of truce from time to time. To exchange information—even though I knew most of that information would always tip to your advantage rather than mine."

"Murphy—"

"Now I'm not so sure about that common enemy. See, I'm beginning to believe that *we* would have been just fine, Duran. If your people had left us alone. If, even, you had just settled down here, integrated peacefully.

"Because psychics weren't so common here before you came and started meddling. Psychics weren't a threat to anybody. Like the odd Einstein or Mozart, psychics came along infrequently. One in a million, even less than that, and a high percentage of those never even knew what they might have been capable of, what was locked inside them. Most passed unnoticed, their potential never realized, their latent abilities unknown even to themselves. Oh, maybe we would naturally have evolved as a race of psychics, given enough time. That has been one of the theories advanced. But even if it happened at all, that wasn't going to happen for millennia."

"You can't be certain," he said.

"Can I not? We've been reaching out to each other, we psychics, remember? Especially these last few years. Sharing information. And it's been . . . a bit of a revelation, what some of us knew."

He was silent.

Murphy smiled, an odd, gentle smile. "We know when you came here. Your people. The first generation. You weren't the first to visit us from another part of the galaxy; that's been happening, if you ask some people, for thousands of years, possibly lots of races. But your people were the first to stay here in any kind of numbers. The first to truly settle here. The first coming. Such an intelligent way to handle an invasion. So quietly and insidiously, causing hardly a ripple in our society. At first. Settling in. Studying us. Even examining us, and crudely at times, especially in those early years."

"Your people have . . . vivid imaginations," Duran said.

"Yes, we do. And you learned to take advantage of that. You learned to take advantage of the very human tendency to create . . . wild conspiracy theories most of us never took seriously. But it was an excellent cover for you, for many of your actions. So you could learn about us. So you could discover, in due course, that some experiments, some combinations just . . . don't work. That there would be no easy path for your people. That reaching your goal was going to prove costly in many ways."

"Murphy—"

"And that whatever progress you *could* accomplish was going to take time. A lot of time. A lot of time and a lot of trouble—and a lot of failures along the way, bad ones. Sometimes the kind of failures you couldn't keep quiet. Failures that caused your superiors to push you even harder for results."

"That is my job," he said.

"And has been most of your life. Something you dedicated yourself to, body and . . . soul."

That last word was not . . . quite . . . a question. But it was a hint that Murphy, at least, questioned the existence of Duran's soul.

Which bothered him a lot more than he wanted to admit.

"As you've dedicated your life," he said. "To your cause."

"Yeah, but my cause is protecting the often most vulnerable of my people from deadly predators."

He knew he stiffened, hard as he tried not to. "And mine is to save my people from extinction," he said coldly.

---

She looked at the long and, perhaps, still-growing list of people who had called so early on this slightly chilly June morning, people who had used the contact number given to them, sometimes long ago and sometimes for the first time.

Driven to call. To report. To ask what they could do.

Because of the babies. Because they had known what had happened. They had felt it.

"Bonded pairs," she murmured, wondering if the murder of babies, deliberate or not, had been a catalyst the other side could never, surely, have imagined. Wondering if, out of the brutal crucible of that fire, something extraordinary had been formed.

A youngish man came into the room just then, his thin face serious, and stood before the old table she was using as a desk. "It's confirmed, Madam Secretary," he said quietly. "The Bishops are on their way straight back to Charleston, since they'll report to Murphy. Our sources say a private jet, unmarked."

"And in Charlotte?"

"First responders are there. House fire, the structure totally engulfed. They won't be getting in for a while. No sign anyone escaped. We can know with a high degree of certainty that none of the women made it out alive."

"I see. Jordan?"

"Yes, Madam Secretary?"

Mildly, she said, "I realize you intend only respect, and that old habits are hard to break. But we have discussed this. That title belongs in the past."

"Yes, M— Yes, ma'am."

"Thank you," she said.

He nodded and retreated to another room.

She sat there awhile longer, thinking. Glanced at the clock on the wall that reminded her it was still before dawn. Murphy was likely still out, because she'd had things to do, as usual, in the dark watches of the night. Seeds to plant, if possible.

After a moment, she used the landline on her desk,

the very special landline that would call another very special phone Murphy routinely checked every four hours.

The phone on the other end rang twice, then there was a tone, but no identification or invitation to leave a message.

She left a message, brief and to the point.

"Murphy, call in when you get this."

---

Murphy shook her head, her gaze remaining fixed on the still, silent man standing before her.

"To save your people from extinction. But is that what you're doing, Duran? I mean, I'm sure it started out that way. A long . . . long time ago. But all that time has passed. And you're so far away now. From home. You've been so far away for such a long time. So I have to wonder. I have to wonder if you've asked yourself what's been happening during all the time that's passed back home, so far away, where there was surely an enemy. Once upon a time. But maybe not now. Maybe you're too far from . . . home . . . to even know that enemy came and went while some of your people left to find help. Have you considered that, Duran?"

There was a long, long silence.

"Yes," he replied finally, "I have."

Softly, she said, "Then you must have wondered if there's even anything to go back to by now. After all this time. More time passing there than here, if I understand the theory of relativity and the . . . difficulties . . . inherent in faster-than-light travel. Maybe an awful lot of time has passed. Back home. Maybe you'd better think about that a bit harder. Maybe you'd better consider . . . all the possible unintended consequences for your own people."

She didn't say good night or good-bye, she simply faded back into the darkness, and within seconds he knew she was gone.

*Unintended consequences.*

There had been more than Duran liked to think about, on virtually every level of this, and from the very beginning. Failed experiments. Assumptions that had turned out to be incorrect. *Unintended consequences.* Because Murphy was right about the human need to be free, the unwillingness to merely serve, to be subjugated.

Oh, some could be, certainly. Psychopaths and sociopaths like Astrid, who had made her choice quickly and easily because it was something new in her life, an adventure. An adventure in which she could play an important, pivotal role. A role that gave her power, at least over many others.

She liked that.

There had been a few like her. And others who, for their own reasons, had chosen to, in essence, betray their own people. And in so doing also revealed an inherent weakness in their characters.

In the beginning, there had been a few.

But not enough, not nearly enough, and all of them flawed. Not enough to serve the purpose. Especially once they had discovered what Murphy and her people must have, by now, understood as obvious. Murphy had said it.

That some combinations simply don't work. That nature fights back. That biology fights back.

How many of his own people had died in those early years? How many of Murphy's?

How many were still dying even now, for what might well be reasons that no longer even mattered? Perhaps even no longer existed? And even if the reasons still existed, still mattered, what of the cost?

Had the cost been, already, too high? Or, as Murphy had suggested, had so much been spent on . . . a useless attempt to stop what had already happened?

Had he spent his life, his entire life, in service to a cause that no longer mattered? No longer even existed?

Truth? A kind of truth? Or simply the stalling tactic she'd needed to get her people into place, set up the necessary safe houses or clinics or other outwardly normal places. Places where young women, their minds already irreparably damaged and their bodies changed in ways those doctors and scientists on Murphy's side might be able, now, to understand and even to remedy, waited to give birth to an entirely new generation of born psychics.

Born with the potential of . . . extraordinary abilities, or such was Duran's hope.

Murphy had had time enough to at least have a plan in place, because Duran's people had had time enough. Barely. Much of their previous network of homes and clinics and other facilities had been compromised or could be, so the decision had been made at the highest levels to move those valuable assets, mothers and babies born and still in the womb, to other, safer locations.

A move scheduled to begin in the next few weeks, because finding and readying suitable places and suitable caretakers had taken time even for someone with Duran's resources.

He had no idea how far Murphy's side had progressed with plans of their own that had to involve relocating pregnant women and their unborn babies. Plans to keep them safe and healthy.

He was not even certain if Murphy and her people had truly grasped the realities of any planned rescue. Damaged women and unborn children those women would simply turn away from after birth. Infant orphans in every real sense, psychic orphans who would, to say the least, require specialized care.

For a long, long time. Perhaps for life.

For the first time Duran wondered if the resistance could have, by now, discovered the true scope of the eugenics operation. Was that even possible?

It had taken Duran and his people decades to set up the houses and clinics, each with a cover story, each intended to be in use for only a few years before closing down. Decades to get that operation up and running smoothly. They had been careful. Very, very careful. And for the past three decades and more, the operation had remained a secret from the resistance.

Until Tasha Solomon had been located by them. Until Duran's superiors had begun pushing, hard, for faster progress. Until he had followed the instinct of the moment and pointed Murphy in a direction she might never have explored on her own.

But that had been only weeks ago.

Even with the technical and researching genius of someone like Tucker Mackenzie, *could* they have found all the houses and clinics currently operating?

All of them?

---

Tasha stirred slightly, raising herself on an elbow to look down at Brodie. He opened his eyes and smiled faintly, startling her just a bit because she had so rarely seen him smile. And never like that.

"John—"

"No regrets, Tasha."

"No. I mean, not from me. I just don't want you to feel—"

What he felt flowed through their connection, all the warmth and the certainty and the love. And was met instantly with the depth and certainty of her own feelings.

Tasha smiled, and made herself even more comfortable at his side, pillowing her head on his shoulder. "You were right. This connection of ours is very handy and saves a lot of time. And words. I thought I'd have to argue."

"It does save time. But there was never anything for you to argue against, Tasha."

"You've always wanted to stay as closed up as you could, we both know that. To not share yourself with anyone else, unless a psychic needed to read you, trust you. And even then, you had to force yourself to invite that kind of pain. And these last weeks, you've always been so . . . so adamant about being my Guardian. I thought that was all you wanted to be."

"Now you know better."

She did, and knowing that was a warmth and strength she wanted to wrap herself in. And just be. Be only a man and a woman who had found something neither had ever known before. A man and a woman, connected now, with the time and leisure to explore that connection, to become familiar with it and with each other.

That was what she wanted.

But there was a world outside. A war outside.

Tasha was aware that their connection was there, both sides open but not as widely as they had been even moments before. Instead, it was . . . as though doors had been quietly pushed almost closed.

"For privacy?" she asked, knowing he'd understand.

"Partly. Because even though we never have to be alone in our own minds again, sometimes solitude is necessary. And because it's new. Because we'll have to find a balance that suits us. That fits us. Because we don't yet know what we're capable of."

"You know you're psychic now. That you've been psychic ever since Duran was testing me with that maze thing and you pulled me out."

He was silent for a moment, then said, "I know I'm psychic with you. That I can know your thoughts and emotions through our connection. I don't know if it goes beyond that."

"I do. There's something else in you, John. It isn't telepathy or empathy, not what you feel through our connection. It's something else. Something so deep inside you that you can't see it yet. Can't use yet. Something that hasn't been . . . triggered."

"Do you know what it is?" he asked almost idly, one arm holding her against his side, the fingers of his other hand stroking the arm she had flung across his chest.

"I caught a glimpse when I was in that maze. But . . . just a glimpse. Almost more a sense. A sense of something really powerful."

"Negative? There's been a lot of negative in my life the last ten years or so."

"I'm not sure," she said slowly. "There was a lot going on just then, but whatever it was it didn't scare me. Didn't make me feel wary or frightened. If anything, it . . . gave me the sense of something strong and sure, something certain I could hold on to if I needed to. I don't see how that could be anything negative."

"Then we'll wait and see," Brodie said wryly. "If I've learned anything from you psychics over the years it's that it's never wise to force a psychic ability."

"It'll come when you need it. Be triggered when you need it."

"Or when I least need it and probably don't want it," he said with a low laugh. "We both know there's a downside to every single psychic ability we're aware of."

"True enough. So we wait and see."

"We wait and see."

Tasha wanted to hold on to this warmth and comfort as long as she could. Wanted to shut out the world and all the dangers there. Wanted to forget, if only for this peaceful time with him, that there was a war—and they were both soldiers.

Wanted to forget what had awakened her in such agony. It had brought him to her, and she could never regret that. But what had happened only hours ago . . .

Quietly, he said, "If you need to talk about it, it's okay, Tasha. We have to, sooner or later. And with the others as well. Some of them, at least."

It was the last thing she wanted to talk about, to even think about.

Not now. Later. They could talk about it later.

Couldn't they?

He hesitated, his reluctance to put her through any of this obvious, but said steadily, "When you woke up, it was because you'd heard the ones in the house screaming."

She nodded without lifting her head, wondering if the echoes of those awful sounds would ever not lurk somewhere in her mind. "The babies. Just the babies. I only heard them."

"None of the adults? Not the mothers or any of the caretakers?"

"No. Only the babies. All of them. The infants only days or weeks away from being born—and even the ones months away from being born. But no adults."

"How can you be sure? Because it was . . . wordless?"

"More than just wordless. I got the sense they didn't even have language, not yet, especially the ones barely into the third trimester. It was . . . primitive. Raw emotions. They felt threatened, then terrified. Helpless. They had power but no focus. No way to save themselves, even though they cried out for help."

Brodie frowned, not liking any of the thoughts flitting through his mind.

"You had no sense of when it started? Of how long the house had been burning, or what might have started the fire?"

"Who," she said instantly. "Who started the fire."

That was what he'd feared she would say.

"It was arson?"

Tasha lifted her head from its comfortable resting place on his shoulder and looked down at him, realization dawning on her face. "Yes. Someone set the fire. Someone deliberately destroyed those women and babies."

"How do you know?" he asked her quietly.

"Because . . . they knew. The babies. They knew someone intended to kill them." She frowned. "That's how the nightmare started. I mean, I didn't see them. I wasn't even sure who they were at first. What they were. I'd been dreaming some silly dream about being back in school and knowing I couldn't graduate because I'd somehow missed a final exam."

"Typical anxiety or panic dream," he noted.

"Yeah. I even remember knowing it was a dream and telling myself to snap out of it. Then I sort of drifted . . . and then I felt a sense of being threatened."

"You were frightened?"

"I . . . felt like I should be. Then everything just sort of faded around me, and . . . I was floating. But it was dark, and I couldn't see anything. Before I could figure that out, things shifted again, and I wasn't really floating anymore. It was still dark, and I felt like something was wrapped tightly around me, so I could barely move. But I wasn't afraid of that. That made me feel safe. And I heard a sound. Sort of a thumping. With a rhythm."

"Like a heartbeat," he suggested.

# SEVEN

Tasha drew a breath and let it out slowly. "Yeah. Yeah, like a heartbeat. Just one at first, then more than one, like echoes, because it wasn't the same rhythm. But I knew there was more than one. A lot more. And I was trying to listen past the heartbeats, because all of a sudden, I felt so threatened. I knew . . . there was danger. Close. I knew there was some*one* close. Someone bad. Someone who was afraid of me. Someone who wanted to hurt me, to . . . destroy me."

"You were feeling what the babies felt. Even before the fire started."

He didn't sound surprised, but Tasha was finding it a bit difficult to accept. "But . . . I didn't get the sense they heard anything to disturb them. Not a threatening voice or sound. Nothing to explain what they were feeling, not then, not at first. Everything was peaceful, and then . . . they were afraid. Some more than others. Some of them *knew* there was a threat close by. Others were just . . . afraid. Wordless and growing stronger."

"What about their mothers?"

"Sleeping," Tasha answered immediately, faintly surprised that she really had sensed anything about the mothers. "Not uneasy. Not afraid. Not . . . aware of any threat. Not even dreaming. Just sleeping."

"The babies knew that?"

"I think so. I don't think I would have picked it up any other way. I think . . . more than one of them tried to reach out to their mothers. It would have been natural for them to try, especially being psychic. But the ones who tried knew their mothers couldn't help them. Couldn't save them. Couldn't even hear them."

"Did they know who wanted to destroy them?"

Tasha shook her head slowly. "No sense of identity. No name. No words. No language. They felt . . . danger. They felt threat. And an enemy. An enemy who wanted to destroy them. Raw, primitive emotions, not words. If they knew who it was, they didn't have the ability to communicate that to anyone else. At least, not to me."

"Did *you* get any sense of who it was?"

"No. No, by the time—by the time I felt their absolute terror, heard their screams, the fire had engulfed the whole house. Whoever started it had to be long gone by then."

"What about the caretakers? We know there are caretakers, at least one nurse and usually two. Someone else at each place; Tucker says it is probably administrative, which makes sense in that sort of setup. All of them living in the house. Any daily help, anyone who came every morning to cook and clean, that sort of thing, didn't live on-site. But the nurses did. Whoever was in charge did. Were they gone, or do you think you just couldn't sense them for some reason?"

Tasha frowned, then shook her head. "I just don't know. I don't know how reliable my senses are when it comes to knowing how many people might have been there."

"Why?"

"Distance, maybe? Or just being blind and deaf to everything except the babies. It was . . . horrific, what was happening to them. Their terror and agony. Maybe that blocked anything else I might have sensed."

Brodie's arm tightened around her, but his voice remained quiet. "You couldn't help them. You were too far away."

"I wish that made me feel better," she murmured.

"You heard them," he said. "We might not have even known otherwise."

"The Bishops know."

"I'm betting they don't know as much as you do. They saw the fire, maybe they even picked up on the screams of the babies telepathically. But you know what they felt."

Tasha drew another breath, this one shaky. "Then I hope that makes a difference somehow. I hope it helps. It's . . . not something I ever want to go through again."

"I know."

There was, she realized then, a real comfort in *knowing* that he really did understand. Because he had felt her pain. And theirs. She let herself be comforted by that, knowing he was aware of how she was feeling.

"There will have to be an investigation, an official one," Brodie said. "It's the law. Though I have to believe

Duran has someone inside law enforcement to . . . shape the story he wants the media to have."

"Maybe Bishop can get someone inside for us," Tasha said after a moment.

"He's probably the only one we know who can. And if everything I've heard about him is true, he's already working on that angle. And quietly. I'm betting he and Miranda were gone by the time the fire trucks arrived."

"They hadn't planned to go into the house or stay any longer than necessary, and they wouldn't have changed the plan. They got there too late to do anything to help, I'm sure of that. But they must have seen."

"Then Bishop will already be working to get someone inside the investigation so we're able to get our hands on the report before Duran has time to replace it with his own version of what happened." He frowned again. "That could bring Bishop too far out into the open for my taste."

"With psychics taken by Duran's people calling out to Bishop in that last, desperate moment, and his own psychics involved in snatching those people, I doubt very much that Duran isn't totally aware of the Bishops."

"Aware is one thing and being certain they're actively working against him is something else."

"He must know, or at least suspect, how Bishop would react once he found out about this. That he wouldn't just stand by while psychics, any psychics, are being hurt. And that would go double, triple, for psychics he's been keeping tabs on for years who just vanish—especially when their last psychic scream of fear is his name." She shivered without being aware of it.

---

They had not raised Miranda's shield after the fire because neither of them had wanted to be alone after that, so she heard it as loudly as he did when the telepathic cry came through so strongly that it actually caused Bishop to jerk.

*Bishop!*

*Help me!*

*Don't let them get me . . . please . . . don't let them—*

And then it ended with chilling suddenness.

In the near-silence of the jet's cabin, Miranda looked at her husband, not needing the stark pallor of the scar twisting down his left cheek to tell her how upset he was.

"Do you know who?" she asked quietly. "I didn't get a sense of identity."

"Emma Garrick." His voice was beyond grim. "A telepath with an amazing amount of potential. But from everything we've learned, everything we've been told, I didn't think she'd be a target."

"She's a born psychic?"

"Yeah. But latent. Completely latent. I talked to her not three months ago, and nothing had changed."

"If she's latent—"

"Then the abduction itself must have triggered her abilities. Did they know it would? Is this something new—or just something nobody noticed until now?"

Miranda shook her head slightly, her gaze steady on his face. "We have to find her. Emma. Henry, Katie, the others. We have to find all of them. Even if Murphy and the rest don't believe they can be found, saved, we have to try."

"I know."

"There's more, isn't there? What is it, Noah?"

"Emma. She's . . . Miranda, Emma is only sixteen years old."

---

Brodie managed to get them both completely under the covers in a few economical movements, without once losing his comforting hold on her.

It was a warm cocoon with him in it, but even as she relaxed again, Tasha murmured, "We have to be up soon anyway. It's getting light outside. And the others . . . We need to tell Murphy at least, don't we? About the fire?"

"I'm betting the Bishops will, if she doesn't already know about it. But we still need to talk to Murphy. With that fire being caused by arson, we need to start considering who would have done it."

"And why."

"Yeah."

"The Bishops were physically closest," Tasha noted. "And both were sensing as much as they could in those last moments, I'm sure they were. One or both of them might have picked up something I didn't, since I was so focused on the babies."

Something in her quiet voice or just something he sensed in her made Brodie pull her an impossible inch closer. "What?" he asked just as quietly.

"There's something else I think we need to consider." Her eyes were very dark. "How many of us heard those screams. The Bishops were close, and powerful telepaths, so no surprise if they did. I don't know if we had anybody closer. But, me? It's, what, a couple hundred miles between Charleston and Charlotte? Sarah and Tucker are between here and there, but hardly a mile from here; did they hear the babies? Did a nightmare wake *them* up? Where was Murphy, and did she sense anything? Do we have any other psychics who sensed what happened in that fire?"

Brodie was watching her intently. "And if we don't?"

"Then maybe I didn't feel what I felt, didn't hear their dying screams only because I'm psychic. Maybe I heard their dying screams because they were connected to me."

"Tasha—"

"I'm in the first or one of the first successful generations of their eugenics program, we're fairly sure of that." She was vaguely surprised she could say that in a steady voice when just the possibility of it still totally creeped her out. "Whether I was the *lucky* but entirely natural product of two born psychics they paired or else something in them or in me was manipulated to *make* me a born psychic, we don't know."

"Tasha, it's all just supposition."

"But that's just it, John. We don't know what's only supposition and what isn't. Which guesses are right and which are wrong. All we *know* is that I was adopted, that I've been watched over in a very creepy way by creepy smiling people with creepy unnatural shadows probably my whole life. Which is weird enough to make me believe that particular supposition is on target.

"And—" She drew a deep breath and let it out slowly. "There must be others in my generation, other generations, even if we don't know who they are or how they were produced either. I can't be the only one. The only success. They never would have set up so many of their—their breeding houses if they weren't very sure the expense and commitment of so many of their resources were worthwhile."

"That makes sense," he admitted.

"So they found *something* that proved to them it was possible to breed psychics. Another supposition, but I can't see anything else that makes sense. Whether it was something genetic or something else, we don't know. But they found something. They know something about this that we don't know."

Brodie nodded reluctantly. He hated giving the other side any kind of advantage at all, far less one so close to the very heart of whatever this was.

"Whatever it is, we need to find it. I know doctors and scientists on our side of things are testing my blood and anything else I was willing to give them," Tasha said.

He had to smile at that, however faintly. She had been very disgruntled and not a little indignant about some of the requests.

Tasha knew what amused him and managed a smile, even if it was brief. "And I know Bishop has some really good private lab he uses running a complete genetic test on me. But he's already told us that genetic tests have been done on every born psychic in his unit *plus* born psychics he's monitored for years—plenty of . . . specimens . . . tested—and so far doctors and scientists have found absolutely nothing at the genetic level that is in any way different from nonpsychics."

"Yeah. Nothing they recognize, at least."

"So we don't know if any of that—*any* of it—will prove anything at all. And what else do we have? Not even Tucker has been able to find paperwork on me beyond the fact of my birth and the bare statement that I was adopted by a perfectly normal couple who never said a word about it to me *or* kept any documents concerning an adoption." She shook her head a little, still baffled by that. "And no luck at all in tracing ownership of that—house—I was apparently born in."

"No paper trail," Brodie murmured.

"It makes supposition less likely to be wrong, doesn't it? I mean, too many of our guesses seem to be way too close to possible not to contain more than a grain of truth."

"Probably. But we still have no proof of any of this."

"No, but maybe we have a better idea of where to look now. And we definitely have to find out whether one of Duran's people went rogue and burned that house or somebody else did. We have to know why it was destroyed. Why they were."

Brodie thought about it for a few moments, frowning slightly, then said with clear reluctance, "As much as I hate so many of us being in one place at the same time, I think we need to call Murphy—and I believe she'll want those of us here in Charleston most closely concerned in this all to come together. There's no good reason I can think of for Duran to do it, not like that. Whether one of his people went rogue, or someone else did it for reasons of their own, we have to understand why it was done."

He didn't get the chance to call Murphy.

She called them.

---

"There was nothing to be done by the time we got there," Bishop told the others, wrapping up his brief but succinct report on the fire only a few hours before. They were gathered together in the building that had been recently converted—at least outwardly—to luxury condos only a mile or so from Tasha's building. Bishop and Miranda, Tasha and Brodie, Tucker and Sarah Mackenzie, and Murphy.

They were in the penthouse condo, where Tucker and Sarah Mackenzie had been living for the past weeks, and the meeting had been called by Murphy just as soon as the Bishops had arrived back from Charlotte. It was still very early morning, no one had taken the time to eat breakfast, and they all had some version of coffee near to hand even though none of them needed the caffeine to be wide-awake.

Miranda said, "Even the neighbors were only just being awakened when we heard the first sirens, though the house was completely engulfed and must have been burning for at least ten to twenty minutes by then."

Bishop said with a frown, "And there was something odd about the dogs too. We saw a dozen or more in the neighborhood while we were approaching the house, and not a single one was barking. They were awake, alert—and totally silent and still. Both inside the houses we could see, and outside in the yards. Most of them had to be able to both see and hear the fire."

"I'd call that creepy," Tasha said. She had been rather subdued since she and Brodie had arrived, still clearly shaken by what had awakened her, what the Bishops had seen. But it was also clear to everyone in the room that she and Brodie had turned a corner in their relationship; they weren't touching, but they remained close to each other.

Brodie, frowning as Bishop had, asked the fed, "Can any of your people control animals psychically?"

"Control, no. I have one agent with a canine partner

she raised and trained, and they communicate telepathically almost as easily as we're talking now. There are a few others either in Haven or on our watch list who have shown the ability to communicate with animals at some level and in limited ways. But not control, not like that."

"The dogs should have reacted," Tucker said.

"Especially to something like a house fire," Sarah agreed. "No matter how they start, they aren't exactly quiet, and they are very, very visible in the night."

Miranda said, "An explosion would have awakened the neighborhood, and we would have been close enough to hear it. So it wasn't a gas line, or anything else that would have roused anyone in time to get into the house before it got too bad. Especially when none of the dogs sounded the alarm—and the smoke detectors and other fire alarms inside the house had been disabled."

"You're sure of that?" Brodie asked.

"Positive. We'd been monitoring the emergency services radios and scanners, and re-ran the recordings on our way here. No one was alerted to the fire until a neighbor, one street over, got up to let his dog out, and called it in because he could see the flames through the trees. It had to be arson. It was set to go up like a bonfire and that's exactly what it did."

Saying aloud only one of the dreadful possibilities that had been chasing each other through her mind, Tasha said, "One shadow breeding house deliberately burned, and it wasn't empty. Maybe because something was going wrong there? With the program?"

"Did you feel anything—else—wrong?" Murphy asked her directly.

*Other than babies burning alive.*

"No. It was—only the fire. It's like I told John, I *felt* the babies, when the fire was—was burning, their terror and agony. I have no way to be sure, no proof, but there didn't seem to be anything else wrong with the babies. Nothing I could sense."

"The opposite, in fact," Brodie said quietly.

Tasha looked at him, then nodded. "The babies . . . I think *they* knew it was deliberate, knew that they had an enemy. Some of them, at least, probably the ones closest to term. They were psychic. I don't know if they were telepathic or clairvoyant or what, but I know they were already psychic. Not latent."

"In Duran's mind," Brodie said, "unborn babies already showing signs of psychic abilities would be a huge plus."

Miranda said, "That fits with what we picked up, at least in part. We got that the babies were psychic. Nothing more specific than that in terms of their abilities, but definitely psychic."

Murphy nodded. "So, highly doubtful Duran and his people were . . . culling. Destroying failures and all the evidence of them. This place, at least, sounds like it would have been a win for Duran. Especially at this stage, when we're reasonably sure they've already had some success, and for long enough to have learned what works and what doesn't, at least in their eugenics program. Besides which, it's too obvious and too . . . messy a way of dealing with problems, if there even were any. Too many bodies to get rid of after a very public tragedy."

---

Emma Garrick still wasn't sure what had happened. She was cold, and afraid beyond anything she'd ever felt before, but she wasn't a weak girl or a stupid girl, and every instinct told her she needed to understand what had happened.

Wherever she was now was dark and quiet, silent even, and that didn't make her feel better. That didn't make her feel better at all. She couldn't open her eyes, couldn't move. In fact, her whole body felt weirdly numb, the way her face did after the dentist shot her up with novocaine.

So all she could really do was think, to try to understand and get it all straight in her head. She had been . . . What? At school? No. No, she'd been . . . There had been a party at Gary's house. A party that hadn't even *started* until after midnight, but Toby was going to be there, and she'd badly wanted him to see her in something other than her school uniform.

So she'd sneaked out after her parents were asleep. And she'd gone to the party, which hadn't been as much fun as she'd hoped because two other girls had taken turns plastering themselves on Toby, which he'd seemed to enjoy. A lot.

She'd nursed one beer for more than two hours, disliking the taste but wary enough not to either drink something with a lot more kick or set her red Solo cup down so somebody else could have slipped something into the beer.

Being a cop's kid wasn't usually a good thing; Emma knew way more than she wanted to about how quickly and easily kids got themselves into trouble.

Like sneaking out. And everything that followed that fairly minor rebellion.

Her dad was going to kill her.

A new car, her *first* car, and she'd run the damned thing off the road sneaking home at dawn.

Jeez.

*He's gonna kill me. I'm gonna be grounded until my eighteenth birthday. Maybe my twenty-first birthday. Dammit. Goddammit.*

It was only beginning to get light as Emma struggled to pull herself out of the little car that had slid inexplicably if gently off the road and into a not-so-little ditch. And it hadn't been until she'd done that and stood on the side of the road looking around that it had occurred to her she didn't know where she was.

Nothing had looked familiar. Which had been weird, because it wasn't like she lived in a big city. She would have sworn she knew practically every inch of this small town in Kentucky. But nothing looked familiar.

Nothing looked familiar at all.

And it was real quiet, not even crickets.

The first chill had crawled up her spine then, so icy cold that her instinct was just to run like hell. No matter where, *just run*. But before she could obey that instinct, she started to feel even colder, and she was puzzled because it was getting darker, not lighter like the sun was coming up.

It had gotten darker, and colder, and she thought she heard whispering, or maybe it was leaves rustling, but that almost never happened in June. And then she'd caught something from the corner of her eye, movement, and—

Shadows.

Just before the darkness closed over her, she'd seen

them, seen the shadows. Twisted, ugly, looming. Monsters. Not human.

*Not human.*

That was when she knew there was trouble a lot worse than just sneaking out to a party and wrecking her car. That was when the careless teenage certainty of invincibility left her all in a rush, like the strength flowing out of her as her knees buckled.

That was when she'd screamed out silently to the only mind she instinctively knew might be listening.

Bishop.

Now, eyes closed but aware she was somewhere else, somewhere that was not at all better than stranded on the side of a weirdly unfamiliar road in Kentucky, Emma Garrick understood that she had been taken, abducted.

All the things her dad had told her about why teenage girls got abducted roiled through her mind, icy-cold. Rapists. Human traffickers. Serial killers.

But none of those possibilities was the worst. Emma hadn't known the worst, not until now. She hadn't known there were worse things than even her dad knew about.

She hadn't known there were real monsters that came in the dark.

*Bishop . . .*

# EIGHT

Tasha held her voice steady. "Whatever the reason, what if this is the only one we know about because Bishop and Miranda were nearby, because I sensed the babies? What if . . . if other houses burn?"

"None have so far," Tucker said immediately. "Not, at least, any we've been monitoring. We're using a mix of different electronic devices and some of our people who are keeping their distance but able to do a thorough recon. Both our people and our devices register an automatic check-in every hour; anyone misses the check-in or reports something going on, we're alerted immediately." He nodded toward the far corner of this enormous living area, where a very complex-looking computer system was set up, with rows of equipment on shelves as well as on the large desk.

Equipment far too advanced to be available to anyone in the private sector. Or, possibly, even the military.

"Nothing unusual has happened except at that one

house—where we'd held off installing any kind of electronic surveillance until Bishop and Miranda could check it out. We also didn't yet have any of our people watching. We'd only discovered that house two days ago, and the ID was iffy at best."

He added, "It's taken most of our available resources, but we've kept the heavy surveillance on the other houses and clinics we've found so far because we knew we'd be moving the women and babies within the next week."

Quietly, Sarah said, "Maybe Duran knows that too. Maybe keeping them away from us was more important than keeping them alive."

"I'm not really one to give Duran the benefit of any doubt," Brodie said rather needlessly, "but it just doesn't fit with his usual methods, *or* his goals as we understand them."

Tucker glanced at his wife, then said, "Sarah picked up something that suggested the fire may not have been sanctioned. Maybe one of Duran's people is off the reservation. It's not like it hasn't happened before."

"True enough," Brodie said.

Murphy was not easily driven to temper. In her work, she could hardly afford the luxury. But what had been done on this early June morning—and what might be threatened in other places, not just in that one quiet neighborhood in Charlotte, North Carolina—drove her as close as she ever wanted to come to pure, absolute, white-hot murderous rage.

Not that she allowed it to show. Much.

"Duran virtually always keeps close tabs on his people, his assets," she said, her voice utterly calm. Still, she let some of the anger show because it was expected—and there were too many telepaths in the room to try to shut it out. Completely out, at least.

Underneath a dozen walls she had built over a lifetime to shield the most secret parts of her mind, she wondered if Duran could possibly have *known* what was happening, what had happened, when they had met unexpectedly and talked before dawn.

Could he have known?

Could he have ordered that done?

And if he had, could he have stood there talking to Murphy without giving away a sign of it? Could even *he* have managed to hide that from her?

She briefly considered what she wanted to do, weighed the risk, and then added it to the list in her mind with boxes to be ticked where he was concerned. And to hell with the risk.

"It doesn't make sense if it *was* sanctioned," Tasha Solomon said quietly. "For someone like Duran, the sheer waste alone should have stopped him. They want psychics, they've taken psychics, and somewhere along the way, they learned how to—to breed psychics. Once that worked for them, even if it was only in a small way at first, even if there were more failures than successes, they obviously put a great deal of effort into building that program. Time, money, manpower. What I felt this morning . . . They were incredibly close to having a dozen more psychics under their control, to be raised and trained by their side, just in that one house. Every single pregnant woman was carrying a child with psychic abilities."

"Maybe he knew somehow that they *couldn't* be controlled," Brodie suggested reluctantly. "We all know plenty of psychics have problems, both inherent to them because of their lives and personalities and because of abilities they can't control. Very powerful psychics can wreak a lot of havoc, with and without control over their abilities. Do we even know anything about unborn babies already reading as psychic? At an age so early there isn't much besides instinct, do we know what they can do? I mean, aside from trying to reach out for help, the way at least some of them did to Tasha?"

Murphy looked at Tasha. "You think they deliberately reached out to you?"

"I think they reached out. Cried out for help. And I know I heard them."

Murphy's gaze remained steady. "Did you believe then, or do you believe now that they were reaching out to you personally?"

It was an oddly formal question, and it caused Brodie to look at Murphy with slightly narrowed eyes.

"I think . . . there was a connection," Tasha answered slowly. "Far as I know, I never met, never connected with any of those women in person, far less their unborn babies. But . . . we were akin somehow, those babies and me. Alike. I felt that."

"You were part of the program," Murphy said. "Maybe it's only that."

Tasha had been thinking about that as well, and the likely conclusions she had reached were chilling. "Which argues the possibility that those babies and I *are* in some way connected . . . biologically. Maybe at the most basic level possible. DNA. Even molecules, atoms. Something like that. Maybe that's what Duran and his people eventually discovered through years, decades, of their *experi-*

*ments.* Maybe they've been doing a little scientific tinkering with the genetic code."

"If so, it's beyond anything we can do," Bishop said. "We've barely mapped the human genome."

"Yeah." Tasha nodded. "I kind of figured they had to be way ahead of us to do something like that. Especially if it started with my generation, thirty years ago. Or, at least, started to be successful that long ago. Maybe while science on our side has been using that research to look for cures for diseases, Duran and his people have been searching for a way to . . . create psychics. Maybe even to create very powerful psychics. And maybe they found it."

Sarah said, "More than scary, if so. But they're still taking born and triggered psychics, we know that. As recently as just a few weeks ago, Bishop lost some of the psychics on his watch list."

"More recently than that," Bishop said quietly. "On the flight back here, Miranda and I both heard a mental scream for help. From one of the youngest people on any of my watch lists. Emma Garrick. She's sixteen."

Murphy was frowning at him. "They've taken kids," she said slowly, "young people. Before now."

"Have they taken latents?"

"She was a latent?"

"Until they grabbed her a few hours ago she was. I'm fairly certain that now she's a full-blown telepath with enormous potential. The question is, did they know that?"

---

Duran dared not look up from the open folder on the blotter of his desk to meet the undoubtedly nervous gaze of the man who had just reported in. He didn't trust himself.

"What did you say?" he asked softly.

Vargas kept his gaze fixed somewhere above Duran's dark head, hoping to hell he wouldn't have to meet those strange, greenish eyes. "I said—there was a fire. Before dawn. In Charlotte."

"And?" Duran's voice was still soft, his gaze still apparently fixed downward.

"There were no survivors."

"Why did our surveillance system not alert us that something was wrong?" Duran asked after a moment.

"The fire did a great deal of damage, but as far as our people could tell, our devices had been removed, or replaced by what appear to be faulty smoke detectors."

Duran lifted his gaze at last. "What about before the fire started? We had no warning? Our surveillance system recorded nothing out of the ordinary in the data transmitted here during the night?"

Vargas had been right. Meeting those greenish eyes squarely was difficult. Very difficult.

"No, sir. I viewed the recordings myself. No one came near the house. No movement at all was recorded by any of the exterior cameras. One moment all was well, and the next a wall of flame shot up."

A very slight frown drew Duran's brows together. "A wall of flame. In front of each camera? Simultaneously?"

"Yes, sir."

"The fire won't be ruled an accident."

It hadn't been a question, but Vargas replied anyway. "It was too obvious that some accelerant was used, I'm afraid."

"And the women?" Unlike most of his people, Duran resisted calling them "subjects." He was uncertain in his own mind why he did so, since they most certainly fit the far more clinical term.

"All killed."

"None tried to save themselves?"

"No, sir. Their conditioning held: They were programmed to follow a careful schedule. The schedule called for them to go to bed at a precise time and go to sleep, without wakening, until their alarms went off."

"So they slept to their deaths."

Vargas wasn't entirely sure he understood Duran's tone, but knew better than to question it. "Yes, sir."

"And the fetus each woman carried?"

Vargas blinked. "None survived, sir."

There was a slight pause, and then Duran said gently, "My question is whether the programming of the mothers also affected their unborn babies."

Wishing anybody else was standing where he was, Vargas searched for words that would answer but not anger his superior. Which was often difficult.

"That programming, as you know, sir, is psychological at its core, and the physical changes provide only a basis for a more ready acceptance of that programming. We have seen no evidence that either is something passed through the placenta to a fetus. And since the conditioning takes place before the subjects become pregnant, there would be nothing external that a maturing fetus would hear."

Duran was silent. Expressionless.

Hoping there would be no more inexplicable questions, Vargas said, "Our people were able to remove the bodies of the subjects closest to term, and replace three others with deceased male bodies clearly burned to death. The remaining subjects will show no signs of pregnancy at autopsy. The cover of a minor nursing facility providing short-term care for people recovering from various surgeries is solid. Nothing will be found to dispute that."

"I see. I want all reports and interviews on my desk before noon."

"Yes, sir." Vargas knew a dismissal when he heard one, and was more grateful than he wanted to admit to himself that he was able to leave the room.

Duran leaned back in his chair and fixed his gaze once more on a report he didn't even see on his blotter.

The fire hadn't been set by one of Murphy's people, he knew that. They might well have set fire to an empty house after removing the women and anyone else they found there, but they would never wantonly destroy people. Not psychics or nonpsychics.

And most certainly not pregnant women.

One of his people.

One of his people had deliberately destroyed one of their operations, killing three caretakers and a dozen pregnant women who carried in their wombs some of the most powerful psychics they had ever managed to produce.

*Unintended consequences.*

The phrase dropped into his mind so clearly he could almost hear Murphy's mocking tone, and he had to wonder if the destruction of the Charlotte operation had been just that. An unintended consequence.

Of failure?

Or of success?

Had one of his people guessed or discovered what

only he and a handful of his healers had been almost certain of? That among the group of unborn babies in the Charlotte house had been quite possibly the single psychic mind they had been working for so many years to locate or produce?

The term whispered only among the few who knew was The Supreme. A psychic born with almost unlimited abilities—and with total, *instinctive* control over those abilities.

It was no more than a few short minutes after Vargas had left when Duran touched the intercom on his desk.

"Yes, sir?" his assistant responded immediately.

"I want to know the exact location of every one of our people here in the southeast during the last twenty-four hours."

"Yes, sir." She sounded neither surprised nor dismayed by the order.

"Before noon," he added.

"Yes, sir. I'll see to it."

Even with their technology, it would not be a quick or simple process; Duran had a number of teams operating in the southeast at the moment, performing a variety of tasks. Some in areas not at all easy to access.

*Unintended consequences.*

Someone had betrayed him, and that someone was going to pay dearly.

---

Murphy's frown deepened. "You have psychics on your team able to sense others, right? Even latents?"

"Yes. But they have to know who they're sensing. Get close enough. A latent's mind is quiet, doesn't produce an unusual energy signature. We don't have anyone who could . . . scan an area and know there was a latent psychic there."

"How did she end up on your watch list?"

"Her father got in touch with me. He's a cop, and his family line has produced a number of psychics. He has some mild ability himself, more of heightened intuition than actual psychic senses. In any case, he's more than usually open to the idea. And since he saw more than one family member struggle with their abilities, he wanted to know if Emma might have to face that sort of issue."

"So one of your psychics able to determine it scanned her and found latent ability?"

Bishop nodded. "I told him what we'd found, he and Emma's mother talked it over, and it was decided that it was something Emma needed to know about. Her dad's made a practice of being honest with her, warning her about the dangers he sees on the job. She's their only child. He wanted to protect her, and to a cop knowledge is protection."

"Yeah, he's right about that. Mostly. You talked to her, I take it."

"A bit later. She was barely twelve when he asked me to find out if there was a chance she could be psychic. We both knew that adolescence sometimes triggers latent abilities, so he wanted her to be prepared before the hormones really kicked in. He told her about his own family members, and about the unit and me. Made sure she understood both the positives and negatives of being psychic. I talked to her for the first time about a year later. I've kept in touch with her ever since. Talked to her last a couple of months ago. She was still a latent."

"Where was she abducted from?"

"Kentucky."

"Right out of her bed?"

"No, her car. Apparently, she sneaked out after bedtime to go to a party, one without parental supervision. She's a good kid, always has been. But . . . I take it she expected a boy she liked to be there. She's sixteen."

Murphy nodded, saying somewhat ruefully, "How well I remember."

"Okay, another weird thing," Brodie said, clearly thinking along other lines. "Her father is a cop? They don't usually abduct psychics with family ties in law enforcement. Just too damned risky."

Murphy had kept her gaze on Bishop's face, and saw the scar on his left cheek whiten. "They arranged an accident for her?" It wasn't really a question.

"Just after dawn this morning. According to the police report, she was taking the long way home, in the new car she'd had barely three weeks. Lost control at high speed, and wrapped the car around a light post. The car caught fire. They removed a body from the wreckage. Female, probably mid-teens. The right height and weight. Wearing Emma's clothes, her watch. Her cell phone was virtually destroyed, but recognizable."

Bishop drew a breath. "So, around seven o'clock this morning, Matt and Jody Garrick were notified that their only child had died in a fiery single-car accident investigators believe was caused by a combination of inexperience and alcohol."

"Those poor people," Tasha said.

Looking at Murphy, Bishop said, "This is one we can't walk away from. We know she's alive, that she was abducted only hours ago. Nobody in Kentucky is going to be looking for her, not even her father."

"So you have to."

"We've been looking for the others anyway. I had notified a dozen psychics from all across the country on . . . another list I keep . . . to let me know if they sensed anything unusual."

"I thought you said areas couldn't be scanned," Tasha said.

"Not for latents. But for active psychic ability, they can be. If the psychics scanning areas are strong enough. These people are."

"Not from your unit or Haven?" Murphy asked.

"Two are Haven operatives, currently not on a case. They don't know each other, and they don't know about your group or the other side. None of them do. All they know is that I've asked them to use their unique abilities to probe as far as they can reach and let me know if they sense anything unusual around them. It's a request I've made more than once in the past."

"Ah." Murphy nodded. "I wondered how you built up that watch list of yours. This is one of the methods."

Bishop nodded. "One of many."

"Any luck so far? This time, I mean."

He frowned slightly. "A clairvoyant in Colorado believes he picked up something unusual yesterday. He's in Boulder, but he said it didn't feel like whatever he sensed was close."

Tucker spoke up to say, "Speaking as a researcher, I have to say that's a little vague for a place to start."

"Agreed," Bishop said immediately. "Which is why I have people moving into the surrounding states to probe.

Each of *them* has better control and more experience in using their abilities."

Murphy said, "I take it whoever you have closest to Kentucky didn't sense anything, say, around dawn this morning?"

"As a matter of fact, she did. Shadows. Dark, twisted, inhuman, colder than anything she's ever sensed before. They were there—and then they weren't. That was less than an hour before the report of Emma's accident came in."

# NINE

After a long moment, Murphy nodded. "Well, you don't need my permission to look for people on your watch list."

"No, I don't need that," he agreed. "But I think we both need to be aware of what's happening when it comes to psychics. Yours and mine. I also believe that *when* we find Emma and the others, we'll also find that wherever it is they're being held is very important to the other side."

"What you find," she warned, "could be the kind of laboratory chamber of horrors you see only in the movies. We *know* they've hurt psychics, Bishop. We know they've tortured them, very probably conducted god-awful experiments on them. We know that we've never been able to recover an abducted psychic, dead or alive. We don't know how many have died over the years, but we're positive plenty have."

She glanced around at the others, and added, "That said, you're almost certainly right that wherever they were taken, wherever they're being held, is important. The fact that we've never been able to come close to finding it is pretty much a gilt-edged guarantee that they have more there to protect than abducted psychics."

He nodded. "That was my thought."

"Yeah. So . . . fresh eyes can make all the difference, especially when they belong to powerful psychics trained to investigate. I really hope I'm right about that, you're right about it, and they can find what's eluded us all these years. But—if any of your . . . roving psychics can home in on that lab, we definitely need to know about it. *Before* you move against it."

"There might not be much time to plan," he warned. "You just said it. Torture, experimentation. Emma's only been gone a few hours, some of the others a matter of weeks. I have to believe we can save them, perhaps even others taken longer ago. And that means that as soon as we have even a *possible* location for that place, we'll have to move."

"Were you thinking of using your own people?"

Bishop immediately shook his head. "If this place is what we both think it is, no, at least not primarily. There could be intel there to help you win this war, intel your people need to see, to use. I don't want to do anything to hinder your efforts, Murphy. I don't want to take this war public. I just want to get those abducted psychics out of their hands. *And* make them think very, very hard before they ever again try to use the body of a dead teenager to fake the death of a living psychic they plan to torture."

There was a long silence, and then Murphy nodded. "Good enough. I assume your roving psychics can contact you directly?"

"Yes."

He didn't offer anything else, and Murphy smiled faintly. But her voice was serious when she said, "I don't know how they knew about Emma. We may never know. But what we do know is that they don't waste much time before they start . . . working on an abducted psychic. Tell your people they should probably hurry."

"I already have."

"So that's one front," Brodie said into the silence. "I hope like hell your people find that lab, Bishop. I'd love to be able to take the war to them for a change."

"We all would," Tucker agreed.

"Yeah."

Sarah said, "If we have assets we haven't tapped, now's probably the time."

"I'll say," Tucker agreed ruefully. "Good thing we've spent the last months getting a bit more organized. Who's idea was that, by the way?"

"The boss's," Murphy replied.

"Did she see this coming?"

"Maybe. She gets a rare vision now and then, I believe. Before anybody asks, I have no idea how much that guides her decision-making."

"Well, it seems to have been a good call," Bishop observed. "Because it definitely feels like a number of things have . . . reached critical mass." He was frowning slightly.

"Bothered by that?" Murphy asked.

"No, not that. Or maybe it is part of that. Our shield was down on the jet, which is probably why Emma's cry for help came through so clearly. But even when we're buttoned up tightly, we always . . . leave a window open just a bit."

"To maintain contact with the other members of your unit?" Murphy's voice was mildly curious.

"It isn't continuous contact," he explained. "A sort of sense of where everybody is, but no direct thoughts unless somebody's trying to reach us or we're trying to reach them."

"I get that. And so?"

Bishop glanced at his wife, then looked back at Murphy. "Ever since the fire, we've both been aware of . . . connections. A stronger and stronger sense of them. As if we can . . . almost . . . touch the connections of other psychics we've never even met."

"I take it that's unusual." It wasn't really a question.

Bishop was nodding. "For us, yes. We tend to be aware of the connections between people we know. Especially bonded pairs. But this is . . ."

"A *lot* of connections," Miranda finished. "Almost like . . . a honeycomb coming together, more sides touching all the time."

Murphy tilted her head slightly and looked at them both. "It's always male-female, isn't it? The bonded pairs?"

"Yes, so far, at least," Bishop replied. "And usually mates, or two people on their way to becoming mates. Though there's certainly nothing to say a same-sex couple couldn't also forge the sort of connection we're talking about."

"Bonded," she murmured almost to herself. "Mind, body, and soul." Then she blinked and looked around the room, adding dryly, "Well, you're all safe from him."

"How sure are you?" Brodie asked, seemingly not at all disturbed by everyone's awareness of his still-new closeness with Tasha.

"Positive you're safe from Duran, safe as long as he's the one calling the shots. Off his list as potential recruits, at least."

"But we're still enemies," Bishop said.

"Oh, yeah. I doubt his superiors feel the same way. And there's always danger if one of his people goes off the reservation. Or if his superiors just decide a change in tactics is in order. But Duran showed his hand in this thing long ago. He avoids open battles, and he doesn't send death squads to kill psychics in the night. Take them sometimes, but not kill them. Not even his enemies."

"Yeah, but why?" Brodie demanded. "It would be to his advantage to get rid of us. He's killed some of our soldiers along the way. Maybe not with his own hands, but we've had pretty good evidence they were killed by his people, following his orders. And at least a few of those killed were psychics. What makes bonded psychics, connected psychics, enemies he's reluctant to kill?"

"Are we of value to him somehow?" Sarah mused. "Or are we dangerous to him or his plans?"

"Maybe it's because we can see them coming," Tasha said. "Not necessarily individual psychics, but . . . Look, I know I'm stronger bonded with John than I ever was alone. I *know* that. And I know Sarah feels the same way about her bond with Tucker."

"Absolutely," Sarah said, as Tucker nodded.

"Same here," Miranda said. "Noah and I were both pretty strong as individual psychics, but together . . . Well, it's been an adventure."

"And then some," Bishop added gravely.

Murphy smiled. "Yeah, I can see how it would be. And Tasha may be onto something. She was, after all, able to actually *see* unnatural shadows attached to people she thought she'd known. A few of us have caught glimpses, out of the corner of our eyes, but Tasha saw a lot more. And that was just one quick experiment, before her bond with Brodie was complete."

"Wonder what I'd see now?" Tasha murmured with a glance at Brodie. Before he could say anything to that, she added, "When I was in that maze and knew I could get out, when I knew John and maybe somebody else was helping me, I . . . tried to see Astrid."

"She was actually there?" Murphy asked.

"No. Well—not in the flesh, of course. I mean, we were all . . . really . . . inside John's head. More or less."

"Can we move past that part?" Brodie requested.

"Takes some getting used to," Tucker told the other man with some sympathy.

"I'm fine with Tasha in my head," Brodie said calmly, surprising at least two of the people in the room. "And I can handle being scanned by a psychic who needs to trust me. But Astrid's a sociopath and having a dark and very weird maze dropped into some part of my mind as well as her was . . . disturbing."

"I very much doubt it'll happen again," Murphy told him.

"Why not?" he asked. "If it's worked for Duran before—"

"You and Tasha came out of that little experiment of his with the beginnings of your bond. Pretty sure that's not at all what he had in mind." Without waiting for a response to that, she immediately returned her attention to Tasha. "How were you able to see Astrid? Very few of us have. And none psychically, as far as I know."

Tasha frowned. "I didn't see her, really. I mean, even though I bet I'd recognize her voice, I don't have a clue what she looks like. But I knew she was surrounded by those cold, strange shadows. I was trying to figure out who she was, and—"

Without warning, memories washed over her. Memories of a kind of conversation.

*Shadows. Shadows all around you. I can't see you. But you're there, aren't you? Hidden by the shadows. Protected by them.*

*Well, I wouldn't go that far. Hidden, yes.*

*But not protected?*

*Hidden because it suits them. Can't you feel them, Tasha? Don't you know what they are?*

*No. No, just . . . shadows. Sliding away whenever I try to get closer to them.*

*Just as well, I suppose.*

*Why? Why is it just as well?*

*Because they're killing you, Tasha. Right now, this very minute, they're killing you.*

---

Henry had lost all track of time. The cell where they left him after each of their little . . . tests . . . was a whitewashed cinder-block prison, tiny and claustrophobic. The cot was narrow and lumpy, the single chair bolted to the concrete floor, and the sink-with-toilet arrangement a stainless steel blister on all the whiteness.

There was no window, the single door had no handle whatsoever on his side, and even though he knew air circulated in the room and there was clearly artificial light, he hadn't been able to find a sign of a fixture or vent, or any other kind of opening.

He had looked, at first. Tried to find a way out. Before he had grown so utterly weary he almost didn't care anymore.

Almost.

*Are you there?*

*I'm here, Henry.*

He was lying on the cot, where they'd dropped him, in a sprawl that would have been uncomfortable if there had been anything left in his world that was comfortable.

*You haven't told me your name.* He thought idly that he was getting pretty good at this mind-talk stuff. For a medium, anyway.

*You wouldn't know it.*

*So? You know my name. Fair is fair.*

*Yeah, okay. I'm Juno.*

*Pretty name.*

*Thanks. Henry, you have to stay strong.*

*I don't feel very strong.*

*You are. You've . . . you've lasted longer than most.*

He thought that probably should have given him a chill, but he was just too tired to think further than that.

*I don't feel very strong,* he repeated. *It's . . . getting harder to think about things.*

*What things?*

*Things . . . before. Things outside.*

*You mean your life before they took you.*

*Yeah. That. It feels like I'm losing that. I think I loved old houses. I think I loved working with my hands. Do you like working with your hands, Juno?*

*Sure.*

*Maybe, if there's a time after this, we can build something together. Will there be a time after this, Juno?*

*I . . . hope so. Henry, there was another name in your mind the first time I touched it.*

*Yeah. Bishop.*

*Did you call out to him?*

*I . . . maybe. Maybe I did. I'm not exactly sure. Everything happened so fast. I've always been alone, and I just . . . Before, when they took me, I wished I hadn't been so alone. So maybe I called out to Bishop. Maybe I thought he could help me.*

*Don't you still think so?*

*I'm really tired, Juno.*

*I know. I know, Henry.*

*And I think Bishop is very far away.*

*It doesn't work like that. Not if you connected with his mind even for just a few seconds. If you did that, Bishop is close enough to still hear you.*

*You know Bishop, don't you?*

*Yes. Yes, Henry, I do. And I believe Bishop can help us. But I . . . never connected with him. I think you did. I think you can reach out to him, call out to him, ask him to help us.*

*But I'm so tired, Juno. Can't I call out to Bishop tomorrow? After I sleep? I need to sleep . . .*

Juno lifted her head from her raised knees and stared across her cell at the featureless cinder-block wall. Henry was sleeping now, she knew. Exhausted. Beginning to let go.

She was exhausted herself. Beyond exhausted. And cold down to her bones. Because she thought Henry was probably her last chance to get out of this place alive.

And she wasn't at all sure he had the strength to save them both.

She wasn't even sure he had the strength to save himself.

---

"Tasha?"

She opened her eyes, realizing that Brodie was holding one of her hands. And that everyone else was looking at her very intently.

"Wow. That was . . . intense. And unexpected." She glanced at Brodie, knowing that even though their connection remained narrowed as it had been before, he still had some idea of what she had experienced.

She described the "conversation" to the others, adding, "That last bit was mostly Astrid being nasty, I think. Or, at least, I think that's the way she meant it. But there was a part of me that believed if it hadn't been for John I never would have come up out of that maze."

Murphy didn't allow her to dwell on that. "And when you tried to see Astrid, all you saw was the shadows?"

"Yeah. I couldn't see her, because the shadows around her were . . . around her. I think they're always around her. Almost like guards."

"Interesting," Murphy said slowly. "Very interesting. Because my bet is that Astrid was entirely willing to throw in her lot with them. Others must have been too."

"Then why the guards?" Tasha wondered.

"I don't know. Maybe even willing they have to be watched. Or maybe it was only then, when Astrid was trying to draw you to the center of the maze. That's what she said, right?"

"Pretty much."

"So maybe while she was connecting with you, she needed the shadows. Maybe as guards. Or they could have been helping her somehow, even shielding her from the psychic she's testing. I've never been in the thing myself, but as far as I've been able to gather, that maze serves two purposes for Duran. It's a sort of test of the strength of a psychic's abilities, and it's a kind of lure. It seems to be important to them that they at least try to bring psychics willingly to their side at first. So the idea is, the psychic finds the center of the maze—and that's where the deal is. Where we're offered a choice of some kind. After that . . ."

Nobody really wanted to think about what happened after that, but Sarah spoke again, quietly.

"When they were after me, when Tucker and I were on the move last year, we met a psychic who'd been acting as one of their . . . tools. But he wasn't able to do what they wanted him to do. Bring me over to their side. I know he expected to die because of that, that he disappeared right afterward. And . . . I know whatever deal he made with them cost him more than his life. Maybe his soul. Whatever it is that makes us all unique. He lost that. When he made the deal. And lost his life when he wasn't able to turn me."

"Duran doesn't tolerate failure," Murphy said.

Brodie was the first to break the long silence. "Well, if you ask me, somebody failed Duran badly last night. He would have had that house wrapped tight in terms of security, no matter how unthreatening it appeared to the neighbors."

"Their electronic security is beyond state-of-the-art,"

Tucker agreed. "And it's pretty much hell to hack into it. I've been trying to get into that other place of his here in Charleston, the one he thinks we don't know about. They haven't even finished installing the security system, and I still can't get in."

"Unless Duran burned it or had it burned himself, he must have believed the security was solid," Brodie said.

Tucker said, "And yet somebody managed to get in without setting off any alarms. To have either an unknown enemy or one of his own people gone rogue for some reason burn down one of what looks like his most promising shadow homes should at least put Duran on alert."

"I would say so," Brodie agreed. "It would sure as hell put me on alert."

"You mean more alert than he has been?" Tasha managed a faint smile. "Is that possible?"

"Unfortunately, yes," Brodie told her. "If there is a traitor inside his own house, it may pull his focus a bit—but not for long. Nothing pulls his focus for long."

"True," Murphy agreed.

"We plan with that in mind?" Brodie asked.

Murphy frowned. "We continue on with plans we've already put in place, especially when it comes to the mothers and their babies. We're almost ready to move on more than a dozen houses, simultaneously because it's our only hope of getting through their security *and* of forcing Duran to scatter his forces if he even tries to stop the operation. I say we move on them as planned."

"And then?" Brodie asked.

"Then we keep looking for more, and move to get those women and babies to safety. As many as we can. For as long as we can. One at a time if that's the way we find them. Until that plan stops working, we keep using it."

"Nobody's disagreeing, Murphy," Brodie told her.

"Yeah, yeah. Look, we have a lot going on now, and our resources are stretched thin. But I think we really need to know who torched that shadow house in Charlotte. Because as twisted and evil as some of their actions have been, they still made a kind of sense. That fire makes no sense at all. And whoever set it has dropped down into a whole new level of bad."

"We have a couple of good contacts inside Charlotte law enforcement," Bishop said. "Should be able to get you their report, and the fire marshal's report. It's a place to start."

"Good." Murphy nodded again.

Tucker frowned. "There are security cameras all over the place, especially in large cities like Charlotte. And that's a very nice neighborhood, with very nice houses. If any are close enough to Duran's former operation, I might, given a little time, be able to hack into somebody else's security feed. Might see a whole lot of nothing. Or we might see something useful."

"Another good idea," Murphy said. "I say go for it." Then she looked over at Tasha and lifted an eyebrow. "What?"

"Are you reading me?"

"Just your face. I'm good at that."

"She is," Brodie agreed dryly.

"So I know something's bugging you. What is it, Tasha?"

# TEN

"It's just . . . a worry, I guess. The thing is, for me to feel that connection with those poor unborn babies now, today, has to mean that whatever . . . biological manipulation was needed to produce babies with stronger psychic abilities is something they've had to be working on for a long time. Maybe they hadn't perfected it early on, but it must have been a part of Duran's eugenics program more than thirty years ago."

"Not necessarily," Murphy said immediately. "Or at least, not knowingly. According to our information, they tried different methods, a lot of them. For years, maybe decades. We don't know if *they* knew what worked and what didn't, not at first. Maybe not for a long time. Maybe they didn't have either the tech or the psychics decades ago who could scan unborn babies. Maybe those early unborn babies didn't read as psychic until they were older. That's more typical—isn't it, Bishop?"

He nodded. "Most tend to be born latent, and are

triggered when they're older. Some are triggered at various ages due to trauma. Though some psychics, especially when the abilities run in their family, can remember psychic experiences when they were very, very young."

Miranda added, "Sometimes imaginary playmates are spirits. Night terrors are visions. That sort of thing. Considered by the nonpsychic to be fairly ordinary parts of childhood. Though most very young psychics learn to hide what they can do when they're still young, just like Tasha did. A defense mechanism."

Murphy said, "There's no way for us to know for sure when *Duran* knew you were a success."

"I was watched from childhood," she reminded them, her voice very steady.

"And maybe that was simply their standard operating procedure. Maybe all the babies born healthy and with psychic potential were watched from childhood, especially if they showed any signs at all of possessing abilities. In fact, I'd be surprised if they weren't."

"That's at least potentially a lot of resources."

"Well, if he's proven anything at all, Duran has proven the stakes in this are very high. For him, at least."

Quietly, Bishop said, "Tasha, most of your test results are in. And there is absolutely nothing abnormal in you. From the DNA out. The only thing that separates you from a nonpsychic person is just that. You read as psychic. We tend to have a higher-than-normal amount of electrical activity in our brains, often in areas that appear to be unused in nonpsychics, and we just as often carry a stronger . . . static charge . . . in our bodies than other people. So we're more likely to screw up ATMs, and other simple kinds of computers, and we have trouble with magnetized keycards and credit cards. Cell phones tend to die on us a lot faster than on nonpsychics. But as far as our DNA goes, our brain cells, the cells of our bodies, all that is perfectly normal, just like any nonpsychic. And that's all."

"You mean that's all we know right now. All we *can* know."

---

Annabel half woke up, conscious of dim, almost inaudible voices on the other side of the condo from her bedroom. Even half asleep, part of her wanted to probe, to make *sure* those visitors were unthreatening. Because she was still wary.

*Don't worry.*

*Are you sure?*

*Yes. Friends. People who care about you.*

Annabel was faintly surprised, and not at all sure she believed him. She'd never had even two people to care about her, really care about her, and was still a bit wary of reaching out to Sarah and Tucker even though they'd been so kind to her.

*Annabel, you're safe. And you need to rest.*

*I think I've been sleeping a long time. Mostly. Mostly all night, I think.*

*Yes. But you're still very tired, and you still need to rest. Sleep. I promise I'll keep watch. Always. Keep you safe always. Go back to sleep.*

Relaxing, smiling, Annabel rubbed her face on her sweet-smelling pillow, and drifted back to sleep.

---

Brodie looked at Tasha, beside him on a large sectional in the room, not needing their connection to know she was still thinking about being among the first successful generation of Duran's eugenics program. The shock of that was still with her, and all his strength or comfort could not change that.

Still, his fingers tightened slightly around hers, because other kinds of connections mattered too, and she sent him a quick smile before going on steadily to the others. "I assume every other psychic's background has been checked out, on our side, I mean?"

"Checked and triple-checked," Murphy said dryly. "Duran got cute and put the idea into Brodie's head that we might have a traitor among us, so that last check was only a few months before you joined us."

Brodie didn't waste a glare.

"Then I'm the only one on our side," Tasha said. "All of you said that Duran really, *really* wanted me on their side until John and I connected. Right?"

"Yeah."

"I doubt I was the *only* one who survived the program back then and grew up being watched. There must have been others. Are we looking for others?"

Tucker nodded. "One of the things the crackerjack researchers on this side are working on now. Some are mapping the current houses, but quite a few are searching out any that existed over the last thirty-five years and digging into their history. We're also trying to find other babies that might have been adopted from the house where you were born, Tasha. It wasn't in operation very long so there aren't that many names—but since they apparently favor using as their phony names some of the most common, we're hitting a lot of dead ends. We'll keep at it, though."

Tasha didn't know whether to be relieved or more anxious. "I'm glad. I think."

Tucker shook his head. "I have to say, I thought the other ways Duran and his goons were getting psychics were pretty damned elaborate, what with all the fake disappearances and real dead bodies replacing those of kidnapped psychics, but this eugenics program is something else."

"And we don't know how successful they've been at it," Murphy said. "Or how long. How many . . . mistakes . . . were made along the way."

"Not a good idea to mess with Mother Nature," Tucker agreed. "We have way too many examples in history to prove that. I hope they're aware of some of those. I mean what *not* to do."

Murphy, slumped down in the chair that enabled her to see everyone in the room easily, muttered several curses almost under her breath.

She could have been any age, Tasha thought, studying the other woman really for the first time, but she looked younger than anyone else in the room, so much so that she likely got carded at any bar or club. Her oddly youthful punk look of camo army jacket and army boots, plus at least two colorful tattoos partially visible on her neck above her black tee-shirt and on one wrist just peeking from the cuff of her jacket marked her as someone who wore her individuality like a shield.

The overlarge and very worn leather bag she carried

with the wide strap slung across her body, never mind her extremely short, very spiky, and usually blond but occasionally multi-colored hair also gave her appearance a youthful slant.

The scowl marked her as somebody who was visibly furious, an occasion as rare as hen's teeth.

"Don't lose it," Brodie warned her, a warning about her very rare but scary temper.

He had known her the longest, but Murphy had never been known to take comments like his in an accepting spirit.

"Don't lose it? Do you know what the list of current shadow houses and clinics is up to now, Brodie? Tucker told us before you two got here. He and our other crackerjack researchers have been busy these last few weeks. They've found over a hundred. So far."

Tucker murmured, "And those are mostly in the southeast. We're spreading out from here, cautiously."

Brodie's was a face that rarely showed emotion, but shock crossed his hard features briefly. "I knew there were a lot of them, but—"

Tasha spoke up then, her voice unsteady. "Whoever burned the Charlotte house . . . they won't burn others, destroy others. Nobody on Duran's side would do that, would they? It represents at least decades of work for them, we know that, and if even half of what we think we know is right, then they've finally figured out whatever it was they needed to—to breed true and get the results they want. To breed psychics a high percentage of the time. At least . . . we know they did at that house. So why would anyone on Duran's side destroy it?"

---

Sebring moved almost carelessly through the almost weirdly deserted industrial jungle of broken pavement, rusting fences, and abandoned buildings with broken or boarded-up windows. She wasn't worried about being seen in any sense of the word.

She had long ago found herself a couple of psychics who kept her shielded whenever she was on the move or involved in an operation.

Something Duran should have thought of.

It was only a glancing scorn, easily set aside. He had his own methods, and they apparently served his masters well. And if Sebring took care to stay out of his way just as he took care to stay out of hers, it was simply because their objectives were as different as their methods.

Sebring served her own masters well.

So when one of her contacts reported that a very strong psychic mind had been sensed probing near a certain very important building in Chicago, it was her responsibility to check it out. Her responsibility to track down that mind, that psychic, and determine the level of threat.

To destroy that threat.

She reached the meeting place just then, coming upon him suddenly as she turned a corner and entered what had once been the service area of an old gas station. It wasn't a particularly secure location in the sense of hiding either one of them from any potentially watching eyes, but she knew herself to be hidden and didn't really care if he was.

"Good morning," she said, intentionally making him jump.

"Jesus. Where did you come from? I didn't hear a thing."

"You weren't supposed to," she reminded him with a wholly deceptive pleasantness.

"Right. Right." He was very nervous, and it showed. "So, you got my message?"

Sebring didn't bother with an impatient sigh. "The psychic you sensed in Chicago. Who is it?"

"Shit, I don't know that. Just—strong. And she was looking for something or someone, I got that."

"You're certain it was a woman?"

"Well—yeah. Sometimes I don't get that much, but I did this time. A woman, powerful telepath, maybe more than that."

"What do you mean?"

"I mean I was surprised when I looked down at my arm not to see her hand on it. It was like she was touching, not just sensing." He struggled visibly for words. "Reaching out with more than her mind. It was weird. Different."

"So she's a threat."

"I gotta say yes. I didn't get anger from her, and I'm not sure who or what she was looking for, but she was really strong. *Really* strong."

"Did she find who or what she was looking for?"

"I think so," he said cautiously. "Because right after I sensed her, she was . . . gone. Just shut it down, that's how it felt. I roamed around the area for a couple hours after that, but never picked up anything else. I don't think she stuck around."

"Would you recognize her if you felt her sensing again?"

"Oh, hell, yeah."

Sebring considered for a moment in silence, aware that it was making him even more nervous and not caring.

"All right," she said at last. "I'm going to send you down to Charleston. I want you to cover that area for at least twenty-four hours. See if you can pick up that same psychic's touch."

He half nodded, but said, "I heard Duran was in Charleston."

"So?"

"Well . . . he has Astrid."

She waited, brows raised.

"It's just . . . Some of us have run into her before, been in the same area. She's mean. Tries to get in your mind just for the hell of it, and that is *not* something you want. It's like she thinks of you as a fly, and wants to pull your wings off."

"So it wasn't her mind you sensed in Chicago."

"No, definitely not. But if Duran is in Charleston, then so is she. And none of us can really shield against her. I reach out to probe, she's gonna know I'm there. Know I'm looking for somebody. Maybe even know why."

"And she'll report that to Duran."

He looked uncertain. "Hard to say, with Astrid. Way I hear it, she likes knowing things Duran doesn't know. Things she doesn't report to him, I mean. So maybe she wouldn't tell him. But she'd know. Do you want her to know?"

"I don't think I care either way," Sebring said reflectively.

He looked miserable. "Oh. Okay."

"Go to Charleston," she told him. "Do your job. And report back to me *any* psychic contact, whether with the target, Astrid, or anyone else. Understand?"

"Right. Got it."

"Good," Sebring said.

---

"I don't know why someone on his side would have burned that house." Murphy's voice was hard. "If I had to guess—and wanted a hopeful guess of sorts—it would be that, sanctioned or not, destroying that particular house was a warning."

"A warning to us?" Tasha asked.

"Because the Bishops were close?" Brodie said.

"Because *we* were close. Because we knew too much about that part of their master plan, and they wanted to make sure we also knew how . . . ruthless . . . they could be if they had to. Ruthless and efficient. An army burning its munitions before the enemy could get their hands on them."

"Living munitions," Tasha murmured.

"Yes," Murphy said. "To us. But maybe not to them. Maybe it was meant as a warning to us. Or maybe somebody's stepped up their timetable, and they can't afford the time for the babies to be born and grow, even if they are psychic. Hell, maybe somebody's just cut their fucking budget."

She sounded vicious.

And looked it.

"They have too much invested in this already," Tasha insisted. "More than thirty years of working at this?

Houses like the one I was born in gone now, who knows how many others came and went since then, how many babies were adopted out, now toddlers and school kids and teenagers and adults? And what if there are survivors of the program like me, but who've already married and started families? Maybe that's part of the program too."

"Maybe it is," Bishop agreed. "I'd assume it was. They'd need to know if the psychics they produced could pass on the abilities to the next generation. In fact, it almost has to be a multi-generational plan."

Tasha said, "Something that vast, that established, has to represent billions of dollars over the years. Would they just throw away all the potential in the Charlotte house?"

"As a warning?" Bishop shook his head slightly. "Costly gesture, as Tasha said."

Brodie half nodded, but said, "Cost aside, I would have expected something less destructive from Duran. Besides that, for it to be a warning . . . Why? We haven't gone out of our way to show too much of our hand. We haven't made a move against any of those places yet, haven't made any attempt at all to get the women and babies away from him. In fact, we've been as careful as we know how to be to make certain Duran doesn't know we're onto them."

Murphy's smile was thin. "We've also been very, very careful to hide those of our assets and allies who've been waiting secretly on the sidelines to do something, anything, to help. Our active cells, those Duran knows exist, may not have the resources to take care of countless young Stepford mothers and their offspring, but I doubt he realizes we have enough allies who do. And will. Our best use of those still undercover assets and allies may well be to protect those women and their children."

"We need a few more days if we agree we can stick to the plan," Bishop said. "By Sunday at the latest, we'll have enough people and equipment in position to very quietly raid at least half those places on the same day or night, as closely as possible at the same time, as per the plan. Not just a dozen, but closer to fifty. And we'll have the safe houses to take the women and babies to, with caretakers already waiting. I know we don't have a long-term plan yet, but crippling that breeding operation has to be a win for our side."

"But," Miranda said, "once we make that big move, then Duran knows without doubt that we're aware of the program and are determined to stop it."

Brodie half shook his head. "Granted. But how much could he assume we know *now*? It's new intel, and we've protected it. Tucker, the other researchers, everyone in this room has been as careful as we know how to be. Every psychic mind is as protected as we're capable of making them with all the different ways we've learned to shield, psychic and nonpsychic."

Bishop said, "Only a handful of us had any knowledge of the eugenics program. And we've been keeping our distance, even when using surveillance. We've used people we're sure Duran wouldn't recognize as our soldiers, and in every team waiting to move we've got at least one psychic with a strong shield."

Brodie nodded. "So, until we move against the houses and other facilities we've found, how could Duran be aware of how much we know? I mean, to the point that he'd decide to burn one of the houses as a warning to us?"

"But if it was someone else," Tucker mused, "and unsanctioned, then how did they breach all that security? That can't be intel that Duran hands out to even one more of his people than is absolutely necessary."

Murphy's hard voice dropped into the silence. "No matter how much I don't want to believe it, no matter how much we all know he values psychics and how well he guards his assets, it had to be Duran."

"Murphy—"

"I told him." She stared at Brodie and Tasha with hot, glittering eyes. "I told him. I told him we knew. I told him it would stop. That there'd be no more genetically selected women matched with genetically selected males to produce genetically perfect little psychic babies. I told him to shut it down, weeks ago. It's why he pulled his people out of Charleston—at least for a while. So if Duran did this, if it was sanctioned, then it's on me."

Slowly, Brodie said, "How could you have expected him to do that? To force him? No matter what you said to him?"

Murphy was silent, staring into space now, her green eyes still hot and glittering.

It was Tasha who said finally, "He already knew the Bishops were close, that they were searching for missing psychics. It's what spooked him weeks ago, we figured that out. A new player in the game, a team like Bishop and Miranda, with so much power, so visible, so able to hurt Duran and his people in more ways than he can probably count. He knew about the threat they pose. Murphy . . . what other new threat is there?"

"What have you got on him?" Brodie asked, his own voice hard. "What have you got that was important enough to him, that mattered more to him than their eugenics program? Important enough that you had the leverage to even believe you could force him to shut it down?"

Tasha looked at him, then at Murphy, realization suddenly on her face.

"It's . . . it was that threat?"

"What threat?" Brodie demanded.

"It had to be something huge," Murphy said, ignoring him, her gaze on Tasha now. "Something that in the grand scheme of things would pay off for Duran and the rest of them. Pay off big-time, giving them more of the kind of power they need to keep operating. Pay off faster and with a lot more certainty than the potential of babies still in the womb. It'll take years for that investment to really pay off, just the babies we know about."

"Yeah, but . . . just our knowing about another of their operations isn't that much of a threat to it, right? All we had was the one name, just that. All we knew about was Eliot Wolfe."

# ELEVEN

"We could have used that knowledge to make a very big, very public mess," Murphy said. "Just what we knew was enough."

Tasha drew a breath and let it out slowly. "Okay. Then maybe it's time," she said.

"Whatever this is, I'm not going to like it," Brodie muttered.

"Instinct?" Murphy demanded, her gaze still on Tasha.

Tasha nodded slowly. "He has to know. And that part of it's over now. Eliot Wolfe is dead and buried. And Duran knows—I'm out of reach now, useless to him. You said it. And it's true, right? Even if he found someone else like Wolfe?" Her voice was steady, but her eyes were shadowed, worried.

"Yeah," Murphy said. "It's true. You don't have to worry about that, Tasha, I promise. You and Brodie are bonded now, and you're safe from any more plans like that."

"Who was Eliot Wolfe?" Brodie demanded, not quite

so harsh now because he was realizing that answers kept from him for some time now were suddenly in the offing. He had been as patient as he knew how, had not even looked for answers when the connection with Tasha had likely made that possible, but every instinct he could lay claim to had screamed at him that whatever this was, it was bad.

Tasha's hand felt cold in his.

"I should probably tell him," Tasha murmured.

"No," Murphy said. "I tell him. It was my decision to wait." Her eyes were on Brodie now.

Miranda immediately said, "The rest of us can leave, go for breakfast, make some calls. Since it's been a few hours, we should check in with the psychics Noah has moving in around Colorado."

Sarah was nodding. "Annabel is still in bed on the other side of the condo; she'll sleep for hours yet, and deeply. She does every night now. Still catching up on decent rest, poor little thing."

Brodie said nothing, and never took his gaze off Murphy.

She returned the stare, but nodded slowly. "I think maybe you guys should leave Tasha, Brodie, and me alone for an hour or so. Because even though you'll need to know part of it, I don't believe all of it needs to be discussed even within this cell."

"You've got it," Bishop said, rising as the others did. "We all understand information shared on a need-to-know basis. Want us to bring back breakfast for you?" His tone was casual.

Murphy smiled oddly. "You live up to your reputation, Bishop, and I can't say that about many. This cell is stronger with you and Miranda a part of it." Without a pause, she added, "Any kind of breakfast burrito would make me happy. I doubt Brodie has a preference."

"That's fine," he said shortly.

Tasha almost winced, but looked at Bishop with a nod. "Same for me." She wasn't hungry and her stomach was decidedly unsettled by nerves, but in the last weeks Brodie had impressed on her the need to eat and rest when she could, to the point that it was now all but automatic.

She was only distantly aware of the fact that she had completely closed the door on her end of the connection, not sure if she was trying to protect Brodie—or herself—for as long as possible.

Some truths were painful. Very painful.

She could feel Brodie looking at her, but kept her gaze fixed on Murphy as the others left the condo.

"Tasha?"

She half nodded, still not looking at him.

"Some things are better faced alone?"

That jerked her gaze back to his face, because something in his voice told her that her abrupt withdrawal had hurt him. His face was as impassive as it had been when she'd first met him as a stranger, but it didn't take seeing the hurt to be sure it was there. "I don't know," she said slowly. "I really don't know, John. But . . . you should have that option."

"I do. That's why the connection has two doors. I can shut mine if I need to."

Murphy spoke before Tasha could respond, her voice matter-of-fact. "Secrets are tricky beasts. Especially when they're someone else's."

Brodie looked away from Tasha at last, returning his gaze to Murphy. His face remained impassive—but his voice was strained. "You two made it plain there was something I didn't—need—to know these last weeks. So did the boss. I trusted all of you that it was the right call."

*I trusted you.*

He might as well have said it out loud, because that's what Tasha heard.

"It *was* the right call," she told him quietly before Murphy could. "You didn't need to know. Even more, you knowing . . . too soon . . . was dangerous."

"Dangerous to who?"

Murphy replied, "To you. And to the rest of us, probably. We can't know for sure, but even Duran knew the dangers of it going public, in a very . . . visible way. A very nasty way. One way or another, we would have lost you. For good. That's certain. And in losing you, we would have lost so much more."

"Murphy—"

"I should have asked them to bring me a latte," she said, her tone suddenly absent, even evasive.

Tasha wondered if even Murphy was having a hard time figuring out how to tell Brodie. It made her feel a little better about her own anxiety. A little better.

"Sarah got that," she told Murphy, not exactly stalling but willing to help the other woman stall.

"Not from me," Murphy said, half a question.

"No, from me. Sorry."

"Christ, don't be sorry. Just tell me not everybody finds me as easy to read as you do."

"They don't. You've been in my head, remember? Even as a conduit, you left bread crumbs. They seem to be a pathway I can follow almost without thinking about it."

Curious, Murphy said, "Sarah mentioned that. She left bread crumbs too, didn't she? Even though I was the conduit. That's how she reads you so easily."

"Yeah, but . . . she left more than bread crumbs. She left . . . something else. Not sure what, but it's stronger than anything I've ever felt. Except . . . what I feel with John."

*What I'm not letting myself feel now. Or him feel. Dammit. Just . . . dammit.*

Getting more than a little tired of being ignored, and on edge as any man would be who was expecting to hear things he really didn't want to hear, Brodie snapped, "I'm not invisible."

Murphy looked at him, brow rising. "Really? And here I thought you could blend into the woodwork, scowl and all."

"Murphy—"

She lifted a hand to cut him off. "Yeah, yeah, I know. Sorry. It's just that it should be painfully obvious to you that neither Tasha nor I is really looking forward to this."

"Because I'll be angry," he guessed, hoping that was it.

Tasha shook her head silently even though he wasn't looking at her.

Murphy said, "No. You'll be mad later, probably. At least I would be. And if you are, be mad at me, because it *was* my call to keep you in the dark this long. You might even understand the reasoning—and agree with it—but probably not at first. And right now . . . this is going to hurt, John. It's going to open old wounds."

He drew a deep breath and let it out slowly. "Then it's about Elizabeth," he said flatly. "About her murder."

"Yeah. Some of this I can't really explain, and Tasha can't either, but just know we both believed it then, and believe it now. That psychic test of Duran's, the maze? After you pulled Tasha out, you two had that first kind of connection. Not like now, but there was something new. In you. And in Tasha."

He nodded silently.

"We think it was more than the connection forming between you. Or maybe part of that. Christ, who knows why new doors open, why new abilities are triggered. Something happened hours later, Brodie, when you thought Tasha was asleep."

"She was asleep," he said slowly.

"Yeah, at first. But then something woke her up. Something very quiet you weren't aware of. For the first time in her life, Tasha had a mediumistic experience."

"Who came through?" The strain in his voice was showing now on Brodie's face.

"I think you know. It was Elizabeth."

Brodie didn't speak for a long moment. But then he looked at Tasha, the strain still showing, and said, "Open the door."

"John—" She was somehow surprised that he was still holding her cold hand.

"It's the quickest way and we both know it. You kept that memory, that experience hidden from me—and I don't know how I'll feel about that later on. But I do know you can share the entire experience with me now, in a matter of seconds. And that's what I need, Tasha."

She barely heard Murphy murmur something about

checking on Annabel as she left them alone. She was too busy being afraid one incredible memory could change everything between her and the man looking at her with such a still, strained face and eyes that were diamond-hard.

"We knew what you'd do," she whispered. "Even I knew, and I hadn't known you any time at all then. We knew what you'd do, and—and it would have meant losing you. Elizabeth didn't want that either. She's the first one who told me you didn't need to know—yet. That I should listen to my instincts and they'd tell me when the time was right."

"Open the door, Tasha."

Brodie hadn't known himself how he'd react to what Tasha had to tell him. When she had first requested a private meet with Murphy, all he'd been able to *know* was that Tasha had been deeply upset, shocked somehow. And even then, even with their connection so very new and unfamiliar, he had sensed or known somewhere deep inside himself that it wasn't time for him to ask.

But their connection was strong now, he knew that, and even though he believed Murphy that this would reopen old wounds, he also knew it was something he needed to know, both because of the war and because he had to somehow say good-bye to the first woman he had loved in order to move forward with the woman he loved now.

"Tasha. Open the door."

She hesitated, nodded, and then closed her eyes. Visibly braced herself. And opened the door on her side of their connection.

The first thing he felt was her fear, cold and painful,

that this knowledge she had to share would somehow change things between them. And he wanted to respond to that, to reassure her, but just as it had been before, when she had first looked into his mind, his was filled with images. Only this time they were images of Elizabeth, as beautiful as he remembered, sitting in a chair in Tasha's bedroom and quietly, softly, telling a story.

He didn't hear every word. He didn't need to. He knew the story in seconds, the whole story, as he'd expected to. He learned how she had unknowingly lived a life designed for her, had fled the psychic mate chosen for her to build a new, far more secretive life for herself.

He learned how she had fallen in love with him, how happy she had been, how their life had been on track, their future something she had looked forward to. Until she had reached out to use her psychic abilities, gentle, giving Elizabeth, driven to help others.

He learned who Eliot Wolfe had been. He learned that the soulless man who had murdered Elizabeth because she had refused again to be his mate had been one of Duran's people. That he had gone unpunished for his crime then, even for murdering a valuable psychic, because other, more *important* plans had been in place even a decade ago.

And then he learned who Eliot Wolfe had become, who Duran had planned for him to be. And he learned what Murphy and Tasha believed, that she would have been Wolfe's next intended mate, possibly always had been. That Duran had wanted her badly for that reason, because she was an adult and a born psychic able to control her powerful abilities, something that would have been a decided asset to a political puppet Duran's side had groomed to go far and attain another kind of power they wanted.

Political power.

And right there at the end of it all, he felt Tasha's surprise because Murphy had, clearly, sent her part of the story to Tasha to pass on. And now, in real time.

He saw her meeting with Duran at the coffee shop across from Tasha's condo. Saw her tell Duran he would lose his political pawn no matter what. That Brodie would kill him when he discovered what Wolfe had done, resulting in chaos on both sides, that she would lose a soldier she could not afford to lose, and that Duran would lose much more, because his superiors were even less forgiving of mistakes than he was, and Wolfe had made many. With Wolfe dead and Brodie likely jailed, too many things were likely to go very, very public.

So she was doing them both a favor by warning him to get rid of Wolfe on his own, permanently, no fake body or new identity. Dead and buried, with as little fuss as possible.

And in return for warning him so that he could avoid a very messy situation, there was something he would do for her. She told him he would stop the eugenics program. He would stop it or they would, she'd told him, deliberately giving him a heads-up that they knew and would not stand idly by for much longer and allow him to breed psychics.

He would find a reason or an excuse to stop that program. Or, her strong implication was, maybe Brodie would find out who had murdered his wife.

And go after Wolfe.

And cause a very public mess.

Duran, for that reason or reasons of his own, had done at least that part of what Murphy had demanded. He had arranged a traffic "accident" that had killed his promising political candidate.

Elizabeth's murderer dead.

Just as Tasha had said.

Dead and buried.

To say it was all a lot of information to take in would have been a vast understatement, and there was a moment when Brodie was conscious of his own soul-deep rage that his first love had been brutally taken from him and he had not been allowed to avenge her. But even as that rose in him, he was abruptly conscious of a gentle touch, familiar even though she had never touched his mind like that when she was alive.

A gentle touch from Elizabeth that was a confirmation she had told Tasha to keep the truth from him awhile longer, and apologies, and thanks, and her happiness that he had found a new love, understanding that he was bound to Tasha in a way he never could have been with her, a way that would make them both so much more than he could now imagine. And her certainty that this war would finally be over, sooner than he realized, and that he and Tasha would be able to build a happy life together.

Connected. Bonded. Soul mates.

Then Elizabeth Brodie said a final good-bye to her husband, and he felt her leave, felt her move on to someplace that was warm and bright and welcoming. He felt her happiness in that, her peace. And her happiness helped to drain what remained of the rage from his soul.

Brodie sat very still, looking down at Tasha's hand,

aware only then that he had continued to hold it—and in too tight a grip. He loosened that grip instantly, sorry he had hurt her even in that small way, and looked up to find that her eyes were still closed, her face tense, mouth vulnerable.

"Thank you," he said quietly.

Tasha drew a shaky breath, then slowly opened her eyes and looked at him. She was clearly still worried, anxious, her eyes a little wet, darkened and uncertain.

"That was Elizabeth in those last moments, wasn't it?"

Tasha nodded hesitantly. "It—it felt like her. The way it felt that night, when she came to me."

"And told you everything."

"John, I wanted to tell you—"

He leaned over and kissed her. Not briefly.

When she could, and a bit dazedly, Tasha said, "Your door. It's open. Wide open."

"You really thought it wouldn't be?" He smiled at her. "I don't need to handle any of this alone, Tasha. I may still be getting used to it, but our connection means everything to me. And the rage and grief I felt over Elizabeth's death have been slowly draining away since the first time I touched you. It's gone now."

---

"All settled?" Murphy asked briskly as she returned to the room and reclaimed her chair.

"I ought to shoot you," Brodie told her.

She eyed him, taking note of his calm but relaxed face, his faint smile—and the somewhat blissful smile Tasha wore.

"You two need to get a room?"

Tasha blinked, then frowned at her. Ignoring the question, she said, "You got in my head again. You explained about that planned political future for Wolfe, all the stuff you told Duran."

"Yeah, sorry to do that without asking. But it does seem to come awfully easy with you. More than bread crumbs left by a conduit. I'll have to think about that awhile."

"Right now, there are other things you need to think about. Because you're going to talk to us." Brodie's voice was still uncharacteristically mild. "For one thing, you've been having secret meetings with Duran. How long has that gone on?"

"You don't need to know."

Very gently, Brodie said, "Yes, Murphy. I do need to know. You need to tell me."

She eyed him steadily for a moment, then sighed. "The boss said you'd have to know, and probably now. I'd choose otherwise but, hey, just another foot soldier."

"I don't think so," Brodie said. "I don't think you've ever been just that, Murphy. You did a hell of a job wearing that hat, but you came into this to be something else, didn't you? Something a lot higher up the chain of command than just another foot soldier."

"I don't know what you're talking about."

"Yeah, right."

Murphy sighed again. "Brodie, wherever I am in the organization, I came into this to fight just like you do, any way I can. And my background, like yours, has been examined under a microscope, and both the boss and, apparently, some panel made up of very smart people on our side who don't know each other but get to weigh in on these things, all decided I was good to go. I also, like you, report straight to the boss, and she always knows what I'm doing. Always."

Tasha didn't really mean to, but since their connection was wide open on both sides and Brodie was thinking about it, she knew for the first time who "the boss" was in all this.

"Wow," she murmured, eyes wide.

"Forget you know that," Brodie told her, but with a sidelong smile.

"It's forgotten." She wondered if it could be, but then Murphy spoke again and answered the question for her. Sort of.

"I really hope none of Duran's psychics can read you, because open or closed, this connection with Brodie seems to have opened a window or two in your shield," Murphy told her in a wry tone. And then she frowned, adding, "Astrid. Astrid is going to continue to be a problem."

"Bread crumbs?" Tasha said.

"Yeah, she's left too many pathways into too many of our people, and she *is* a powerful psychic. It's not just that, though. Brodie said earlier that she's a sociopath, and I agree. Possibly a psychopath or even worse. She's dangerous. And though Duran believes he can control her, I'm not so sure she doesn't have an agenda of her own."

"Duran," Brodie said. "You meeting up with him was sanctioned?"

"Well, of course it was."

He stared at her, waiting.

"Brodie, I'm not going to just spill my guts about him. Ask a specific question, or let's change the subject."

"How long have you been meeting him?"

"Nearly three years."

"That long? Jesus Christ, Murphy."

She considered him with a faint frown, then said, "Okay. Let me put things in perspective for you. The tip I got about looking into Tasha's parentage? That came from Duran."

It was Tasha who said slowly, "But . . . that led us straight to the eugenics program."

"Yeah," Murphy said. "It did."

"He couldn't have known that's where we'd end up. It doesn't make sense," Brodie said slowly.

"It makes sense if you accept and understand one very simple fact."

"Which is?"

"Duran doesn't agree with his superiors. About a lot of things. I'm not sure he ever did. But it took him a while to work his way up through the ranks and get himself into a position of authority, and he still has to be careful in how and when he . . . interferes in their plans. Very careful. He still has to do ruthless things sometimes. Still has to follow orders and toe the company line."

"Company?" Brodie's voice was quick.

"Yeah, you weren't far off with that idea that they could be using a Fortune 500 company as a front. Because it *is* expensive, this thing of theirs. And it goes back a lot further than thirty years. So they've had time to build some very convincing fronts for their operations. Some very big companies, most of them merged in recent years into just two or three behemoths, often on the cutting edge of technology, or finance, or whatever. Company names we'd recognize doing fairly blameless things—at least in terms of Wall Street—and earning a hell of a lot of money for their shareholders. Shareholders who are, basically, all their own people, from their scientists to their foot soldiers."

"That's how they fund their operations? Completely?"

"Well, that's as much as I've been able to get out of Duran. Trust me when I say he *definitely* does not spill his guts. I've learned a lot from him over the last three years, but it's been in bits and pieces the boss and I've been putting together like a jigsaw puzzle. Duran and I have these tense little discussions. We exchange information."

Brodie opened his mouth, but Murphy went on calmly before he could ask the obvious question.

"No, I don't tell him anything about *our* operations that he doesn't already know."

"How can you be sure of that?"

"I can be absolutely positive. But *how* I can really is not something you're cleared to know. Sorry."

# TWELVE

"Goddammit, Murphy."

"Hey, you know protocol and why we're set up the way we are. They're good reasons. None of us should know . . . more than we should know."

"Can you read him?" Brodie was still frowning.

"Not his mind, at least so far, and I can't tell if he's psychic. But I can tell you that his mother was psychic, and that she did something extraordinary. Something that protects him to this day."

It was Tasha who guessed. "She built a shield for him?"

Murphy nodded. "When he was very young. No psychic I've ever encountered has been able to explain to me how it was even possible, but according to Duran she somehow constructed a completely organic shield for him, one that exists almost independently of him, not something he controls or even has to think about. In fact, he's certain she began building it when he was hardly more than a toddler. And she added layers to it over a period of several years, until not only was his mind protected from the probing of any psychic, even his personality was hidden. She knew people like his own father were hurting psychics, and even though she couldn't tell if he'd inherited any of her psychic ability, she still wanted to protect him. So she did."

"His father?"

"Born into the company, so to speak. That's one reason he was able to rise through the ranks the way he did, on the fast track. And his mother is another of the reasons his loyalties are . . . divided."

Tasha asked, "Are his parents involved in his life?"

"His father never really was, from what I can tell. No idea why, at least not when Duran was a kid; he was apparently killed in some kind of field operation when Duran was in his teens."

"And his mother?"

Murphy frowned and answered slowly. "When we agreed to meet the first time, after sort of running into each other a few times in field operations, I told him I needed to know why he thought I could trust him at all, why I should believe he was willing to help our side in even the smallest ways. He told me that while he was away at college, his mother was supposedly killed in a car accident. He believed that at the time, but after years in the field, he began to suspect that either because they mistrusted her or needed her abilities, his mother had been yet another psychic taken. He was certain she was dead by then, but a lot less certain she died in a car accident. And he provided enough details so the boss was able to corroborate what he'd told me."

Murphy added calmly, "And, yes, we know the name

he was born with and where he went to school—Ivy League, by the way, very impressive. Top of his class. Duran is the name he took when he formally joined up and—in what is apparently their protocol—more or less detached himself from the life he'd had until then. Duran's life began when he graduated from college; the life of the man he was before then simply stopped at that time. Which is why we've never been able to run background checks on any of the field operatives we've run into, using the names we've heard and what photos we've been able to take."

Brodie was frowning, but said almost absently, "Yeah, that makes sense. I guess you've pushed him as hard as you could for intel we could use."

"That better not be a question. Of course I have."

"Maybe it's time you pushed harder. If Bishop's people really are closing in on the abducted psychics, we need every bit of intel we can get our hands on. Because wherever they're being held *is* bound to hold a lot more secrets than missing psychics. Secrets that could help us win this war."

Murphy studied him for a moment. "Okay, I'll see if I can needle him into revealing a bit more the next time we meet. Sometimes that works very well."

"I'm not surprised," Brodie retorted.

---

When the others returned to the condo just over an hour after they'd left them alone, they found Brodie calm but fairly expressionless and with eyes thoughtful rather than hard—and he was still holding Tasha's hand, which seemed to indicate that whatever the news finally related to Brodie, it had clearly not affected their relationship in any negative way.

"No news from your psychics yet, I take it?" he asked Bishop.

"No, not yet. I notified a few more to head west; there's a lot of wilderness they have to cover, and even scanning broad areas is going to take some time." He sounded like a man with infinite patience, but it didn't take a telepath to know that Bishop was more than driven to locate his missing psychics, especially since teenager Emma Garrick had been taken.

Murphy sent him a quick but searching look, but didn't comment on that. Instead she provided a brief need-to-know summary of what they had missed.

"Duran's people showed the first signs of political ambition we've been absolutely sure of, running one of his born psychics for a major state office—with the plan, though he never admitted this part—to pair him with Tasha. Which partly explains his very intense interest in Tasha. I had enough serious dirt on his candidate to force him to pull the guy out of the race—and get rid of him."

"Car accident?" Miranda asked mildly, remembering a newspaper headline she'd noticed weeks back.

Murphy nodded. "I have a hunch he knew the guy wasn't going to work out long before I told him, because Duran was the one who had, earlier, tipped me off to check into Tasha's parentage. Hell, I probably did him a favor giving him a good reason to off that particular candidate.

"As for the breeding operation, I'd been getting the feeling he was ready to start winding that up and wouldn't mind a push from us. Maybe because this possible *Supreme* he thought he had was one of their ultimate goals, or maybe just because whatever his medical people and scientists had to do in order to turn those women into Stepford moms bothered him almost as much as it bothers us."

"Supreme?" Bishop asked.

"Sorry, forgot we hadn't discussed that. The ultimate psychic. One born with unlimited potential and absolute control. It was just a whisper for a long time, but we've confirmed that was at least one reason for the abductions. And experimentations. Looking for that ultimate psychic."

"Have they found or created that psychic?"

"I honestly don't know, and I haven't been able to persuade Duran to either confirm or deny. But it's possible."

Bishop said, "On a need-to-know basis, is Duran secretly playing for our team, or just a source whose information you triple-check before you act on it?"

She chewed a bite of her burrito thoughtfully before answering, saying finally, "He has divided loyalties, but understandable reasons for that. I think he'd stop this if he could, but it's way too big for that now. So . . . he minimizes damage when he can, and offers the occasional tip or snippet of information. And lets me push him around from time to time if I've got a good enough reason."

"Lets you?" Bishop smiled faintly, then turned to Tucker and added, "If you don't already have it, I can get you into a data bank that'll give you access to real-time satellite photography able to pinpoint Wi-Fi signals or pings off cell towers. Anywhere in the country. I can also offer software that will allow you to use that data to pinpoint any security systems hardwired or wireless—*and* allow you to hack into those systems remotely."

"Is that legal?" Sarah asked dryly.

"No," Bishop answered simply. "I have to get a warrant or get permission to obtain in any way private security system information outside the scene of a crime. But once the software is downloaded into Tucker's system, there'll be no sign he's in possession of it, and no matter how much he uses it, there'll be no detectable sign it's been . . . unofficially used."

"Suits me," Tucker said.

Sarah murmured, "Why does that not surprise me?" And smiled when her husband grinned at her.

Bishop said, "It should show us pretty quickly if any of the neighbors have security cameras that might have caught at least a few frames of what went on at the Charlotte house before the fire."

"I would love to add that to my toolbox," Tucker said agreeably, and they both headed for his large desk.

Miranda reclaimed her chair as Sarah went off to check on Annabel again and the others worked on breakfast.

When Sarah came back only a few short moments later, she was laughing softly. "Annabel is still asleep, and I'd swear Pendragon opened his eyes just long enough to glare at me and make the point I wasn't wanted. That's one strange cat."

"Didn't you say he's turned up in more than one odd place in all this?" Miranda asked as Sarah sat in another chair close by.

"I'll say. He first turned up in Richmond not too long

before I met Tucker. I asked around, but nobody admitted he was theirs despite his collar and tag. So I fed him and he stuck around, coming and going on his own schedule. Then everything sort of hit the fan, and Tucker and I were on the move, heading north, stopping at different places along the way. And then Pendragon turned up for just a brief minute or two in the middle of a sort of rescue operation when one of Duran's goons tried something definitely unsanctioned. And that was way up north, in Maine." She frowned briefly. "I never could figure out how he got out of that old church, since it was burning. But he's done stranger things, like turning up here in Charleston and bringing Annabel to us."

Miranda, who knew as well as her husband the questions *not* to ask, merely said, "I remember Annabel said he slept with her at night out on the streets when she didn't want to go back to that hellhole foster home. That he kept her warm."

Sarah nodded. "And whispered to her, she said. Told her he would take her to a place where she'd be safe and where people would love her. Which is what he did."

Miranda shook her head. "First Richmond, then Maine, and now here. I know cats can wander pretty far, but that strikes me as extreme. And very . . . specific. There is definitely something unusual about that cat."

Sarah said, "I agree he's a cat of a different sort. I've never encountered one quite like him. And he's stuck close to Annabel since he brought her to us. She hasn't said much about it, but I'll swear those two really do talk to each other."

Miranda smiled. "You're going to adopt her, aren't you?"

"If she'll have us, yes. A judge and Social Services gave us temporary custody and guardianship once they saw that damned foster *home* and how the other kids were treated. I just wish they'd been able to jail that couple and get the other kids into safe places sooner."

"Some things have to happen just the way they happen," Miranda said. "We've learned that the hard way."

Sarah nodded. "Yeah, after everything that's happened since my abilities were triggered in that car accident, I really believe that's true. It seemed like a curse at first, even a death sentence, but . . . I met Tucker. And we found psychics good and bad, and people who weren't psychic but wanted to help, and were part of this, people like Brodie, and others."

Emerging from her post-breakfast bliss, Murphy said, "And Sarah's spent these last months learning more about her abilities and how to control them."

"Also making some public noise," Miranda noted with a smile.

"Tucker's book about me." Sarah looked a bit rueful. "Given a choice between hiding and going public, there really wasn't a choice to make. Plus, we both wanted to stay in this thing, help all we could. I have to admit, though, that the decision to relocate here in Charleston was partly because of all the attention focused on us back in Richmond after the book came out. Tucker has the well-known habit of vanishing for a while whenever he's researching a new book, so we told a few people we knew would spread the word that was our reason for leaving Richmond—indefinitely."

"And you got a break from the spotlight," Miranda said.

---

On the other side of the quiet condo, Pendragon opened his eyes and his other senses briefly, then released an almost human sigh. He was perfectly comfortable cuddled up beside Annabel, and content that she was sleeping in peace, not cold or lonely or afraid. He'd chosen well for her, he thought.

She would have a happy life.

But there were things to do first, Pendragon knew that. Important things. Necessary things. The humans talking so quietly on the other side of the condo knew that, and were slowly working their way toward knowledge and understanding, as humans tended to do.

Adding up bits and pieces of knowledge, of speculation. Asking themselves and each other questions. Pondering . . . possibilities.

Pendragon could have offered a shortcut or two to help them along, and thought he might need to do that. Maybe.

But the fragile little soul beside him was his main concern. Because they would need her help as well, and his, though they didn't yet know it.

But they would.

Soon.

Pendragon closed his eyes and drifted back to sleep.

---

"Yeah, a nice break," Sarah said. "Plus the chance to help out with what was going on around Tasha. We were both being so careful at first about being so near one of Duran's operations. Neither of us realized then that me being connected to Tucker, bonded the way we are, protects both of us."

"Recent intel," Murphy agreed. "After Bishop first made contact, we naturally took a closer look at the Special Crimes Unit. He offered us some fairly bare facts about his teams, and one thing that struck me was the number of personally paired psychics, all of them male-female and most of them married to each other."

"Including us," Miranda murmured.

Murphy nodded with a faint smile. "Each of you powerful on your own, but a *hell* of a lot stronger together. Bishop said that was true of all the bonded pairs. So I started to wonder about that."

Brodie, his breakfast finished and his attention on the conversation, said slowly, "We've come across a few bonded psychics in the last ten years that I know of. All male-female."

"Yeah," Murphy agreed. "More than a few, once I started looking into it and counting. A few of the pairs joined the fight and are still in it. Others, usually because they'd started their families or for other reasons, elected to stay put and be really visible. And not a single bonded pair that we know of has been a target of Duran or any of his people once that bond formed."

"Because we're stronger?" Miranda suggested.

"It could be partly that, but I think it's something else too. I don't know what that is or why it matters, but I know from one of my tense little meetings with Duran that none of the psychics he's taken or turned, and none produced through their eugenics program has managed to bond with another psychic. Not, at least, any he still controls."

"People like me," Tasha said.

"Yeah. This whole eugenics thing is so new to us that so far you're the only one we know about who *did* escape Duran's control. There could be others who were good, or lucky, or both; he certainly wouldn't share that. Now, with you, it's clear that the connection between you and Brodie happened, or at least started happening, when you first met. I honestly didn't know if Duran would move against you before the bond was complete—but he didn't. He knew Brodie was your Guardian, and I'm fairly certain he has a healthy respect for Brodie and his abilities, but I don't think that's what stopped him."

"You *had* run him out of Charleston," Brodie reminded her dryly.

"So to speak. And he had other things to occupy him. Troublesome political candidates to get rid of. Probably a few carefully crafted explanations to his superiors and delicate questions about whether they *really* wanted to get into politics, given that very bright spotlight and all the potential problems. Decisions to make about his eugenics program. But he's back here now, and he knows Tasha is out of reach."

"Why's he back here?" Brodie was frowning.

"Well, I haven't asked him because I'm pretty sure Tucker's right and he doesn't know that *we* know about that new base of theirs here. But—I'm also pretty sure he knows we've turned this building into a base of our own. And if I had to guess, which at the moment I do, I'd say he's bothered by a few things."

"Such as?"

"All these years, we've gone out of our way to be mobile; even though some of our cells cover a specific area, most of our people stay on the move. Even the boss. So the fact that we've committed considerable resources in turning this building into a highly secure base probably bugs him. Resettling Sarah and Tucker here, if he knows that and I'm pretty sure he does, would definitely bug him. Because they're a bonded pair. And because they're not only powerful in terms of psychic abilities, but Tucker has mad skills as a researcher and is a technical genius."

Miranda glanced over at what was clearly an extensive technical command center, where Bishop and Tucker were both intently working at keyboards, and said, "Yeah, I can see how that would bother him. Just in the last few years, technology has improved so much that the ability to uncover information has taken more than a quantum leap forward. It's almost impossible for anyone to hide anything—at least not for long."

"Maybe we're catching up to them technically," Tasha offered.

"Could be," Murphy agreed. "As Tucker said, we have a few more geniuses, some researching and others working on the purely technical end of things. We've managed to get our hands on some of the gadgets Duran's people have used over the years, and reverse-engineered a few of them. And designed a few of our own using the knowledge we gained from them. That's one reason why we felt we could actually make this a secure base, one Duran's people won't be able to just waltz in and out of."

"They got into my building," Tasha said ruefully.

"This building is way more secure," Murphy said simply.

"Wow."

"Cost a bundle, but we have background assets more

than willing to contribute, and it's an investment we hope will pay off in protecting whoever or whatever we need to protect, including the intel we've been able to collect and will continue to collect. We've been building some pretty impressive files on Duran's operations and his people."

Brodie said, "I'd settle for knowing what their endgame really is. It's tough as hell to be tactical in your general strategy when you don't know the ultimate goal of the other side. Beyond their apparent need for psychics."

Ruefully, Tasha said, "It just seems we keep on getting pieces of the puzzle and still don't know what the whole picture is supposed to look like."

Smiling faintly, Brodie said, "Ten years ago, the only puzzle piece we had was the certainty that psychics were in danger. And I'm pretty sure our side had only been in existence in any organized way for a few years before then. We've learned more in the last couple of years than in all the time before."

"Yeah," Murphy said, brooding now. "But we don't know enough. We don't know nearly enough. Not yet."

---

Duran was not happy to find that when he had in front of him the list he had requested of the positions of all their people, he could not find a single operative or psychic who had not been where he or she was supposed to be.

And no one had been anywhere near the Charlotte house for at least two days, when they had last been visited by the operative and healer who had been sent to scan the women and their unborn babies. Using technology—not psychic abilities.

More than one of their psychics had said, over the years, that whatever the healers did to heal their various ailments—often the headaches psychics so often suffered—felt very much like an invasion, and a highly unpleasant one at that. But the healers certainly gleaned no abilities or even knowledge from the psychics they healed.

Not that any of that was uppermost in Duran's mind at the moment.

Each of their people had implanted in them a tiny chip that was a GPS locator, a biometric monitoring device, and a passcode, the latter enabling them to pass through the first layer of security in any building of the company's operation. After that, the layers were progressively more difficult.

So Duran knew that the official record showed every last operative and psychic in their individual positions as per whatever orders they were following.

He also knew he had a problem. A very big problem.

Whoever had torched the Charlotte house must have somehow disabled or somehow . . . deceived . . . that very sophisticated and supposedly unhackable chip. In addition, that person surely had a wide range of abilities to have not only disabled the surveillance without being detected doing so but also to—he believed—have recognized the importance of that particular operation. And to want, for reasons unknown, to delay any duplication of that particular project at best—or have it classed as a failure at worst.

He had asked his technical people point-blank if there

was any way the arsonist could have put all the video feeds on a loop, showing peace while destruction was being wrought right in front of their unseeing electronic eyes.

One nervous technician said that anything was *possible* when it came to electronics, but that they'd found no sign as yet that any of the equipment either at the com center or in Charlotte at the house itself had been tampered with before the fire. Just destroyed *in* the fire.

Duran had resisted the urge to cause the nervous technician more anxiety; it was a technique he used quite deliberately but carefully; he wanted his operatives to be fully aware of the fact that he was authorized to simply end them at any moment if he wished.

A reminder of that now and then was a good thing.

Duran did not wish to be loved by his people, he wished to be feared by them. A goal he had accomplished years ago.

And that was one reason why he seldom felt concern about any dissension in the ranks. There had been two or three over the years who had altered some plan of his because they had believed their own ideas better; Duran had made certain that every other operative knew what happened to those with such idiotic impulses.

There had even been a few along the way who had taken a small, simple step out of line for whatever reason; those, too, had been dealt with, less severely but still punishment to be feared.

But something like this . . . He had never faced this sort of betrayal in all his years in command. Had never seen any such thing in the earlier years, when he was working his way up through the ranks, being a perfect soldier.

And he had a double problem on his hands. There was the urgent need to discover who had destroyed the Charlotte operation and why, and there was the equally urgent need to minimize the fallout once his superiors knew.

Depending on how much he told them, of course.

His only luck there was that they had not been aware of his belief that among those unborn children had been at least one that could have been The Supreme. And Duran had been very careful to keep that possibility confined strictly to the healers who had worked on the project and an operative he trusted.

The question was—who would have been so threatened by the possible birth of The Supreme as to take such drastic and dangerous action?

And how could he identify that person?

# THIRTEEN

Murphy paused on the almost-deserted sidewalk, digging in her bag for one of the burner phones that still had a charge. She checked three of them before finding one with about a quarter of a battery left.

It was enough.

She punched in the number, and when he answered, asked one hard question.

"Did you know?"

There was a brief pause, and then Duran said evenly, "No. It was not sanctioned. At any level."

She almost believed him. Enough, at any rate, to forgo asking the question that had been teasing her mind ever since Bishop had called her only moments after her predawn encounter with Duran. Because if it had not been sanctioned, that fire, then perhaps Duran did not know *why* that particular house had been burned. And *why* it had been destroyed might well be far more important than who had committed arson.

"Do you know who?" she asked, her voice still flinty.

"Not yet. But I will find out."

He would certainly be searching for the person responsible, if it really had been an unsanctioned act. He might even find out who had done it.

But Murphy intended to get to them first. Because anyone who would cold-bloodedly murder a dozen young women and their unborn babies was worse than an enemy.

She ended the call without another word, then immediately removed the cell's battery. And as she continued along the nearly deserted sidewalk across from a dog park, she unobtrusively dropped the battery in one trash container. The phone itself was smoothly dropped into another trash container two blocks farther along her journey.

She changed direction twice more just in case anyone thought they could track her movements by somehow tracking that disabled and discarded phone or pings off cell towers or anything else. Her life had taught her to be cautious, even paranoid. She did not consider either a bad thing, simply her reality.

She needed to find out who had torched that house.

And she needed to find out why.

---

As it turned out, it took three days to receive and study all the reports of the Charlotte shadow house fire. And even though Bishop was certain his inside contacts had gotten the original reports, the first reports, it was quickly obvious that Duran's people must indeed have been prepared for anything.

And had somehow been able to alter the very scene of the fire, the charred remains themselves, because according to the reports, no pregnant women had died in that horrible fire.

No unborn babies had perished.

Just an unfortunate few "patients" who had been recovering from surgery in what was supposed to be a quiet, restful house in a nice, quiet neighborhood.

Male and female patients of various ages.

But no babies.

---

*Do you really believe someone is looking for us?*

*I have to believe it, Henry.*

*I'm so tired, Juno.*

*I know. I know you are.*

*Will they find us?*

*I have to believe that too.*

*Will they find us in time?*

*Henry, you have to keep holding on.*

*Do I?*

*Yes. Promise me. Promise me you won't let go.*

*Do you really believe someone is looking for us?*

*I have to believe it, Henry. I have to . . .*

---

No matter how easy they made it look on TV and in the movies, hacking into any good electronic system, especially a security system and even more especially remotely from nearly two hundred miles away, was not an easy or quick process.

Luckily, Tucker was a genius.

After successfully hacking into those systems, copying hours of recordings from what turned out to be more than a dozen cameras at other houses in the neighborhood providing even a sliver of a dim view of some part of the shadow breeding house property took a bit more time. And Tucker added in four more cameras he'd discovered with views, not of the shadow house or yard, but of the streets in front of and surrounding the house. Two were directly across from the shadow house; the other two were farther down the street in each direction.

Just in case the arsonist had parked some distance away, or walked carelessly across that street.

After all that, and even deciding to work in shifts, with two people always reviewing the tapes to make certain tired eyes didn't miss something important, it was hours and hours of staring at the large computer screens. Examining every frame of the many recordings made that night, from midnight until after dawn, because Tucker thought it a good idea to see the first responders in action, and maybe look over any neighbors who lingered to watch as well.

Because you never knew.

Tucker was somewhat bemused to find out that the Bishops never appeared on any of the cameras near the burning house at any time; he found only a few frames of them slipping across a dark yard and crossing a street two blocks away. And then disappearing into the predawn darkness.

Since nobody doubted the couple had indeed *been* at the Charlotte house, he couldn't help asking Bishop about it. And somehow wasn't surprised when the reply had been simply, "It's a knack we have."

A *knack*.

Tucker was tempted, but didn't push it. He'd been in

this thing long enough to know he had plenty to do without looking for puzzles he didn't need to solve. So he went back to the all-important puzzle of who had started the fire.

It was only on the fourth day after the fire, on Friday morning, that the long, long hours Tucker and others had spent going over all those recordings finally paid off.

It was only a quick glimpse caught by a single camera mounted at the back of a neighbor's garage, actually two houses down and at a sharp angle that showed only a sliver of the fenced backyard of the shadow house. And that quick glimpse of a figure scaling the privacy fence easily—after leaning over it to drop two large plastic fuel containers onto the ground—lasted only seconds.

A few seconds entering the grounds and, then, in the flickering red light of the fire, the same figure carrying clearly empty fuel containers that were tossed over the fence before the figure followed, going easily over the fence and disappearing.

The first appearance was time-stamped just slightly more than half an hour before Bishop and Miranda had arrived at the burning house. The second was time-stamped fifteen minutes later.

Tucker isolated those frames and enlarged them as much as he was able without losing too much resolution, put them through a video enhancement program he'd helped develop, then replayed both scenes on a loop in slow motion. It was definitely a view of a corner of the backyard of the shadow house. And definitely someone slipping into that yard with enough fuel to burn even a large house, if they knew what they were doing. And then slipping away again, job clearly done.

He was able to get a very good image of their arsonist's face.

"Nobody I recognize," he said.

"Somebody I do," Murphy said, digging in her large bag and producing a tablet. "One of my little worries just got resolved. Can you copy that loop to my tablet, Tucker?"

He took one look at her grim expression, said, "You bet," and wasted no time in copying the data to her tablet. "Do we need to know?" he asked as he handed her tablet back.

"Yeah, but not until I get back. I'll explain then."

"Do I need to call the others?" On that particular morning, only the two of them had been reviewing the videos and were, in fact, alone in the condo.

"Not until I'm on my way back, and that could be a couple of hours or longer. I'll call you. And, Tucker—don't mention or show this clip to anybody else, okay?"

"Not even Sarah?" he asked neutrally.

"Not even Sarah. You'll all understand when I get back."

"Got it." Even as Murphy was rising, Tucker was saving the clip to a separate file under an innocuous name, and then securing the rest of the videos in another file.

Within seconds, the screen was showing the multiple boxes of the primary security feed from the building they were in.

"I know we have people doing this," he said absently. "But I like to keep an eye on things."

Murphy smiled faintly for the first time that morning. "Have I mentioned you're a very special asset, Tucker?"

"Once or twice." He smiled faintly himself. "I've got

plenty to keep me busy until you get back. I want to use the new tools Bishop gave me and see if I can help search for that lab. Take care, Murphy."

"Always."

Murphy placed the call when she was three blocks away, and she never stopped moving. As soon as he answered, she gave him the address of an unused warehouse several miles away.

"Be there in thirty minutes," she said. "Bring Astrid."

"Murphy—"

"Bring Astrid. Do *not* tell her who you're meeting. Thirty minutes, Duran."

She ended the call, going through the usual procedure of dropping the battery in one receptacle and the useless phone in another.

She never stopped moving.

---

Murphy got there early, as usual, and scouted the area carefully, using every sense she had to probe into shadowy corners as she circled the big warehouse cautiously. She was always careful when meeting Duran, but this time she took extra care. She made absolutely sure no one was nearby, then slipped inside, checked out the interior just as carefully, then chose her vantage point.

Then she settled down to wait, raising every shield she had, every wall, every layer of protection she had learned to not only shield her mind, but make herself virtually invisible.

An idea she'd gotten from Duran. She thought he would appreciate the irony.

She had to wait less than five minutes before Duran

and Astrid entered the warehouse. Duran was dressed a bit more casually than usual, with no tie or suit jacket, which caused Murphy to idly wonder if he planned to do something non-work-related for the weekend. Something not stealthy.

She supposed even Duran had to unbend occasionally. Either that or he'd wanted to make it obvious he was not armed.

She would have put money on the second possibility.

Astrid was dressed even more casually in jeans and a summer blouse, and looked extremely wary, her thin face tense and sharp eyes darting around. Duran didn't normally take her to this sort of place, and Murphy knew very well that the other psychic was using every sense *she* had to probe.

It was what she'd expected.

Knowing herself to be invisible, Murphy waited serenely for the other two to move to the center of the warehouse near her position, where there was an open space surrounded by giant but defunct machines that had once produced some useful product. There were two big wooden crates, one half open and showing machinery parts, the other still nailed shut and abandoned. Both the crates were about waist-high to a tall man like Duran.

They reached the center of the big warehouse, the "center" of any building being always the default agreement between Murphy and Duran unless some other area of a meeting place was specifically designated.

Duran leaned slightly against the crate that was nailed shut, his very handsome face expressionless except for the slight smile that tended to unnerve just about anyone who saw it.

Astrid was unnerved.

"Why am I here, Duran?"

"Why don't you tell me, Astrid?" he suggested pleasantly.

She never got the chance to respond.

Murphy came out of nowhere on silent feet, her weapon raised and leveled. The silencer emitted only an almost apologetic sneezing pop as she shot Astrid in the head.

The other woman dropped like a stone.

Duran barely changed expression as he looked down at his dead psychic. "I assume you have a reason," he said in the same tone he had used with Astrid.

"Yeah. I have a very good reason. See for yourself." Murphy held her gun down at her side, pointedly not putting it away, and with her free hand produced her tablet. She didn't hand it directly to Duran, but placed it on the crate and pushed it toward him.

He picked up the tablet, opened it, and silently played the very short video clip. He played it a second time. Then he closed the tablet and, as Murphy had done, placed it on the crate and pushed it toward her.

"I must be slipping," he said mildly. "It hadn't occurred to me to have my people hack into any security systems other than our own."

"We're learning fast," Murphy said. "And we have some very bright boys and girls now with some *very* mad skills when it comes to finding whatever it is we're looking for. Finding Astrid was really very easy. It just took a little time."

He didn't comment on that, but merely said, "I would have liked the opportunity to question her first," he said.

"To find out why she torched the Charlotte house? My

guess would be that it was about that dozen unborn babies. They would have been born with all their abilities fully realized. But, even so, it would take time for those babies to grow up, to learn to control those abilities, and to become useful. Maybe to replace Astrid. Right, Duran?"

He didn't say anything.

Murphy hadn't expected him to. Not yet.

"But I'm betting that Astrid somehow found out that at least one of those babies was possibly this *Supreme* you've been searching for and trying to produce. A child born with powerful psychic abilities—and the strength to master them completely. A child who could probably become a major asset for you in just a few years. I mean, we've known your side took children. Very young children. But none of them was your very special Supreme. Are any of them even still alive, Duran?"

A very slight but visible emotion crossed his face. "A few."

"How many?"

"Half a dozen."

"Taken when?"

"Most in the last year."

"And useless to you."

"Not useless. Just—"

"Just not your Supreme. And, really, not of much use to you until they grow up. If then." Murphy drew a breath and released it slowly, her hand tightening around the grip of her pistol as she forced herself to continue holding it at her side. "We'll come back to that later."

He didn't respond, merely waited.

"See, I think Astrid felt threatened. She was your pet psychic, after all. The one you called on most often. The one who usually traveled with you in the field. The one with the strongest abilities—and absolutely no loyalties to her own kind. Astrid would do anything you asked, and had. She enjoyed being in that position. Even more, she enjoyed being able to . . . bore into the minds of other psychics. To threaten them. To scare them. To hurt them if she could. It's what sociopaths do. What psychopaths do.

"So there was no way she was going to lose her very important position in your organization to a little kid. There was no way she could allow that child to be born. Even if there was only . . . a chance . . . one of those babies was your Supreme. So they all had to die."

Duran looked at her steadily.

Murphy met that gaze and waited, the faint smile she wore nowhere near pleasant.

"She couldn't have known," he said finally in a measured tone. "Only myself and a handful of others knew there was a *possibility* one of those infants might have been . . . the one."

"A few of your *healers*, maybe? The ones you told me have the ability to help one of your people as well as a psychic who's sick or in pain."

He nodded slightly.

Murphy went off on a tangent suddenly, catching him off guard. "Your healers are very old, aren't they? The only survivors of the first generation. The first coming of your people."

Duran didn't nod this time, merely inclined his head, his sharp eyes watchful.

"I'm assuming there was some . . . medical intervention there. To keep those healers alive and useful as long as possible. Maybe even to clone them. Because your people aren't immortal. You're not even ageless, even if you do apparently have longer life spans than we do."

Some emotion had flitted across his expression at the mention of cloning, but he didn't comment on that. After a moment, deliberately, Duran said, "Whatever was done to the first ones, whatever medical intervention was done to any of the following generations, none of it is effective on your people, Murphy."

"And you'd know that. For certain."

"Yes."

Murphy leaned an elbow on the wooden crate beside him, still holding her gun at her other side. She looked very relaxed now, even amused. "What if I told you that you were wrong, Duran? What if I told you that your biological tinkering changed some things a long time ago? Some people. Some of my people."

Slowly, he said, "Then I would wonder how that happened. And how you could know it had happened when we do not."

"How it happened is simple. Some of your failures weren't really failures. And some of them got away," she said softly.

"Our monitoring system—"

"Is really quite amazing, I agree." Her clear implication was that they knew exactly how Duran was able to track the people on his side. Murphy didn't dwell on that issue, however. "But it wasn't nearly so advanced decades ago. No biometric chips then. Further back, when the first generation was still convinced they could create a successful hybrid in a petri dish, engineering biology. Before you began to see some success in breeding born psychics to born psychics, your people were still tinkering with bloodlines and mixing DNA, and mostly producing freaks or . . . unviable offspring."

"Before my time," he said briefly.

"But you know about it. I'm guessing your people have quite an extensive historical database filled with all the details."

Duran was frowning slightly. "There are records."

Murphy was about to prod him to elaborate on that when a calm voice touched her mind with an ease that had been growing all along.

*Murphy. There's a psychic I don't recognize in Charleston. Probing. Not much of a shield.*

*What's he looking for, Sarah?*

*Not what. Who. He's searching for a psychic whose mind he touched in Chicago not long ago.*

*He's one of Duran's?*

*No. That's the thing. Like I said, not much of a shield, so I've been picking up a lot from him.*

Murphy kept her gaze on Duran as she listened to the voice in her mind, knowing that only seconds were passing and that her own expression wouldn't reveal to him that new information was reaching her, confirming recent intel she and others had gathered.

Then, calmly, she said, "Records. And I'm guessing those records are kept in at least two locations. Necessary when your people split into two factions."

He was silent.

Murphy smiled. "Tell me about Sebring."

# FOURTEEN

With so many of their assets tied up in preparing for the coming rescue operation, the Charleston cell worked long hours doing whatever was needed. Tasha and Brodie had been sent on a trip to scout out a suspected shadow breeding house in northern Florida. The entire trip required no more than twenty-four hours, driving time included, since they came straight back to Charleston afterward, though they arrived very late back at Tasha's condo.

The location had turned out to house another shadow breeding operation, something Tasha had been able to sense with absolute certainty when she and Brodie had still been two blocks away in their car. Only three pregnant women there, but Tasha sensed the babies and knew two of the three had some psychic ability. She didn't believe they were as strong as the babies who had died in Charlotte, but she was certain they had psychic abilities.

Brodie knew what she had sensed, because their connection was even stronger and more secure now, and because Tasha no longer closed the door on her side. For any reason.

She had dreamed that night, uneasy dreams that were not quite nightmares, and though her almost inaudible cries had not awakened her, they had awakened Brodie. He had pulled her closer to him, and she had almost immediately grown peaceful again.

He knew what she had dreamed. A shadow creature, its elongated and otherwise distorted shape looming, had been circling the house they had found, never getting closer but circling, circling. Watching. Hunting. It hungered, and Tasha had felt that, had felt anxious and uneasy because of it.

Which was one reason he looked at her rather searchingly when he sat up in their bed late on the fourth morning to see her coming out of the bathroom having clearly just showered. She was wrapped in a big towel, using a smaller one to attempt to dry her thick auburn hair.

"Dryer's on the fritz," she told him as she sat down on the foot of the bed. "Or else I shorted it out. According to Bishop, as our abilities evolve, lots of psychics find out they interfere with electrical and magnetic things."

Her voice had been as casual and easy as it usually was, but he had to ask anyway. "Are you okay?"

"You know I am."

"Tasha, I also know about the dream you had last night. The nightmare."

She continued to towel-dry her hair for a few moments, watching him, then said, "Yeah, I remember. One of the shadows was circling that house we checked on."

"Circling, watching—but not threatening."

With a slight frown, she said, "Not . . . immediately threatening. Watching. Maybe guarding."

"Do you think a security camera would have caught it?"

"I don't know."

"You only sensed a shadow. Not a person."

A frown flitted briefly across her features. "In my dream?"

"Yeah. What did you sense?"

Tasha's frown lingered. "It was a dream. How could I sense something from a dream? I mean . . . something like that."

"You sensed it was watching. Not an immediate threat."

"Yeah. I suppose so. I mean, I guess I must have."

His voice was quiet. "Did you sense a person? Anything that would have cast that shadow?"

Tasha dropped the smaller towel in her lap and absently finger-combed her hair.

"Think about it, Tasha. Try to remember."

Not angry but curious, she asked, "Why are you pushing?"

"I have a hunch it's important."

"That I dreamed about a shadow?"

"That you may be able to sense more than we thought, even if it's only at the subconscious level for now. In your dreams. Your nightmares."

"I don't much like thinking about them," she murmured. "Since I saw those shadows attached to so many of my neighbors and the people I spoke to every day."

Still sitting in their bed, Brodie leaned forward and covered the restless hands in her lap with one of his. "I know. But this could be important, Tasha."

"Why?"

"We both knew your abilities would change once our connection, our bond, grew stronger. It has. And you've shown some fairly minor changes in your abilities, in the last few days especially."

"I have?" She frowned again.

"Yeah, you have."

"I shorted out the hair dryer?"

"Maybe. And there have been a few other things."

Tasha eyed him. "You aren't going to tell me about those, are you?"

"Tell me about the shadow, Tasha. Did you sense a person there? Any kind of living being?"

She was silent for just a moment, still gazing at him, then said slowly, "No. I felt what we all feel when we sense those things. Something cold and slimy. Something bad. Evil. But . . . not a person. Not a personality. Not anything living."

Brodie's eyes narrowed, but with an inward-turned, thoughtful gaze. "Not anything living. I've never heard that as part of the feeling any psychic has gotten from the shadows. I wonder."

"What?"

Slowly, he said, "I wonder if the type of shadow you sensed, one apparently set to guard, to watch, is . . . nothing more than an illusion, a projection. It's a possibility we've considered."

"They aren't psychic," she objected.

"No. But we know they have some very advanced technology, and if they have something capable of that, it's a cinch they'd hide it well."

"What if it isn't tech?" Her voice was uneasy. "What if it's something else?"

"Something an abducted psychic gave them?"

"That isn't an ability I've ever heard of. And I've done a lot of research about psychic abilities in my life."

"I think most of us in this have. And I agree, it's something I've never heard of. But, Tasha . . . we know they've experimented. Trying to figure out what makes psychics tick. So maybe somewhere along the way they found something they weren't looking for. Maybe they found a psychic capable of projecting a scary image into the minds of other psychics. A psychic or psychics powerful enough to project that scary image expressly designed to keep other psychics at a distance. To keep you rattled, frightened. Even before your dream, when we were there, you didn't want to get close to that house."

"I didn't have to."

His fingers tightened over hers. "I know. But I could feel it in you, Tasha. You did *not* want to get any closer to that house. I think your subconscious sensed that shadow then. I think that's why you dreamed of it last night."

---

"You've never asked me about Sebring before." Duran's voice was measured, giving nothing away.

"New intel." Murphy didn't mind him knowing that; she wanted him to be aware that they were always looking, always seeking information and answers. "She leads field operations for the other faction."

He nodded.

"And that other faction is the one still torturing and experimenting on the psychics they abduct. Your faction gave that up quite a while ago. You really should have told me that, Duran."

"Why?"

Instead of answering, she repeated, "Tell me about Sebring."

"She's intelligent, capable. Vicious. And completely dedicated to her superiors and their goals."

"They still believe they can find a way to make your people psychic. Turn them into weapons able to defeat that enemy attacking your world. That's why they're still abducting psychics and experimenting on them. Dissecting them."

Duran nodded again, his gaze watchful.

"I assume you know what goes on in their operation even if you aren't part of it."

"Yes."

"So which side took Emma Garrick on Monday?"

"This is not something we talk about," he said slowly.

"Things change. Who has her, Duran?"

"She won't be dissected," he said finally.

Murphy didn't let her relief show. "So your side. Did you know she was on Bishop's watch list?"

"We haven't talked about him either."

"Like I said. Things change. Did you know?"

"No."

"Before Monday, she was only a latent. Since when have your people been able to determine latent ability?"

His gaze flickered briefly down to the dead psychic. "Something Astrid was able to do."

"She knew Emma was a latent, but didn't know she was on Bishop's watch list?"

"She didn't tell me she knew."

Murphy appreciated the distinction. "I wonder how many others she lied to you about."

"So do I," he said somewhat grimly.

"Emma's only sixteen, Duran. Bishop's very protective of the psychics on his watch list, especially the younger ones. He cares about all psychics, of course, at least those of us with souls. But those on his watch list . . . Well, he's very protective. I have no idea what Astrid was up to in leading your people to a young latent psychic on his list, but—" She stopped herself, instead asking, "Did you know abducting her would trigger her abilities?"

"It has before," he said after a moment.

"Trauma. It usually takes trauma to trigger abilities in a latent. But you knew that."

"Yes," he said. "I knew that."

"Thanks for the reminder. Your faction may no longer dissect psychics, but you don't mind putting them through bloody hell, do you?"

Duran was silent, still watchful.

"How many die in the process?"

"Only the fragile ones."

For a moment Murphy didn't trust herself to speak. When she finally did, her voice was hardly more than a growl. "Again, thanks for the reminder. He wants her back, Duran. He wants all his people back. Did you really think he wouldn't?"

Duran didn't answer that last question. "Once taken, a psychic passes out of my control."

"And is taken to your lab. Where they *aren't* dissected. Which means there are two labs, then. One where psychics are tested and pushed beyond the breaking point, and the other where they're literally taken apart to see what makes them tick."

He was silent.

"Do you know where the labs are?"

"We operate as you do, Murphy, with information on a need-to-know basis. I don't need to know where the labs are."

"Oh, I imagine you could give us a place to start looking."

After a long moment, he said, "I might, perhaps, be able to do that."

"Is that an offer, Duran?"

"It was a statement."

"Yeah. Tell me something. Would you stop all this if you could? The abductions, the experiments, all the rest of it?"

"My superiors—"

"Never mind them for the moment. Take them out of the equation. If it were just you in charge. Just you deciding whether to continue all those useless programs. Would you stop it all?"

After a moment, he said, "I told you once before, Murphy. I'm fighting to prevent the extinction of my people."

"The original mission."

"It's why we came here."

"Yeah. But it's too late to save them. Back on your homeworld. It was too late long before you were born."

He stiffened. "You can't know that."

"Can't I? The problem with obsession is that it blinds you. And when an obsession is carried over from generation to generation, the blindness grows even stronger. Your people came here to accomplish a goal. A long, long time ago. So long ago that none of you noticed that goal no longer mattered."

---

Bishop came out of his and Miranda's bedroom into the sitting room of their suite, frowning down at the notes on the legal pad he carried. His "roaming" psychics had been searching half a dozen western states, the area almost overwhelmingly huge. They had all reported in at various points, some placing phone calls to him and others simply reaching out to touch his mind.

Today, Friday, for the first time, the search area could be reduced to one state.

Wyoming.

*Bishop. Shadows.*

*On the move?*

*No. Fixed. I think in the northern part of the state.*

*I need an exact location.*

*On it. For what it's worth, the shadows feel like an illusion to me. Not real. Not alive.*

*No threat?*

*Guards, I think. Something to scare away nosy visitors and other troublemakers. But don't worry. I don't scare so easily.*

*Be careful. Don't approach the location. Just find it and report in.*

*Copy.*

Bishop's mind was fixed on that mental conversation, and on dealing with his own desire to call Matt Garrick and tell him his daughter was not dead.

He couldn't do that. Not yet. Not until he could be absolutely sure she wasn't dead. Until he had her safe.

But . . . Christ, they were about to have a funeral for her—

Halfway into the sitting room of the suite, he stopped, caught by surprise. Which was a very rare happening for him.

"Miranda, we have a visitor," he called over his shoulder.

She joined him just inside the sitting room, both staring at the blue-eyed black cat perched casually on the broad arm of a chair at right angles to the couch.

*You usually call her beloved.*

Bishop lifted an eyebrow as he looked at his wife and partner. "Did I imagine that?"

She could hardly help but smile, even as she studied the extremely odd cat. "You don't imagine things like this. And neither do I. Clearly he's an even more unusual cat than we thought. How in the world did he get in?"

*I slipped in when room service was removing your lunch cart. Nothing magic about it.*

Miranda addressed Pendragon directly. "And how did you get inside the building and up to this floor?"

*I'm a cat. We specialize in stealthy.*

A rare laugh escaped Bishop. "Well, he's right. That is an attribute of cats." He paused, adding, "But if you're *only* a cat, Pendragon, then I need to reexamine my knowledge of cats."

*Labels. Boxes. You humans always want things defined, don't you?*

"Afraid so. We find it easier to deal with life that way."

Pendragon lifted his chin slightly, and both humans watching him would have sworn he was smiling. A bit like the Grinch.

*All right. I'm not* only *a cat. I am, as far as I've been able to determine, the only one of my kind to survive and escape those beings you call the other side.*

"Survive what?" Bishop asked slowly.

*Experimentation. The two of you should sit down. It's a long story, and I need you to hear it all.*

---

"You keep coming back to that," Duran said, his voice unusually tight. "The original mission. You're so sure it's already a failure. That what we've done was all for nothing. I'd like very much to know how you can be so sure of that."

"Would you? Hmm. I told you our strongest psychics heard the screams of those taken, sometimes even felt the terror and pain. That's been happening for . . . a long time now. And what our psychics came to realize was that a larger percentage of the psychics your teams reached first did *not* cry out. Did *not* appear to be terrified or in pain. From most of them, all our psychics could read, if they read anything at all, was fear—and surprise. And then nothing except shadows."

She smiled faintly. "A dandy distraction, those shadows."

"I don't know what you mean."

"Oh, of course you do, Duran. It bothered me from the beginning that all the people from your side we encountered were, to all appearances, people. Just people. Like you. If I knew nothing of your ancestry, I'd guess that you were a highly intelligent and successful businessman of some sort. Interesting. Actually very handsome. But just a man."

He waited, silent and apparently unaffected.

"Still, there had to be some physical differences. Minor ones, when all's said and done. Mostly on the surface, but not so many at the biological level. Because what science, what biology tells this very bright mind of mine is that a natural mating is not going to take place between two species as dissimilar as humans—and those shadows our psychics see when they try to look more closely at your people. When they try to read your people. Try to focus on a psychic you're using, the way you used Astrid. Nothing like those shadows could have mated naturally with a human."

She paused for only a moment before asking, "Or were you created in a petri dish?"

Murphy had a fairly good idea that in pushing Duran as hard and as far as she had during this meeting she was risking a lot. Maybe everything. But stronger instincts told her the timing was right, and that the future of many psychics, perhaps including some they had believed lost forever, might well be decided by what she could learn from Duran today.

Even if she had to break him open to learn what she needed to learn.

"No," he said finally. "I was not."

"A natural mating, then. No medical . . . intervention."

"No."

Not betraying so much as a flicker that she was ticking off those boxes in her head, Murphy simply said, "Well, I won't ask for intimate details. Too much information even for me. I'll just assume your parents met somehow, spent an enjoyable night or three together, and you were conceived."

"And so?"

"And so that makes you a rare bird, Duran. A very,

very rare bird. A male hybrid from the original line that stretches back to your first ones. It also makes you living proof that our two species really aren't that different after all." She barely paused. "And living proof that those on your side of the schism didn't view a hybrid as a threat, but possibly as an asset. A face our side can recognize as being akin rather than . . . alien. And no doubt stopped our side from taking that one more step into our imaginations from wondering why you wanted psychics so badly to wondering just what you were. And where you came from.

"I do wonder now, though, if those on the other side of the schism *did* see you as a threat. If, maybe, they eventually looked for ways to undermine your confidence even then, when you were so young and not yet in command of anything."

"What are you talking about?"

"Your mother, Duran. You've always been suspicious of her death. It's the major reason your loyalties have so often been divided, which is perfectly understandable. But once you were in the field, once you reported to those whose goals you understood, you began to see . . . more than they expected you to see."

"Are you getting anywhere near a point?" he asked, betraying real impatience for the first time.

"My point, Duran, is that you began to see signs of a schism you hadn't known existed until you were out in the field. Until we were damning you for torturing psychics when that was never something you had done. Never something you had ordered done. Something you had no knowledge had ever been done. Oh, you were ruthless. Any good commander has to be sometimes."

Murphy glanced down at Astrid's body briefly then met his intent gaze again. "We do what we have to in order to protect our own. Or avenge our own."

It was a long moment before Duran spoke, and when he did it was in a careful tone. "I know very little about Sebring and her operations."

"Just that she answers to the other faction's leaders and is dedicated to their cause."

"Yes."

Murphy frowned slightly. "She leaves evidence whenever possible that it was you, your people. She studied the methods you use to abduct psychics, and she replicates them. Except that the psychics she takes are tested with methods a hell of a lot more invasive and destructive than those your side uses."

"Yes," he repeated.

"Do you know where her base is?"

"That's not something I ever tried to discover. My impression has been that she stays mobile, as I do."

"Your superiors didn't want to know that?"

He hesitated long enough to make it obvious, then said, "They're convinced the other . . . faction . . . will see sense. Eventually. That whatever Sebring and her people do now will be forgiven and forgotten."

"Especially if she can bring them some helpful intel? Some elusive fact found only in torturing and dissection?"

"Perhaps," he admitted. "Probably. They want answers."

"And don't care that psychics are being killed. The subjects of horrific experiments."

"They're single-minded," Duran said evenly. "They believe we'll soon have enough psychics under our control to defeat our enemy. The original mission. Beings with psychic abilities they were able to use offensively defeated that enemy on other worlds. We had proof of that. We wanted to give our own people those weapons if at all possible. Or . . . obtain psychics from other worlds to help us."

"With or without this *Supreme* you're all after?"

Duran nodded once. "A Supreme would have been the ultimate weapon. But . . . lesser psychics would still be effective weapons."

# FIFTEEN

"So the numbers do matter. And then? When you have enough psychics?"

"What are you asking me?"

Murphy considered him for a moment, a slight smile playing about her lips. "I need to know where to find this Sebring, Duran."

"I can't help you."

She ignored that. "I need to know where the labs are. Theirs—and yours. I have a hunch there are probably only two of them, given what goes on in them. And they have to be isolated. Hidden. Secret."

"I can't help you."

"Of course you can."

"You're asking me to betray my people."

"No, I'm asking you to save what remains of your people. I'm asking you to provide a few more bits and pieces of intelligence so that together with you my people can stop a vicious, useless, endless war."

"Not endless—"

"You know what's happening is beyond wrong. To steal from another intelligent race even if you were told it would save your own people. To take innocent lives in that pursuit. You knew that price was too high. You've always known. You would never have agreed to supply even bits and pieces of intelligence to me otherwise."

"Murphy—"

"I've asked you this before. I'm asking again. *Would* you stop all this if you could, Duran? Stop the abductions, the experiments of *your* scientists and healers that destroy psychics and turn women they want to breed into mindless baby machines? The torture Sebring and her people use in order to gain information, destroying psychics utterly in the process? *If you could*, would you stop all that?"

"I lack the power."

"Answer the question. *If you could*, would you stop it?"

There was, now, a faintly arrested expression in his eyes. "My superiors are untouchable," he said slowly.

"Nobody's untouchable. And nobody's asking *you* to move directly against those above you in the chain of command. It won't be any action of yours that . . . changes things. You'll be doing your duty, just as always. Obeying orders out in the field in some operation far away from your superiors as they sit in some boardroom in some high-rise in some anonymous big city. Answer the question, Duran. *If you could*, would you stop it?"

"Yes," he said finally.

Murphy half nodded, unsurprised. "Because along with everything else, you know it's over, don't you? In spite of your protests. You know it was over a long time ago. Whatever your superiors and the remaining first ones believe, there will be no Second Coming. Not of your people. Maybe of your enemy one day, but not of your people. No ship to return in answer to the message I'm sure was sent to them long ago, perhaps every year. Every month. Not even a reply to that message. Year after year. Generation after generation. Only silence. There won't be a Second Coming. Will there, Duran?"

"I can't know that. You can't know that."

"We can both know it. Because those who left the first ones here never came back. Years passed, decades, generations, and they never came back. If there was even a possibility of them returning to reclaim their people and whatever valuable information those people had collected, it would have happened by now. Because the need for information, for knowledge, for weapons, was so great. It was supposed to save your people, Duran. So why were you all stranded here with only exploratory vessels that could never have made the journey back? Why did no one return?"

"You don't know what you're talking about." It was said rather mechanically.

"They were supposed to return, weren't they? Generations ago. Our society was a primitive one then, after all, no challenge for your people. The first ones didn't expect to be here long. Not long at all. Maybe they even sent a signal explaining that. And then more time passed, and they had to cannibalize their ships for the technology they needed. The technology they didn't find here. And more time passed. More generations."

He looked at her silently.

Murphy stepped away from the crate she'd been leaning against, and reached her free hand into the big, worn leather bag she always carried. She produced a thick manila envelope, put it on the crate, and pushed it toward him.

"Some light reading before bedtime," she said.

Duran didn't touch the envelope. "What is it?"

"A year or so ago, I got in touch with someone. An astrophysicist. Not on our side, but the friend of a friend. Someone I trust. And since he's one of the most brilliant minds ever produced by humanity, anything he says is worth listening to. Worth considering.

"I asked him about a situation such as the one facing you and your people. Just theoretically, you understand. A group of beings stranded here so long. So far from home. Brought here by some form of faster-than-light travel, and even then in multi-generational vessels because the journey was so long. I asked him to tell me what he thought of that. What his genius brain and his science told him about that. So he did." She nodded at the envelope. "That's a copy of his . . . report. Read it. Think about it."

"Murphy—"

"You might want to keep it someplace safe. At least until you decide what to do with it. And there's a list inside the envelope too. A few critical questions I need the answers to. And soon, Duran. Very soon. Today, in fact."

"I won't betray my people," he said.

"You're betraying them by believing they have a homeworld to return to."

"No."

"You have my number," she said as if he hadn't spoken. She turned and walked away, leaving the huge defunct warehouse and the man standing silently, staring after her.

---

When Bishop and Miranda arrived at the Mackenzie home and what was becoming the hub of their base, Pendragon was riding comfortably on Bishop's shoulder.

And the federal agents, Tucker noted as he let them in, wore expressions that were both thoughtful—and stunned.

"What's going on?" he asked as they joined him in the den and command center where they always seemed to gather.

"Your cat paid us a visit," Bishop told him.

"He's not my cat, he's Annabel's cat," Tucker said more or less automatically. "What, at your hotel?"

"And our suite. Apparently, he slipped in while the table holding the remains of our lunch was wheeled out."

*Apparently?*

Tucker blinked. "I'm not exactly telepathic, but I could have sworn he said—"

"He did," Miranda said. "We were all very right in believing Pendragon is not an ordinary cat."

"I'm not even sure he's a cat," Bishop began, then winced and added, "Hey, take it easy," as he turned his head and stared almost nose to nose with Pendragon.

Pendragon's tail lashed, and he said, "Yaaah," in a tone even humans realized was profane and *very* catlike, then jumped down from his perch and loped toward the other side of the condo and Annabel's room.

"He dug his claws in," Bishop explained to the others, briefly rubbing his shoulder through the casual dark shirt he was wearing.

"What do you mean you're not sure he's a cat?" Tucker demanded.

"Long story. He said we're supposed to wait for—"

The doorbell rang, and Tucker went with a smothered curse to let in Tasha and Brodie. "I haven't called you yet," he told them rather severely. "In fact, I haven't called any of you."

"Were you supposed to?" Bishop asked mildly.

"I was just about to. Murphy's on her way, and wanted me to get the rest of you here."

Miranda sat down at one end of a long couch and smiled at him. "Well, we're here, Tucker," she said as her husband joined her. "And we have more than one thing to report."

Tasha and Brodie were already making themselves comfortable on the couch across from the other couple.

"Is this about Pendragon?" Tasha asked.

"Beats the hell out of me," Tucker told her, perching on the wide arm of a chair.

Miranda looked at Tasha and Brodie with lifted brows. "Did he talk to you too?"

"We both heard him," Tasha answered. "It was weird, because even though we didn't *see* Pendragon, and even though he didn't sound at all like I'd expect a cat to sound, we both knew it was him speaking to us. Telepathically."

Tucker, whose genius ability to utilize the logical, mathematical side of his brain was matched by an equally genius ability to tap into imagination and creativity on the other side of his brain, didn't seem the least disbelieving, only curious. "What'd he tell you?"

Brodie replied, "To come here. He said it was time we knew his story—and that he'd already told it directly to Bishop and Miranda because they're the only bonded pair among us who're both telepaths."

"I wonder why that matters," Tasha mused. "Easier to communicate clearly with two strong telepaths?"

"Could be," Bishop said.

Sarah emerged from the hallway leading to the other side of the condo, wearing a slight frown. "Annabel is settled down watching the latest animated classic from Disney. And Pendragon just joined her. I gathered I was supposed to come in here."

"He told you, huh?" Tucker said.

"Yeah. And Annabel said very matter-of-factly that he talked to her just like that." Still frowning, she added, "She also said everything was about to change."

Tucker reached out for his wife's hand and drew her to sit in the chair where he was perched on the arm. "I thought I was beyond being surprised, but . . . Do we have to wait for Murphy to hear all this? Because I got the impression she was still a half hour or more away."

"Pendragon says Murphy knows," Miranda said simply.

Bishop murmured, "Secrets on top of secrets on top of secrets. I get the feeling she's been a step ahead of a lot of us for quite a long time."

Brodie scowled. "Dammit."

Tasha, smiling faintly, said, "Probably more need-to-know stuff." Then she turned her attention to the Bishops. "So what is it Pendragon needed all of us to know?"

The couple exchanged glances, and then Bishop began to speak in a measured tone. "Apparently, psychics weren't the only ones experimented on by the other side. According to Pendragon, they also tinkered with the biology of a number of animals believed to be intelligent."

"I don't think I want to hear this," Tasha murmured.

"We weren't crazy about it either," Bishop told her. "But it's important that we *do* know." He barely paused. "Pendragon said they were still interested in psychic abilities, apparently trying to discover, using animal subjects, if there was anything psychic linked to instincts."

"That's reaching," Tucker said.

"Leaving no stone unturned seemed to be their mantra. They extracted DNA from a number of species and studied it, even tried to manipulate it at the molecular level. They also attempted to reintroduce the DNA they had tinkered with back into the animals. As you may imagine, most of them either died or had to be destroyed."

"I knew I didn't want to hear this," Tasha murmured.

Brodie reached over and took her hand, but addressed himself to Bishop. "Was Pendragon the only exception?"

"He believes he was the only feline exception, at least where he was being kept. Said the other animals were kept in different labs at the time, labs he believes were eventually abandoned, destroyed, when that line of experimentation ended. And that before that, when he saw his chance to escape, he did."

Slowly, Sarah said, "Why turn up in my life?"

"Well, according to Pendragon, whatever they did to manipulate his genetic code gave him telepathy—and the ability to see the future. And he saw enough of it, he claims, to have known that you, Sarah, and Tucker would play an important part in the—endgame. He knew the same thing about Annabel, which is why he protected her, and why he brought her to you."

Brodie said, "Is anybody else's head spinning, or just mine?"

---

*Hello?*

Katie wasn't a telepath, so she was startled to be pulled from a deep, exhausted sleep by an unsteady voice in her mind. She came awake, blinking, to find that her captors hadn't turned off the lights this time, or maybe she'd slept through one of the irregular cycles and the lights were back on again—

*Hello? Is anybody there?*

Maybe it was because she was so tired, or maybe something in that frightened mind-voice triggered an ability in her she'd never had before, Katie didn't know. All she knew was that it felt like instinct to reach out with her own thoughts.

*Hello. Who are you?*

*Emma. I—I was afraid nobody would answer.* They *never do.*

*Not psychic,* Katie explained.

*They said there was a psychic in the next room, but so far I've never been able to reach them.*

*Tests. They want to understand how your ability works. Probably have another captive psychic in the next room. Another telepath. Easier for you to communicate to another telepath. I'm Katie, by the way.*

*Katie. If they figure out how my ability works, Katie, will they let me go home?*

*How long have you been here, Emma?* Katie knew she was dodging the question asked.

*I'm not sure. There was a party Sunday night, because a friend's parents were out of town and . . . and so there was a party. It was really late when I drove home. Started to drive home. It was nearly morning. I . . . I don't really remember what happened, except that my car went off the road and . . . and . . . it started to get really dark, and cold . . . So I guess I've been here since Monday morning.*

Katie wondered if they were even in the same week, the same *month*, but didn't ask because that voice was awfully afraid. *How old are you, Emma?*

*I'm . . . sixteen. My dad's going to be awfully worried. And my mom. I didn't know anything bad would happen, Katie. I was just going to a party so I could see Toby . . . and he could see me in real clothes and not the school uniform . . .*

Sixteen? They had grabbed a *kid*?

As tired as she was, as fearful, as depressed and worried as she was, it was somehow good to think about what somebody else was going through—and get mad about it. They'd grabbed a kid? Just taken her away from loving parents?

That was when Katie Swan got mad.

That was when she got mad as hell.

---

"It makes sense in a twisted way," Tucker said. "I mean that they'd experiment on animals. Maybe even that they'd want to determine whether various kinds of animal instincts had any tie to psychic ability, though I still say it was reaching."

"They can't possibly have known how successful they

were with Pendragon," Tasha said. "Somehow, he was able to hide that, or their technology failed them—or their psychics did."

"That's true," Brodie said. "If they'd had an inkling he could communicate as clearly as he can . . . Well, I don't know what they'd have done with him. Or to him. Because we *still* don't know what their ultimate goal is."

"Yeah, we pretty much do," Murphy said, just suddenly there in the living room even though no one had heard her come in. The sudden arrival made Brodie jump in surprise. Which was nearly as rare as hen's teeth.

"I see you started without me," she said mildly.

"Jesus," Brodie said. "Either I'm slipping in a major, major way, or you've learned to fucking walk through walls."

"The latter." Her tone was rather suspiciously solemn. She didn't remove either her jacket or the ever-present large bag she wore slung across her thin body. Instead, she simply went into the living area and sank down in the comfortable chair she favored with a sigh. She looked both tired and curiously alert as she glanced around the room. "Coffee ready?"

"Couple minutes," Sarah said. "I stopped at the kitchen and put on a pot."

"We didn't start without you," Brodie told Murphy. "Except about Pendragon. Which apparently you already knew."

"That he was part of a . . . different avenue of exploration in their eugenics program?" Murphy nodded, clearly not at all dismayed by Brodie's irritation. "Yeah, I knew. The boss has another cat who escaped the program, apparently from a different lab. Not telepathic or precognitive like Pendragon, but amazingly empathic."

"How long have you known about this?" Brodie demanded.

Murphy lifted both brows at him silently.

He swore mostly under his breath. "A lot longer than I needed to know, obviously."

"Decision made at the top," Murphy said, still mild. "Other than the boss, I can't tell you who else knows, though I'm sure some do. At least a few specialized researchers pretty much have to know as much as me and probably a hell of a lot more. We've been putting together a puzzle for years, still are, and there are some pieces I don't know if we'll ever be sure of."

"Psychic animals?" Tucker said. "What use could they hope to make of psychic animals?"

Murphy waited until Sarah returned to hand her a cup of coffee, nodded her thanks, then said matter-of-factly, "Some of them still believed if they mixed just the right molecules or, hell, maybe just atoms, in a petri dish, they'd come up with something that would make their own people psychic."

"That's been their endgame?" Brodie asked. "All this time it's been about finding some way to turn nonpsychic people into psychics?"

"That and how to use psychic abilities as weapons."

Bishop said, "That's a road to hell."

Murphy nodded. "Yeah, we get enough fear and anxiety from some nonpsychics now about what we can do. Being able to use our abilities as powerful weapons would not exactly be the icing on the cake."

"But animal DNA?" Tucker demanded skeptically.

"They've tried everything. Every combination you could imagine and quite a few that would never occur to a sane mind." She shook her head slightly. "Amazing how an utter commitment to a goal can create tunnel vision."

"But what did they create in Pendragon?" Tasha asked.

"Something a hell of a lot more than a cat, that's for sure. And here's the kicker, at least for me. Sarah might feel it stronger than I do, but I'm reasonably sure Pendragon is bonded with Annabel."

"I know they're connected," Sarah said slowly. "I know they communicate as easily as we are now. But . . . we aren't talking about the sort of bond the couples in this room have? The sort of bond that forms between mates?"

"Oh, no. What I do think, however, is that we're going to need to redefine our ideas on just how many kinds of amazingly strong bonds can be formed between . . . two intelligent and unusually gifted beings. Even if they're different species."

Tucker was looking for the salient point in all this. "Pendragon is going to help us in some way? Through his bond with Annabel?"

"I think so," Murphy said.

"She's only ten, Murphy. What can she do—with or without Pendragon?"

"That depends on the . . . elements of the plan we're going to come up with."

Brodie looked at her, brows raised. "We're going to come up with a plan? Go on the offensive?"

"Bet your ass we are. Aren't you tired of playing defense?"

"I have been for a long time, and you know it. So tell me, what's changed?"

"The fire in the Charlotte breeding house," Murphy said calmly. "And our bonded pairs."

"You know who set that fire?" Tasha asked.

"I do. And made sure to verify before any action was taken. It *was* unsanctioned, and Astrid set it. She's dead."

Everyone was and looked varying degrees of surprised, and even if more than one of them wanted to ask for details of just who had taken the action that had cost Astrid her life, none did.

Murphy sipped her coffee calmly, offering no details.

Slowly, Bishop said, "Why that house? Just that house? What was different about it?"

Murphy lifted her bottle in a slight toast. "The right questions. What was different about that house was that Duran believed one of those babies would be born this *Supreme* he and his people have been looking for for so long."

Murphy brooded for a moment, then said matter-of-factly, "Astrid found out what Duran suspected, apparently through contact with one of their healers who knew about it. One of the very few who knew about it, according to Duran. And Astrid didn't want her position as one of his operation's top psychics to be threatened. So she destroyed them."

# SIXTEEN

It did not take Duran long to deal with the body of Astrid, to consider and decide what his report would contain. To assign the various necessary jobs to several of his people, deliberately choosing those who had most intensely disliked Astrid.

Jealousy. Envy.

He wasn't even sure if those traits had existed without the all-too-human influence down through the generations.

Odd that he wasn't sure even about that.

Duran shut himself in his office with orders not to be disturbed, made very sure, as he always did, that no monitoring devices had been placed in his absence, activated the jammer hidden in a locked desk drawer just to be sure, and then settled down and began reading the "report" Murphy had given him.

By the second paragraph, a chill began to settle over him. By the second page, he was watching the nightmarish possibilities that had occurred to him only fleetingly over the years set down in clinical, precise mathematical probabilities.

Though he had no idea how Murphy had been able to give her astrophysicist the all-too-precise location of homeworld.

Or when the first ones had arrived here.

*Or* precisely when they had lost contact completely with their mother ship. When the scheduled return and pickup of their small exploratory vessels had come and gone with no sign or signal from that mother ship.

When years had passed.

Generations.

When no ship ever came.

When no response to messages sent ever came.

Just as Murphy had described.

Possibilities he hadn't allowed himself to think about flowed through his mind now, pausing long enough to be considered.

Habitable planets, for their race as well as humans, were to be found in the galaxy, but they were . . . few and far between, relatively speaking. Scientists here called them Goldilocks planets. His people's desperate scientists had found very few. And all far away from homeworld.

Very far away.

So he had to wonder, looking at cold scientific probability he couldn't ignore, if a decision had been made at the highest levels even as the war had turned against them, to save what they could. If theirs had been less a rescue mission for a world, and more a heroic attempt to save a race.

To . . . seed it on other worlds.

*But why would we not be told that?* Even as the question occurred, Duran thought he knew a likely answer. Because theirs had been a militant race, even their scientists and doctors possessing the inborn nature of warriors, and they would have resisted leaving their world, their people, dying while they went off to find a new home. To save themselves.

But to leave on a search for something, some weapon, that would save their people on homeworld? That, they would have seen as a worthy mission. A warrior's mission.

It explained, as he had wondered more than once, why their "scout" vessels had contained so much technology that had little to do with war and, really, only defensive weaponry. Why the historical, medical, and technological data storage on each ship had been so vast. Why numerous healers and scientists had been aboard each vessel.

Why there had been so many scout vessels aboard the mother ship.

It made sense—if those ships had been intended to colonize rather than visit only briefly. The lack of any response to their signals from their mother ship made sense—if the true mission of that mother ship had been to continue on without turning back, searching for another habitable world or two where another fleet of "scout" ships could be off-loaded.

And left for good, to survive if they could.

Duran wondered, on a curiously calm level of his mind, if their mother ship had even made it to another habitable world to off-load more scouts, if it was still searching, or if some technical failure or mischance had caused those aboard to abandon a dying ship the way they had abandoned a dying planet, finding a new home elsewhere.

Or perishing with their ship.

He wondered if any of the first ones had known the truth of their mission, had even suspected what had in all likelihood happened back "home" even, perhaps, before their journey had ended here.

Had they suspected?

Had they known?

Had they lied?

---

"All those people," Tasha whispered. "The caretakers. The women and their babies. Dying in agony, burning alive. All because Astrid felt *threatened*?"

"Sociopath," Murphy reminded her, still calm. "Or psychopath. They don't have a moral compass. They don't have empathy. They don't care about life except their own. Astrid enjoyed being the one sent to probe the minds of other psychics; it made her feel superior. To . . . bore into them. To attempt to make them afraid. To hurt them. It's what she lived for."

After a long moment, Tucker said, "You went to meet Duran, didn't you? When we found the recording and you recognized Astrid."

"And asked him to bring Astrid, yes. She was a problem for both of us, and I had the proof in that recording."

Tasha was looking at her steadily. "Murphy . . . can you explain all this? Do you really know why they're after psychics? Why they're so . . . driven to turn nonpsychics into psychics?"

"Yes. And it's time the rest of you knew."

"Past time, I'd say." Brodie's voice was a little harsh.

Murphy smiled faintly. "Bishop's mantra: Some things have to happen just the way they happen. Knowing before now wouldn't have done you any good, Brodie. It wouldn't have done anyone on our side any good. Because knowing their goal last week or last month or last year wouldn't have changed how we responded to them. How we fought them."

"And now it has?" Miranda asked.

"Yeah. Because we've had the time to figure a few things out, based on knowledge given and stolen and gained by experience over time—and recently. Because now we're certain we have a weapon the other side lacks. Probably the only weapon that stands any chance at all of stopping them in their tracks."

"Our bonded pairs," Bishop said. "I'm not yet sure what you have in mind, obviously, but Miranda and I have been bonded longer than anyone else in this room, and we've never used that offensively."

"Time to change tactics," Murphy told them. "Maybe learn how to use a whole new tool for your psychic toolbox."

"I want to know the whole story," Tucker insisted. "After all this, I think I've *earned* it. I think we all have."

Murphy nodded slowly. "Okay. I'll tell you as much as I know, which isn't everything."

"But more than we have now?"

"Oh, yeah."

"Then let's hear it."

Murphy frowned slightly, clearly getting her thoughts organized. And then she began speaking slowly.

"Two things you need to know up front. The other

side, as we've been calling them, is actually two sides, two different factions of the original group, both working against us. And against each other in terms of their . . . goals, methodology, and ruthlessness."

"Murphy—"

"Just listen, okay? Duran has been my contact on the other side for about three years, I told you that, and those years have changed both of us in ways I doubt either of us expected. I'm far more aware of goals, theirs and ours. And Duran . . . Duran, I believe began to be seriously torn by his divided loyalties, more and more as time passed. What he was asked by his superiors to do made less and less sense to him. Which is one reason he's been helping us."

"Is there another?" Brodie demanded.

"More than one other. And just so you know, the faction Duran belongs to is *not* the one abducting psychics to study them. Hurt them. Hell, torture and dissect them. That faction, whose field operations are run by a woman named Sebring, is a lot less visible, a lot more secretive, I believe considerably smaller than Duran's faction—and still believes in the original goal of somehow making their own kind psychic."

"What does the other faction believe?" Brodie asked.

"That they can . . . harness . . . our abilities and use them as weapons that way. Which explains the Stepford moms and why so much time and trouble has been expended in the eugenics program. Once Duran's faction accepted the fact that just plucking adult psychics from their lives and trying to control them wasn't working, the idea of grabbing younger and younger psychics and, finally, breeding them, made more sense."

"Not in a sane world," Tasha said.

"No, I think we're all in agreement there. But it wasn't our plan."

Brodie drew a deep breath and let it out slowly. "Adult psychics are still being abducted."

"Yeah, by both their factions. Sebring's is still looking for something in our biology, our DNA, to create or awaken psychic abilities in nonpsychics. Duran's is still working on various methods of controlling psychics, and their efforts have too often had . . . unintended consequences. Like the Stepford moms, who were made pliable enough to control, but to all intents and purposes lost their psychic abilities—and lost who they were."

Very quietly, Tasha said, "Can that be reversed? We have a huge rescue operation planned for Sunday; once the Stepford moms are with us, can we help them?"

"It's possible," Murphy answered. "We won't know for sure unless and until we get our hands on their medical and scientific records and find out just what, exactly, was done to those women."

"Start at the beginning," Tucker urged.

"Okay," Murphy said. "The beginning for us was hundreds of years ago, with the arrival of dozens of small scout ships from a culture not all that different from the one we have now. People who had left their own world fighting a powerful enemy. Halfway across the galaxy."

Then she told them the rest of the story.

---

Murphy let the basics sink in, then continued to explain the importance of psychics and what their visitors had done to reach their goals. "They knew that their enemy back home could be fought with psychic abilities, and the ideal was, of course, to find a way to make their own people psychic. They'd tried everything they knew, and all they had to show for it was failure. None of their females could even carry an embryo that had been altered by human DNA. And when they first tried implanting fertilized eggs into human females, the results were very nearly the same. Horrible birth defects and a lot of dead babies."

"All failures?" Tucker asked intently.

"No, not all. Not, at least, in terms of survival. A very small percentage of the embryos implanted in human women resulted in full-term births. Always girl babies. The boys, if they survived to full-term, were either stillborn or died soon afterward. From no medical cause any of their healers could determine."

Tucker frowned. "Something about the Y chromosome?"

"They suspected something they were doing damaged it, but never really figured out what. And they could find no evidence that most of the girl infants born healthy possessed any psychic ability anyway. Some fell through the cracks, believe it or not, just fell off the radar. Probably due to terrified moms who took their infants and vanished."

"How many?" Bishop asked.

"Impossible to know for sure, so it's just educated guesswork, but chances are good that over the years, especially the early years, there were a lot. If we *can* get access to their historical and medical data banks, we might have intel we can work with, but we won't know unless and until that happens. Hell, you could have descendants in your unit, and you wouldn't know, *they* wouldn't know. Because it's been generations now and, besides, biologically they test as human."

"How do you know that?" It was Bishop again, intent.

"Partly from Duran," Murphy admitted. "Until fairly recently, we couldn't do the kind of genetic testing required to be sure of that. Once we could . . . Biologically, they test as human. Which is really the only thing that makes sense, given that there *have* been natural breedings between their people and ours. Two radically different humanoid species could never have produced offspring."

Slowly, Bishop said, "Does it always hold true that only daughters are born healthy?"

"Seems to, according to Duran. At least when they tinker biologically to try to . . . instill . . . psychic ability. And there have been some other bits and pieces of knowledge we've found, other pieces of the puzzle. When they tinker with their and our DNA to produce psychic offspring, the rare surviving and healthy offspring is virtually always female. Didn't seem to matter what the men contributed to the gene pool.

"I don't know enough about biology to be certain, but I'd assume once enough human DNA is in the mix, after enough generations have passed, the human biological imperative would somehow drive the body even on a molecular level to repair what had been damaged, or adapt to it, and sons could be born and survive. Maybe at least a few already have been. We do need males as well as females, after all, as a species."

"Life finds a way," Tucker murmured. "We tinker, and nature corrects."

"Or they tinker and nature corrects, eventually," Murphy agreed. "No real way to be sure if we've reached that point yet, but it's at least possible given the number of generations of at least some family trees that a few males are walking around as living exceptions to the girls-only rule."

Miranda murmured, "That could explain a few . . . unusual men we've come across over the years."

"It might explain a lot," Murphy commented wryly. "But whether we can ever be certain is a very big question. We have those researchers still looking for information, including every possibility we can think of in terms of naturally born offspring, but you have to remember *where* they're looking. Some alien abduction conspiracy theories really are just theories, wild ones with absolutely nothing to validate them. So weeding the wheat from the chaff has been . . . irksome." She shrugged. "But common sense says more than one woman pregnant by one of them very early on managed to disappear, especially before they developed or at least used any kind of tracking technology. The maternal drive to protect offspring, I'm told, is incredibly strong."

"But no way to really know," Bishop said. "How many there were. How many descendants there could be."

"Not without the sort of intel we're likely to get from Duran's people, no. And maybe not even then, if they never figured out for certain what made psychic humans so different from them. Maybe we'll figure that out, but even if we do, that means mapping the DNA of a *lot* of people to even begin to guess how many could be descendants."

Bishop's pale sentry eyes were even more unreadable than they usually were, but he merely nodded.

"Meanwhile, our visitors kept trying, off and on. Not

an official eugenics program, not for a long time. And I imagine there were some of their people who slipped out on their own and found ways to have a good time, but that would have been very much off the record, especially as far as the males were concerned."

"No visible evidence of . . . extracurricular activities," Sarah murmured.

"Right. If their males are anything like ours—and we have good reason to believe they are, at least in some ways—it could have been like leaving a girl behind at every port. Only they would have made up the ports, and never mentioned the ships they supposedly returned to and sailed away in were alien."

Tucker frowned and said judiciously, "I'd really like to defend my own gender on that, but I can't seem to think of anything convincing."

"That's okay," Murphy said gravely. "Present company excepted, obviously."

"Thank you," he murmured.

"But that could certainly account for a fair amount of their DNA dumped into our gene pool, unnoticed, and over a very long period of time. But . . . on the record, they kept working at it. Pondered and tried this or that. Just . . . experiments.

"How long did they keep trying?" Bishop asked.

Murphy shook her head slightly. "Longer than they should have. But some of them began to understand. Not the why of it, but only the fact of it: They could not produce anything close to a descendant of the first ones who possessed even a flicker of psychic ability. No matter how much they tinkered. I can't know for certain, but I believe it wasn't long after that that the schism happened."

---

Duran possessed the ability to absorb a great deal of information, quickly and thoroughly, and it did not take him much time to absorb the report Murphy had provided.

It took much longer for him to carefully consider what he had learned from that report.

And what he suspected.

He had little memory of his father, but his mother was vividly alive in his mind even after so many years. He had a feeling, always had, that it was because she had made certain she would be. Her smile and soft voice, her quick laughter, the times he had come upon her suddenly to find her sad and silent. Briefly. She had never explained those rare moments of sadness, but he had guessed, even though she had never said anything against his father.

*How could she ever seem inferior to me?*

It was a question asked many times, especially later on when his own training had begun, when he had understood that his mother had been viewed as a . . . necessary evil. A means by which to produce offspring no more than half human.

Like worker bees, he had eventually understood, rare men like himself, some women, the direct and naturally bred hybrid offspring of two races, two species, neither of them born psychic and believed to be sterile, had continued to be produced simply for the traits that ensured there would always be enough commanders and foot soldiers to do the jobs required, enough in the field to carry out the orders of those superiors.

Those like his father, pure-blooded descendants of the

first ones, their own survival on a world filled with new diseases that had killed off so many in the beginning proof that they were strong, had been . . . required . . . to mate with human women, as many as possible, in order to produce more foot soldiers, more worker bees.

Not a eugenics program, simply a . . . necessary evil.

Duran had no idea how many half brothers had been born before and after him. Though he doubted there were sisters. It was an odd truth that males of pureblood naturally mated with human females not born psychic invariably produced male children, true hybrids, while males naturally mated with born psychic human women almost always produced females, fertile ones.

Was he as alone as he had believed since his mother's death, or were there half siblings out there Duran could claim as family?

He wondered if he could ask Murphy for that favor when she did what she would do, what she had to do, and take the knowledge and history stored in the vast data banks of the laboratories. She would have to do that, take that, because no matter how much she trusted him, even if she trusted at all, the only way he and his people could move forward, could make a real home for themselves here, would be to cut all ties to that other world.

To cut away that part of their history.

He didn't know if he could ask for that favor. Or if Murphy would grant it if he did.

What he did know, what this report had confirmed for him, was that they were out of time. Ironically, the only chance he could see for saving his people was integration with the people of this world. Complete integration.

There was no other way for them to survive, not now.

*No matter what happened or is happening on homeworld, our race here will die out.*

The pure-blooded branch of it, at least.

That was inevitable.

There were precious few left, and already signs of inbreeding were becoming apparent as those remaining purebloods obsessively tried to increase their numbers. None of their scientists or healers had discovered a way to broaden their gene pool with so little, now, of the original bloodline to draw from.

*"We keep up this war, attrition on both sides is going to pass the point of no return,"* Murphy had said to him not so long ago, her voice less mocking than it often was. *"For your people, at least. We already have so many more psychics than would have developed naturally, and God knows what that's going to do to our race, how it will affect our evolution over time, even if it's all positive."*

*"Do you expect it to be? All positive?"*

*"So few things are. So, no. But we'll deal with that as it comes. Fight it, or learn to adapt."*

*"Biologically?"*

*"Socially is more likely. There still exists a kind of taboo against biological tinkering for us. Most of it, at any rate. And probably for the best, since as your people discovered, Mother Nature fights back.*

*"But whatever happens with us, we at least have a huge gene pool to draw from. Your people began at a disadvantage, with far fewer of the pureblood race they so prize. What happens when they're gone, Duran?"*

What indeed.

# SEVENTEEN

Murphy wasn't sure whether the silence that greeted the end of her story held disbelief, or just shock. And she didn't reach out to probe anybody and find out.

She'd dealt with it all in her own mind and had reached her own conclusions; the others here deserved the same.

"Even if it wasn't by design," she said, "biologically speaking, integration already started, a long time ago. And, like I said, it could be much further advanced than we know. Because we really *don't* know how much of their blood is already part of our human race. How much of their DNA is inextricably connected to our own. With the right motivation, the right leaders, I believe they could . . . join us. Become a part of the human race. Maybe even become assets."

"Assets?" Brodie sounded a little less grim than he might have a year before. Or even a week before. "There's been bloodshed on both sides, Murphy."

"I know. As there is in every war. But sooner or later,

unless those in charge are bent on annihilation, someone has to decide to end it. To lay down arms and stop fighting. Much better for us, for our war, if both sides do that."

"Who decides we stop it?"

"We do." Murphy met Brodie's hard eyes squarely. "The boss, and that panel of very smart people I mentioned—and us. The soldiers in the field. Those of us who have seen comrades, psychic and nonpsychic, fall. Who have seen the toll this has taken. Who have seen too many psychics living their entire lives in fear, and too many nonpsychics turning away from any chance of a . . . normal, happy life in order to fight for us."

"It hasn't been for nothing," Tucker said steadily. "And normal is what you get used to. All of us have made a difference. All of us have done something productive, even special, with our lives. Our dedication to this."

Murphy nodded immediately. "We certainly have. We've saved countless psychics. Probably prevented the deaths of innocents as well. But finding an end to this, one we can all live with, doesn't diminish any of that, Tucker." She looked around the room at each of them. "It doesn't diminish the years and the sacrifices. If anything, it only helps them mean more. Because all that helped us find our way to this point. This possibility."

There was a long silence, and then Brodie said, "Assuming it's even possible, what makes you so sure Duran is the key? Because you know him best?"

"Partly that. Because of his divided loyalties, and the wedge I've been busy driving between those two factions for quite a while now. And at the meeting today . . . I left him with a request for more information, a list of questions—and a reason why he just might answer them."

"What reason?" Sarah asked.

"Well, that's the thing," Murphy said quietly. "What has brought us, finally, to this place. What may well change the outcome of our war. The ultimate tragic irony of it all." She told them about her astrophysicist. "A while back, I asked him some questions. Posed a *theoretical* problem for him, using what I, what *we* have figured out so far about how the first ones of Duran's people came here. Where they came from, as nearly as we can estimate that. Roughly when they came."

Slowly, Tucker said, "Relativity. The theory of relativity. And even with faster-than-light travel, with multigenerational ships, maybe especially using both those . . . millennia could have passed on their homeworld since they left."

"What?" Brodie demanded, frowning.

Murphy looked at him. "My astrophysicist got back to me. Wrote up a report for me. It's what I left with Duran when I met him earlier today."

"And?"

"They've been here a long time, Brodie. Generations. And it took them a long, long time to get here from the world they left generations ago. Halfway across the galaxy. Unless their people somehow won the war they were losing when those ships set out looking for weapons they could use, then chances are they're gone. Their homeworld taken over by their enemy at best, or an uninhabitable wasteland at worst. And even if their side somehow won, they won't be the people, the civilization, Duran's people left behind so long ago and so far away.

"They don't have anything to go back to, Brodie. For at least the ones in Duran's faction, and maybe to others as well, *this* world became home. Most of them were born here, raised, educated here. Before they even realized it was happening, this became home. They're as much creatures of Earth as we are."

---

It was late afternoon when she reached the prearranged meeting spot, and Murphy took her usual precautions. They were second nature by now, and she didn't give them a thought beyond a vague curiosity as to what she'd do with her life after.

Assuming there was an after.

Within seconds of her reaching the meeting point, Duran stepped out of the shadows to join her in the center of this old warehouse that had been apparently abandoned in the middle of some sort of re-purposing project, possibly for lack of funds. There were still a few discarded tools and various supplies here and there, including stacks of lumber like the one Murphy leaned against.

"You're late," he said.

"Only by a minute or two. We've had lots to talk about. Lots to consider."

"And the consensus?"

"Still working toward one. It's been a long war, Duran."

"And yet you seem to believe I can turn my people on a dime, stop all this."

"You can. Don't let it swell your head or anything, but you're probably the only one on your side who could." She barely paused. "So, did my friend's report offer a few unsettling probabilities?"

"What the bloody hell do you think?"

It was an amazingly rare outburst from him, but Murphy didn't flinch, and she wasn't surprised. She was, in fact, more sympathetic than she allowed to show.

"I think you're a smart man, and that the report only . . . solidified . . . a lot of possibilities you've been considering for a very long time. Long before I started bringing them up."

He was silent for a moment, frowning slightly. Dressed casually as he'd been that morning, he was visibly less tense than he had been then, but also visibly more . . . Well, in anyone else, Murphy would have said upset. With Duran, she wasn't sure. But either way, she didn't let down her own guard.

"I told you this morning," he said finally, abruptly. "With my superiors in place, Sebring and her superiors, there's no way I could even begin to end this."

"Well, just for the sake of argument, let's say we could do that for you. Leave you basically in charge, certainly of your faction and even of Sebring's—assuming you can win her people over once she's out of the way. With no superiors to obey or answer to."

"Murphy—"

"There would, of course, be conditions. That no more psychics are abducted, or deliberately created or otherwise . . . interfered with at any level. That any of our people still alive are returned to us. And, of course, most importantly of all, on the condition that our little war is over, a permanent peace declared and committed to by both sides. What would you do, Duran? How would you redirect the energies and talents and goals of your people?"

"What makes you believe I may have considered that?" he asked slowly.

"You wouldn't be you if you hadn't." She smiled faintly.

After a moment, returning her gaze, he said somewhat abruptly, "Many if not most would be best suited to work similar to what they do now. Security. Research, investigative work. Perhaps . . . for a business of some kind. A new company begun by us in which they would have a stake. A reason more than a salary on which to focus their efforts."

He definitely had been thinking about it, she noted.

"What sort of company, Duran?"

"A company such as the one I described. Not mercenaries, guns for hire. Not a military contractor. In fact, I don't doubt you have . . . assets . . . in your organization who would see to it that our interests remain far from anything involving either your military or your government."

Murphy's faint smile remained, and her shoulders lifted in a shrug. "Well, there was that thing with Wolfe. I had to take note. And I don't think I'd go broke betting that there are other potential, if not actual, political candidates your superiors have been grooming."

He nodded once.

"Of course, we couldn't let that go on."

"Of course," he replied expressionlessly.

"One day, maybe. When your people have fully integrated with ours. When nobody's thinking about . . . conquering or ruling over an inferior race."

"You believe that was the endgame of the political

maneuvering of my superiors," he said, a slight frown between his brows.

"I believe your fearless leaders had that in mind. Maybe because of a superiority complex. Or maybe just something that too often runs in the bloodstream of an over-militarized, tightly structured society. That breeds more than a desire to be in power. It breeds a desire to conquer. To rule."

"I have no wish to do either," Duran said.

"No?" She reached out suddenly and, for the first time, touched him, her long, warm fingers closing around his wrist. Tightly.

He didn't move so much as a muscle for a long moment. And then his eyes widened a fraction before narrowing.

Murphy released his wrist and slid her hand, both hands, into the front pockets of her jeans, still smiling faintly, perfectly at ease. "No," she said. "You don't. Which I count as something very much in your favor."

"No one can read me," he said slowly.

"Well. I'm special. So was your mother. She did a very good job, you know. Weaving that unique shield around you. I was always curious about why she did that, especially starting when you were so young."

"To protect me."

"Mmm. She was a telepath, wasn't she?"

"Yes."

"And knew you had inherited that."

For the first and what she suspected would be the last time, Murphy succeeded in visibly surprising Duran. Something flickered in his eyes, his face tightened, and he actually paled slightly.

"No. She wasn't born psychic."

"Sure she was. She just didn't tell your father that." Murphy's thin shoulders lifted in another faint shrug. "She read him all the way down to his soul. Knew who he was, what he was. Knew what his people intended. She even knew what you were meant to be. Just another worker bee, another soldier, maybe rising to be a commander in the field if you were good enough."

He stiffened.

"Yeah. It's what all you so-called first-generation hybrids were supposed to be. Crossing two species together directly like that, even if we were so very similar, tends to have a predictable result. You were supposed to be sterile. Not even close to psychic. That's what all their testing showed them. Perfect worker bees. No way to pass on their precious genetic material, to fuck up their grand plans. Just there to do all the dirty work."

Duran shook his head slightly in a very controlled gesture. "I'm not psychic."

"Everything I just told you *came* from you—and from the information your mother wove into that amazing organic shield, maybe thinking it would take . . . someone special . . . to find it. You're a telepath. A powerful one, I'd guess, though it may take you the rest of your life to learn to find a way through your shield. On your own, I mean. Psychics who struggle alone tend to make their shields stronger, not learn to punch holes or . . . open doors."

"What are you saying?"

"I'm just telling you the truth. What you choose to do with that truth is up to you. You might want to give it some thought. You have, after all, seen both the pluses and the minuses of being psychic up close and personal."

"Yes. I have."

"Your mother gave you a shield for a reason. It kept you safe but, even more, it gave you a choice. Choose wisely."

Abruptly returning the discussion to the beginning, she said, "We were talking about those obstacles standing between you and the end of this war. Were we not?"

"Yes," he said after a moment.

She allowed the pause to lengthen, then said, "I believe we can . . . remove those obstacles for you. Your superiors."

He looked at her sharply. "How?"

"Ironically, by being the weapons your people always thought we could be."

"Your people don't kill without reason."

"Did I say anything about killing them?"

"Nothing short of a bullet will stop Sebring. And possibly not even that. Or her closest lieutenants."

Murphy considered, then shrugged. "Well, if we can't remove her and her boys any other way, you know I'm perfectly capable of killing them. Sebring is, after all, responsible for abducting psychics her faction likes to turn inside out. Literally. All in the name of science. That's more than reason enough for me. For others on our side. And the same thing goes for the scientists and . . . healers . . . who murdered so many psychics, all in the name of their quest for knowledge."

"I can live with that," he said finally.

Murphy merely nodded. "I need the information I asked for, Duran. And, in the meantime, you don't go anywhere near those labs or those high-rises. You don't do anything to raise suspicion. You don't do or say anything that might tip them off. Anything."

"Agreed." He hesitated, then said neutrally, "There is one favor I would ask. A . . . personal . . . favor."

"Ask away," Murphy said.

---

*Henry? Are you awake?*

*I don't really sleep now. Juno . . . I don't think I can take much more.*

*You have to hold on, Henry.*

*I don't think anyone's coming to help us, Juno.*

*They will. Bishop will.*

*Are you sure?*

*Just hold on, Henry . . .*

---

"You really believe your—roaming psychics—can find those labs?" Brodie asked Bishop after the fed told them the status of the search out west, which narrowed with remarkable speed to only one state.

One vast state.

"I believe they can. And Wyoming makes sense. It's one of the ten largest states, and the least populous. I think you could hide more than a couple of labs there for a very long time."

"Assuming the labs of both factions are in the same general area."

"Yeah. And they may not be. But, so far, everything my people have sensed has been there."

"They sensed shadows."

"Which also makes sense. They'd want the labs as protected as possible by security, but even before that they'd want to make certain psychics on this side would be warned off by those shadows."

Brodie eyed him. "You're a lot more tense than you let on, aren't you?"

Bishop didn't deny it. "Matt and Jody Garrick believe they're burying Emma today. And I don't dare offer them hope that they aren't, not until we know for sure."

"Would they expect you to attend the funeral?"

"Probably, but I doubt either will notice at the time. I hate every minute that I can't call and tell them what I know. What I feel is certain. That Emma's still alive."

Brodie hesitated, then said, "If I'm getting all this, her chances are a lot better if one of Duran's field teams abducted her."

"Yeah. Though, in the early hours and days after an abduction, it doesn't make all that much difference to the victim why they were taken and by whom. The emotional and psychological damage begins immediately. Emma is a strong girl, but she's a teenager, and teenagers feel things . . . very intensely."

Tasha, who had been listening silently, nodded to that. "Especially teenage girls. But it won't be much longer, Bishop."

He looked at her. "How do you know?"

She blinked. "I—just know."

"Another door open?" Brodie asked her.

"I guess." Tasha frowned a little. "It popped into my head when Bishop was talking. I hope I'm right," she added a little uncertainly.

"So do I," Bishop told her.

But the hours dragged past, and no word came from any of his "roaming psychics" searching the vast state of Wyoming. They all worked throughout the afternoon, looking over the research that came in continually and helping Tucker continue coordinating Sunday's rescue missions.

Murphy left twice during that time, each time for no more than about forty-five minutes, and no one asked her where she went.

They sent out for supper, and when it was delivered they gathered at the big table in an equally large room filled with windows that could be used for dining or for a board meeting it was so huge.

Annabel emerged from her room, Pendragon at her feet. Annabel was shy and sweet; Pendragon was . . . a cat.

He wasn't talking to anyone.

The others forced themselves to be relaxed and casual when the still-fragile little girl was in the room. Bishop, always comfortable with children and with the knack of winning their trust instantly, talked to her while they ate. Her small, still-thin face seemed to glow from within as she responded to him with no trace of shyness.

At the other end of the long table, Brodie kept his voice low when he said to Tucker, "Say Duran's people headed back to their homeworld. Do you seriously believe thousands of years could have passed on that world?"

"Jesus, I don't know. Einstein thought so. Some of the best scientific minds we've ever produced agree. And

I'm guessing the trip back would take a lot longer than the trip here did. From what Murphy said, the ships that landed here were relatively small craft, intended to meet up with a mother ship. That would have been the fast ship; the smaller ones were probably never intended to travel from one world to another."

Tucker looked around. "Where *is* Murphy?"

"Slid out about fifteen minutes ago. You didn't see her?"

"No. Though, to be honest, it's easy to lose track of Murphy when she wants you to. Probably went to check in with the boss. Plenty of new intel to share."

Tucker frowned. "Do you guys get the same feeling I do? That things are moving all around us, whether we see them or not? That we're seriously closer to the end of this thing than we ever expected to be at this point?"

"I've barely been in it," Tasha said. "The fight, I mean. But knowing I was watched and monitored my whole life and that my life was never even what I thought it was, that part of it all makes me angry. All those women and their babies dying makes me . . ." She drew a breath and let it out slowly. "I'd like to be at the end of this. I'd like to be able to stop all the bad things happening because of this."

Brodie's fingers tightened on hers.

"I don't mean I want to quit," she added, mostly for Tucker's benefit. "But it would be nice to feel that at some point our lives will be normal again."

Tucker smiled faintly. "We're all bonded pairs of psychics," he reminded her. "Our lives will probably never be what most people would consider normal."

"I'm not psychic," Brodie objected. Then he met Tasha's gaze, and added, "With you, but otherwise . . ."

Tucker said to him, "Take it from me; you're more psychic than you know, and it's only going to get stronger."

Tasha, watching Brodie, was glad he wasn't at all upset about that. She could feel his calm and his certainty.

"Our new normal," he told the other man dryly.

"That is certainly true. For us more than most, normal is what we get used to."

Their attention was caught by a motion at the other end of the table, as Annabel closed the box her supper had come in, said something to Bishop that made him smile, then rose with the box and her silverware in one hand and her glass in the other and looked inquiringly at Sarah.

"Just leave that stuff on the kitchen counter, sweetie."

"It was really good," Annabel said earnestly. "Sarah, is it okay if I read for a while? Those books you got for me this morning."

"Of course it's okay." Sarah smiled at her.

Pendragon, who had sat in a chair at the table like people and eaten his own supper delicately from a bowl, glanced around at the humans, then jumped down and followed Annabel from the room.

Somewhat uncertainly, Sarah said, "I think I heard him thank me. Did anyone else hear that?"

Everyone else shook their heads, but before Sarah could question, Bishop said, "I'm pretty sure he has the ability to focus well enough to reach only the mind he wants to communicate with."

"Is that a good thing?" she asked wryly.

"No idea. I've never known a telepathic cat before," Bishop told her in all seriousness.

"He's not a cat," Tasha reminded the fed. "I mean, he looks like a cat and walks like a cat and sometimes even sounds like a cat. But . . . everything about him is unusual."

# EIGHTEEN

When they returned to the study/command center, Murphy was in the chair she had occupied earlier, her legs stretched out before her as she finished the last bite of a donut. After washing it down with what was undoubtedly a latte in a tall cardboard cup, she said, "That coffee shop on the corner will be the death of me. Donuts. Can't resist them."

"You left during supper," Tucker said, not quite accusingly.

"Yeah. Needed to check in with the boss. She already knew most of it, because we'd talked about some of this stuff before and because I checked in this morning after I met with Duran. Knew I was going to give him that report. So I mostly filled her in on our speculating today. And on how Duran reacted to that report."

The others were taking seats around the room, pairing up as usual as if by instinct.

"And?" Brodie demanded. "How *did* he react? Or is that a need-to-know thing too?"

Murphy smiled. "Still sure you want to go on offense?" She looked at the others as well as Brodie. "Take the fight to the other side in a major way? Because once we make that choice, we're committed. If we plan and execute this right, it should be a final decisive battle in every way that counts. If we fuck it up . . . Well, things could get worse."

There were decided nods all around, without hesitation. Clearly, everyone was ready to go on the offensive.

"Good. Since we were reasonably sure you'd all feel that way, the boss has been contacting every other cell, and it seems everybody's ready to do something proactive." She was smiling.

Brodie eyed her. "We're scheduled to send cells—and some extra assets, thanks to Bishop and a lot of other people who've been standing by wanting to help—to fifty of Duran's shadow breeding operations day after tomorrow, on Sunday. Most of us have been working on the final coordination of that. Rescue the women and any babies and get them to our safe houses. That's easily the most proactive operation we've carried out to date."

"It gets better," Murphy told him. "Not only will we get those women and their babies to people who really *can* take care of them, even fairly long-term while we figure out how best to help the Stepford mamas and raise those babies safely and happily, but the operation should serve two more purposes. It'll be a dandy distraction for most of those on the other side, *both* factions, and it should draw all the high-level leaders of both factions into emergency meetings in their not-so-ivory towers."

"We know where those are?"

"Yeah. New intel. We know where they'll be right down to the right rooms on the right floors of the right buildings."

"Where we plan to blow them up?" Brodie asked, something in his tone telling them all that was a line he wasn't at all sure about crossing.

"No, something a lot less violent—and a lot more certain, at least for us. Look, this kind of monster is like a Hydra; if we chop one head off, another grows in its place, sooner or later. We can't go after the leaders individually, allowing them time to fill a power vacuum. We have to render them useless to their . . . cause."

Slowly, Bishop said, "And how do we do that?"

As if she were saying something utterly ordinary, Murphy said, "We use the abilities of some of our bonded pairs to turn those so-called business moguls into just that. We remove the indoctrination and the memories of their mission. We remove everything, in fact, that isn't simply the knowledge needed to run those companies just like regular human robber barons do."

Before either Bishop or Brodie could say something, which both looked ready to do, she added, "Even more, because these monsters posing as greedy business suits in giant corporations will become just that, we have to make sure the money stops flowing for as long as possible—*and* that plenty of very suspicious people are peering over their shoulders. Any company or companies as huge as these, especially designed to make money for their 'shareholders,' are going to have a lot of . . . creative bookkeeping. We can tip off the IRS and SEC, the attorneys general in the states where their businesses are located. And anyone else we can think of to cause those giant companies a series of giant headaches that'll drag on for years."

"That's neat," Tucker said approvingly.

"The boss's idea. All that confusion should also drive those from both factions in these *businesses* further down the food chains to get out of the companies and go get real jobs. Or at least be prepared for new jobs. Most of them, anyway. We may have to deal with the others one on one, if Duran can't. *And* just to make very sure those a bit further down the ranks, the field soldiers running both Duran's breeding operation and the other faction's hellish biology experiments, get the point that all this stops, we do two more things.

"First—and I'm counting on Bishop's roving psychics coming through on this one—we hit their labs on the same day, at virtually the same hour, while all the bosses are coping with disappearing pregnant psychics and psychic babies from a big chunk of their operations—and also forgetting they were ever anything but Fortune 500 executives.

"No matter what, putting those labs out of commission permanently is a major, major goal. They have to be utterly destroyed, no matter what it takes. We *have* to make it impossible for them to experiment on our people any longer. Not by selective breeding, and sure as *hell* not by dissection. Which means the buildings and all their equipment are totally trashed. In fact, obliterated. And we'll metaphorically or literally salt the ground so nothing ever grows there again."

Intently, Tucker said, "I hope we're planning to grab as much intel as we can going out the doors and before all that equipment is destroyed."

"We certainly are. Their data banks will be emptied into flash drives and other data storage devices our teams take with them. We will also, of course, search for any psychics still surviving, and rescue them if at all possible. There will be at least one EMS-trained medic on each of the teams going into the labs." She knew Bishop gave her a steady look, but ignored it to add, "We have to destroy the only *true* aliens left in both factions, the healers."

"I wondered about that," Tasha murmured.

"Yeah, they're all either first ones, somehow medically modified to have way longer life spans than us—or else they're clones. A possibility that seemed to shake Duran when I suggested it. Either way, when the labs go, they go."

"We're sure they'll all be at the labs?" Miranda asked. "Don't they usually help with field operations, or stand by in case Duran or other team leaders need them?"

"Some do, yes, but we'll make sure they're all at the labs Sunday. And when those first ones go, so will the shadows, which means they lose *that* line of defense. I'm hoping there's intel about how the first ones developed and projected those shadows, but if not, so be it. Our world's better off without those illusions."

"And we're certain they're illusions?" Bishop asked. "I know one of my own people reported that was the sense he got, but as far as I know he'd never been exposed to them before, so he could have misinterpreted what he sensed."

"Not sure if they're illusions or projections or something else, but they aren't real. Not at all what our alien visitors look like, not even the first ones. Defenses. They've had a lot of time to build their various defenses. A lot of time. We're still playing catch-up. And even after we take Sebring out, I don't know that all of her field people will be willing to rethink their mission. Or to follow Duran. We'll have to wait and see about that."

"You're banking an awful lot on Duran," Brodie observed in a carefully neutral voice. "On the information he offers being accurate."

She widened her eyes at him. "Yeah, I am, aren't I?"

Tasha was frowning. "I still don't get how my ability to see the shadows—no matter whether they're real—is going to help us destroy them. Whatever they are."

"You don't know the power of your own abilities, Tasha."

"Is that supposed to be an answer?"

Brodie spoke before Murphy could, saying, "You can't be sure they're only illusions, especially if you have only Duran's word for that."

Murphy grinned at him. "Oh, come on, Brodie, you've been considering the possibility ever since we found out Tasha was able to see those *shadows* attached to people she'd thought were perfectly normal. All those people, all those assets tied up over so many years, we thought. What we didn't realize was that those people *were* perfectly normal. Oh, they were definitely keeping an eye on Tasha. And as disgusting as that was, I find it even harder to excuse them knowing what I know now. That they were more of Duran's tools. Human people doing a job they didn't ask any questions about because they were being paid very, very well."

"They were like us?" Tasha demanded now. "Human?"

"I take issue with the idea they're in any way like us, but human somewhere deep down inside their disgusting souls. They might not have known exactly what Duran was, or that they were betraying their own people, but they had to know what they were doing was wrong. You don't get paid the kind of money Duran admitted he was paying them for doing good works."

"Dammit," Tasha muttered.

Murphy looked at her with a certain sympathy, but said, "Look, we've always wondered how Duran managed to run such a massive and scattered field operation. We knew he used tools, people he paid or blackmailed or just scared into doing the jobs he needed to be done. We just didn't know that *most* of his field operations include a lot of people paid to do jobs they don't understand—or don't really want to question."

"Criminals?" Bishop guessed.

"Probably, at least some. Especially involved in the more . . . unsavory jobs like carrying bodies into buildings and then setting them on fire. They didn't need to know those were replacement bodies for abducted psychics. Probably wouldn't have believed it anyway. Or cared."

"And the bodies?" Bishop's voice was even. And they all knew he was thinking of the body buried today with Emma Garrick's name on the headstone.

"I'm betting some cadavers. But since so many had to resemble the psychics who supposedly died . . . probably few cadavers. So far, I haven't gotten Duran to admit in so many words that innocent people died to provide those bodies. Homeless people, hookers, runaways, loners without family, others like them who wouldn't be missed when they disappeared, those were the most likely targets."

Murphy met Bishop's gaze steadily. "I don't doubt Duran has blood on his hands. And I don't know if there'll ever be a reckoning for that. On this side of hell, anyway. But I do believe he's the lesser evil we can use to save countless psychics now and in the future. I believe he can help us end this war. I've made my peace with that. You'll all have to decide for yourselves if you can."

---

Duran chose to work from his private quarters rather than his office, something not at all unusual late on a Friday afternoon. He took the usual precautions to make certain no one would be aware of what he was doing.

Then he settled down at his desk at a laptop that did not look it but was beyond the state-of-the-art. Even so, he had to use all the skill and knowledge at his command to fulfill the last three items on Murphy's list of *requests.*

He had to locate Sebring and her top lieutenants, and tag their biometric implants so he would be able to track them between now and Sunday.

He had to provide as much intel as he could on the likely security setup of the two labs.

And he had to get as many healers as possible to the labs within twenty-four hours. Without drawing undue attention to his actions or their movements.

Murphy didn't ask for much, he thought wryly.

Still. Little enough, if it ended this war.

Little enough.

---

Leaving the others to decide what they could and couldn't live with, Murphy briskly continued with the—really rather bare outlines of their plan. "We also have volunteers, most former military or cops, ready and willing to move against and target a select few of the field soldiers, in front of others, so they understand only too well that we're no longer fighting a holding action and are willing to kill not only in self-defense."

"Those less likely to follow Duran?" Brodie guessed.

"Yeah, in his faction, and more in the other faction. He has to be left in charge of as many people as possible, field operatives, with their scientists and medical personnel out of the picture, because that's the only way those labs don't get rebuilt. The only way this war ends.

"The other faction we weaken considerably by taking out Sebring, their leader, and at least a couple of her lieutenants, maybe more. According to Duran, that should cripple them, making it at least easier for him to bring them around to his way of thinking. Again, we have people standing by ready and able to take care of that part of the operation; they'll move into position as soon as we pinpoint locations."

"We have people doing that?" Tucker asked. "Pinpointing their locations?"

"Yeah. You were right about the biometric chips; Duran's busy as we speak getting the information we need to track Sebring's chip, and that of her lieutenants. Once we have that intel, other hackers—I mean research specialists like you—will be able to watch them move in real time." She nodded to Bishop. "Thanks for that, by the way. It appears to be yet another decisive tool we can use."

"I'm glad," Bishop said.

Thoughtfully, Murphy added, "Though I don't doubt Duran will find a way to remove or disable his own chip once this is all over. Possibly before. So he isn't confused by anyone with Sebring."

"I don't blame him," Tucker said. "But you said we'd need to keep an eye on him. After."

"Yes. And we will." Without explaining *that*, Murphy merely added, "We'll have people on Sebring and her lieutenants before dawn on Sunday, very close, like white on rice, before they can react to our rescue operation at the shadow houses and clinics."

"We're very ambitious," Brodie noted, not as if it worried him unduly, but still with a note of reservation.

"Element of surprise. We catch them flat-footed with an operation like this, it really should be decisive. So we do all those things. And then we do one more thing."

Brodie lifted his brows, waiting.

"We're also going to completely destroy what's left of their scout ships."

"And we know where those are?"

"Every last one of them."

Somewhat wistfully, Tucker said, "Area 51?"

Murphy actually grinned at him, which was a rare sight. "Sorry, no. If they have any alien technology there, it isn't from Duran and his people."

Tucker pursed his lips. "But still possible they have alien tech there?"

Sarah was shaking her head slightly, smiling.

"Of course. You've looked into the—lore. Conspiracy theories. The so-called mythology. History. Like I've said, we have what could arguably be evidence of alien visitations going back thousands of years. Even evidence some argue means that alien DNA was deliberately introduced into the human race at various points."

"Evidence?"

"Of a kind. There were in our history quite a few times when we made sudden and rather unaccountable leaps in knowledge and technology. Even evolution. At least some science found a lot of that difficult to explain."

Since Tucker looked like he wanted to talk about that, Brodie interrupted to say, "I can't believe I'm saying this, but could we please deal with the aliens in front of us?"

"That's the plan," Murphy told him.

"That's going to take every asset we can lay our hands on and probably a lot more than we have," Brodie noted, reservation still in his tone. "And last I heard, we didn't have a clue where their labs are."

Bishop, his slightly abstracted expression vanishing, said, "We know now. Two of my people just confirmed both locations. And they'll remain just close enough to keep an eye on the labs until we can move against them." It didn't take a telepath to read the tension in his voice.

"Good," Murphy responded matter-of-factly, and before anyone could ask a question, went on briskly. "We have to make sure both factions are too crippled to retaliate in any way, leave them stunned and uncertain what to do next, so they turn to the strongest leader left. Duran. Surprise, especially an overwhelming surprise, is the essence of a successful attack."

Brodie shook his head. "Surprise can also be the essence of being knocked on our own asses. Murphy . . . this *plan* has a hell of a lot of moving parts and people doing things they've never done before. All apparently happening at about the same time."

Calmly, she said, "Our demolitions teams for the scout ships are former military, and quite definitely know what they're doing. And before you ask, they've been on our side through all this, and they know *exactly* what they'll be destroying."

Ever the fed, Bishop said, "If those scout ships are any size at all, no matter where they're hidden, blowing them up, especially all at the same time, is bound to be noticed."

"Not with what we're going to use. Something a couple of the geniuses on our side developed a while back. A few years from now, they might even get a patent and sell it." She frowned briefly. "Or maybe not. Anyway, it's not explosive, but more like a timer-activated acid. Doesn't harm anything organic, just metals—and all those other materials we've found some of their devices made up of. Those scout ships will basically just melt away, without even a puff of smoke. The teams have orders to stand by close enough to watch and make damned sure nothing remains. And to make sure the area looks clear of anything suspicious should anyone pass by in the future."

She looked around for questions, saw several faint frowns that likely heralded them, and went on before any could be asked. At least for the moment. "It won't all be over after this operation, huge though it is. We'll have to be on guard for a while. Maybe a long while. Keep many of our cells active so we can monitor what's happening.

"After that, after all that, Duran really is the key, at least to his faction, and probably most of those left once Sebring and her lieutenants are gone. I believe he's willing to manage his people in the field, to . . . work to alter their goals just enough, or change their minds just enough that they understand hunting us is simply no longer worth their while. We can help with that by proving to his field agents once and for all that they've reached a tipping point, that now we're fighting back. And that they're the ones seriously out-gunned. This operation should do that, and *because* it has so many people and so many moving parts."

Honestly, she added, "There are bound to be some on the other side, the other sides, who will refuse to give up, be unable to abandon the mission of a lifetime. Duran will take care of some of those. Some will probably cross paths with us and have to be . . . dealt with. It's going to take time, and we won't be able to lower our guards completely, at least for a while. We just have to make this plan count, and then give Duran all the time we can to work on both factions, to take control and begin redirecting his people to use their talents in a . . . more positive way."

Tasha said uneasily, "Maybe a stupid question, but even given that Duran can talk his people out of fighting . . . what will they *do*?"

"Yeah, any ideas along those lines?" Brodie asked dryly.

"A few. It's something Duran's considered, interestingly enough, and he has some good ideas. We'll discuss those and decide if we can live with them."

After a long moment, Bishop said, "One favor."

"You want to run the operation to take the labs. Because of Emma. And others who might be there."

"Yes."

Murphy held his gaze. "Understand that the labs *must* be destroyed. We can get any psychics we find out of there, knocked out and in restraints, and assess them later when we have time to make sure they weren't turned. Or broken. And we can get all the intel possible out of there. But the people in the white coats *know* what they're doing is evil. All administrative personnel there know. Everyone inside those facilities knows, just the way the Nazi doctors knew. That they were doing evil, unforgivable evil. Orders or no orders, job or no job. Aside from psychics, there are no innocents. Those labs have to be completely destroyed. And so do the monsters in them."

# NINETEEN

"I've been hunting monsters a long time," Bishop said. "I know—" He looked at Miranda and took her hand, then looked back at Murphy. "*We* know that evil has to be destroyed. That it doesn't belong in a sane world. Evil doesn't leave those labs alive."

Murphy nodded. "That's good enough for me. And what the boss said your reaction would be." Before anyone could question that, she was going on briskly, "You'll be able to hit both labs either at the same time or in quick succession, up to you. How far apart are they?"

"According to my people, about fifty miles."

"That's better than I expected. However you decide to move on the labs, the window we have will be very precise. We don't want the bosses on either side worrying about their labs, just the breeding houses and what happens in the field. We rattle them with those operations, enough so they call emergency meetings in their high-rise companies—which Duran agrees is what they'll do—and don't move against the labs or the hidden ships until those suits are all together and worrying about what's happening."

"Security?"

"About what you'd expect, way past pretty damned good." She dug in her ever-present leather bag and produced a flash drive, which she tossed to Tucker. "Courtesy of Duran. Our Rosetta stone."

Tucker raised his eyebrows. "Their native language?"

"Yep. And translation. Apparently, all their tech at these labs and only at these labs, the computers, other equipment, anything irreplaceable that could be hacked or otherwise stolen, is set up in their native language. Duran showed me some of it. Really looks like symbols to me, like Egyptian hieroglyphs. Only weirder. And since we're literally talking about an alien language, without that translation it'd be a bitch to crack even for a genius like you."

"I'll get right on it."

"Good. You don't have much time. We don't want Bishop and Miranda's teams to storm labs expecting trouble. It's going to be tough enough as it is."

"But," Brodie said somewhat dryly, "we still need all the moving parts moving at about the same time."

"Pretty much. And after you've cracked their security," Murphy said to Tucker as if she had absolutely no doubt about that, "you need to make sure our data storage devices can download and handle all the intel so it isn't gibberish, and make sure that our people on Bishop and Miranda's teams know where to plug in and which buttons to push to make that happen."

"On it," Tucker said, clearly more fascinated than appalled.

Murphy nodded. "Bishop, by tomorrow we should also have a sort of shift schedule for both labs so you can hit them at the best possible time within the window we're trying to aim for. They work and live on-site, living quarters on the second floor; some labs and offices on the first floor—and some kind of holding cells and other facilities I don't like to think about in a basement. Which is probably where any prisoners or . . . subjects . . . will be located.

"According to Duran, early on Sunday is a good time. A more relaxed time. Not because the monsters are at all religious, but because all their operations are geared to look as normal as possible. Just in case anybody's watching. Which means more electronic security than armed guards, according to their protocol. Assuming Tucker can breach their security, getting in should be easy.

"After that it'll be a matter of planning and timing. We have two of our largest cells already on their way to Wyoming, where they'll meet up with you. Each cell is made up of very good monster hunters, tech people, and soldiers, who've been in this thing a long time, and know exactly what the mission is. They're more than ready to go on the offensive. Not hotheads, and they'll follow your lead and your commands.

"Each cell also has one psychic able to recognize other psychics, including the psychics that have been turned or are otherwise working against us in those labs. For the record, I don't believe many if any of those psychics can be saved. But that's a judgment call made in the field, which means it's your call. You'll have dart pistols with tranquilizers, plenty to immobilize everyone, alien and human, which could help you neutralize the armed guards without raising the alarm. Though, again, your call.

"As for the psychics, the tranquilizers will put them down and keep them down long enough to get them out of there so they can be assessed. The medic on your team will see to it that they stay out as long as necessary, since we all know the only reasonably safe psychic from their side is one deeply unconscious."

She paused, then added, "Assuming you do find Emma and other psychics from your watch list, Bishop, I hope they're unharmed or at least in good shape, I really do. But to say they'll be traumatized is an understatement."

"We have an amazing healer who can help with that," Bishop said. "And Haven is as secure a location as we could possibly make it. It was named well, and has been a haven for many traumatized psychics for a number of years now. There's plenty of room. And the compound is remote, in New Mexico. No one there except Maggie and John Garrett will know anything about the situation. No one will ask questions. We can call for jet helicopters to transport the psychics to Haven—and we won't be on anybody's radar."

Miranda spoke up then to say something they'd likely already decided privately. "Noah and I will split up, each take one cell and one lab. We can coordinate for a simultaneous assault without the need for radio or cell signals, or anything else that could be picked up or pinpointed."

Tasha noted the other woman used the word *assault* deliberately and without flinching.

Murphy nodded. "Works for me. As for the two not-so-ivory towers where the suits will be gathering, one's in Seattle, and the other in Chicago. We have people on the move to handle the Seattle office, people chosen very carefully. It's fairly remote, and our people should be able to get in and do their jobs."

"Murphy," Brodie said in a tone indicating extreme patience. "Just what are those jobs? I mean how in the name of hell do you intend to use psychic abilities to . . . rewire . . . a couple of boardrooms full of aliens in suits? The bosses are as much monsters as their scientists are, but I get why we can't just take them out. What I don't get is how we use whatever abilities we have as bonded pairs to fix that particular problem."

Murphy smiled at him.

"Am I going to hate this?" he demanded.

"I dunno. A few months ago, I would have said probably. Now, not so sure."

She was stared at. By everyone.

"Don't make me ask again," Brodie told her.

Murphy smiled. "I finally persuaded Duran to tell me why bonded psychics are safe from his people. And the answer is really simple. Fear. As badly as they want psychics, and as long as they've studied them, bonded psychics both baffle and terrify them. Because even inexperienced psychics, if they're bonded to a mate, psychic or not, are about ten times more powerful than they were alone."

"Ten times?" Tasha ventured.

"Whether you know it or not," Murphy confirmed.

"What can she do?" Brodie asked.

"Not just Tasha. Tasha and you. With the exception of

Bishop and Miranda, who have been very deeply bonded for quite a few years, and so can both operate and coordinate even with fifty miles or more between them, every bonded pair we're using needs to act together, in the same place at the same time. We have two pairs joining the cell in Seattle, and they know what to do.

"In Chicago, we'll have you two—and another bonded pair from the Chicago cell. They also know and understand the mission."

Tucker said, "What about Sarah and me?"

"We need you here to coordinate, Tucker, especially given the difficulties of the alien language, the necessity of tracking Sebring and her lieutenants, and the probability that someone somewhere will need something translated, pronto. And since we don't want any communications picked up, both Sarah and I will stay here because of the strength of Sarah's abilities—and the fact that I can serve as a strong conduit for her to communicate with other psychics."

Brodie had to grin. "You really didn't expect you'd be stuck here out of the action, did you?"

Murphy gave him a look. "I go where I'm needed, just like everyone else." But everyone could hear a faintly disgruntled note in her tone.

"Uh-huh."

"Shut up, Brodie." She returned her attention pointedly to the second-longest bonded pair in the room. "Tucker, we didn't expect this central command center of ours to be used as such this quickly, but so it is. Sarah . . . I need to ask you to do something else."

"Name it," Sarah responded instantly.

"Now, and once all this really gets started, we may

well need information only you can provide—from the crossroads. I need you to tap that source, maybe later but certainly now. I need to know if there's anything you can learn there that could help us. We need every edge we can find to pull this off."

Sarah frowned slightly. "I'm willing to try, Murphy, but that's a pretty broad question. The information there is . . . infinite. And there aren't exactly any maps."

"We can help."

They all looked toward the hall doorway, startled to find Annabel standing there holding Pendragon in her arms. Both wore almost eerily identical solemn expressions.

"We can help," Annabel repeated. "Because I'm connected to Pendragon. And he's connected to them. They made him."

*Well, I wouldn't go that far.*

In spite of everything Sarah smiled. But she had to say, "We had a feeling you might want to help, sweetie, but—"

"I've been to the crossroads," Annabel said simply.

"You have?"

"Lots of times. It's such a nice place, like the library. Huge and quiet and filled with things to learn. I love it there."

"Wow," Tucker said half under his breath. And then, louder, he added, "Can you and Sarah go together?"

Annabel nodded. "And Pendragon. He knows where to look. He knows what can hurt them."

"Them?"

"The bad people who try to scare us with shadows. Especially the ones in the tall buildings."

"You know the shadows aren't real?" Tasha asked.

Annabel nodded again. "I knew even before Pendragon told me. I found out at the crossroads. I was scared one night, because one of them passed by the—the place where I was sleeping outside. It woke me up. I thought I saw the shadow, real tall, shaped all funny, and cold, and scary-feeling. I didn't know if I was having a nightmare, even wide-awake. So I closed my eyes and went to the crossroads."

Murphy, rather uncharacteristically showing her fascination, asked, "What did you find out?"

"That they were like things that jump out at you in a fun house at Halloween. Things to scare you. Only not pretend, like in the fun house. Not to scare you and then make you laugh. Just to scare you real bad and keep you scared. So you stay away."

"Did you find out where they come from?"

"Just not here. Far away. From a star so far away you can't see it at night."

---

Brodie knew Murphy too well not to know she'd be slippery until she wanted to tell them whatever it was they needed to know. He wasn't happy about that, but knew there wasn't much he could do about it. For now, at least.

And Tasha asked only one question, about something more than one person in the room decided they should have considered themselves.

"What about the other shadow breeding operations?" she asked Murphy quietly. "All the ones we haven't found yet, or can't move against on Sunday. What about all *those* moms and babies?"

Not surprisingly, Murphy had an answer ready. "We

will continue to rescue those women and babies and close down or convert to our control all the facilities, one by one if we have to. The existing staff at each facility will be ordered to go on as usual until we can get to them all. Duran's agreed that all his attention is going to be more than occupied with dealing with the . . . readjustments . . . of his people. And it *is* his operation to end, of course. He'll handle any open objections to that, and we'll maintain tight security on all the other facilities during the interim."

"But we haven't found them all."

"We'll have a list by Sunday," Murphy told her. "A complete list. Of every house and facility in operation." She paused. "There are a lot. A hell of a lot. That's why I said we'll probably convert some of them to our control, at least for a while. We'll have to figure out how to handle the on-site staff, who are mostly more of Duran's paid tools, but that may be a lot simpler than we had any right to expect. Seems Duran had his human tools hypnotized and a post-hypnotic suggestion planted deeply. When we give the word, all those people are going to forget all about their parts in the eugenics programs, and lose all knowledge they had or might have had about any of this. And it can be done one facility at a time."

Tasha looked at her, troubled. "But aren't they guilty of the things they did do?"

"They actually didn't do so much any of us would find all that objectionable, I think. Whatever was done to the women happened before they were given over to the caretakers. The worse they believed they were doing was running homes or clinics for unwed mothers who were either slightly mentally disabled or else had been traumatized by their pregnancies."

"Which," Sarah murmured, "would answer most of their questions."

"Yeah, most. It's a neat solution Duran planned for various eventualities, and I think it's one we can live with. About the caretakers, at least. As for Duran and his part in developing and running the eugenics program . . . Like I said, I doubt he'll escape judgment or punishment, just not from us."

That was something they all believed they could live with.

They all had plenty to do in order to get ready for their operations, but all wanted to watch as Sarah, Annabel, and Pendragon attempted to reach the place they called the crossroads, where past, present, and future met.

Except they didn't *try.*

They just did it.

Tucker, sitting in a chair at right angles to the couch where he could watch them all, realized first. Connected to Sarah always, he felt it.

"Damn," he murmured, his eyes unconsciously half closed.

"What?" Murphy asked softly.

"They're there. All three of them.

"Can you see—"

"No. Not exactly. It's not a . . . visible place, at least not to me. A feeling. A sound I can't really hear. But peaceful. Very—" He broke off abruptly as both Sarah and Annabel opened their eyes in the same moment.

Pendragon sneezed, opened his eyes, and began to wash a forepaw.

Brodie looked at Tasha. "Why does it surprise me now when he acts like a cat?"

"I think he does it on purpose."

*Allergic to stardust.*

Bishop said, "I'm almost afraid to ask if he's serious."

"I'm not," Miranda said. "Pendragon?"

*Cats joke.*

"Do you?"

*Fun to tease.*

Miranda shook her head and returned her gaze to Sarah and Annabel, both of whom were smiling slightly and looked very peaceful.

"I hate to interrupt," Miranda said.

"It's all right." Sarah smiled at her specifically. "You and Bishop are going to be very successful. And you'll find two of the psychics you thought lost. Two you can save."

"Only two?" Miranda asked.

"At least two. Possibly as many as four."

Murphy spoke up almost idly. "Cheating."

"No," Sarah said seriously. "They needed to know. It'll help them do what they have to on Sunday, because none of this is without cost. Just as it'll help Tasha and Brodie to know that they don't really need you to tell them what to do in Chicago. They'll know when the time comes."

Murphy smiled.

Brodie looked like he wanted to swear.

Annabel smiled at him. "You should know by now you can't plan around corners."

"I can try," he retorted, but in a mild tone.

"You have to learn to see around them first. Tasha will teach you how to do that."

"I *know* how to do that?" Tasha asked, surprised.

"You will."

"Let me guess. When the time comes?"

"The way of the universe."

Softly, Miranda said, "Some things are meant to happen just the way they happen."

---

Given the distance they had to travel, Bishop and Miranda left first, their private jet taking them to Wyoming without fanfare, where they were to meet up late on Saturday with the teams and equipment they would need for their mission.

Bishop had offered another jet to transport Tasha and Brodie to Chicago, but Brodie had elected to call instead one of their deep undercover assets, who had helped plenty but was still itching to help even more.

To Bishop, Brodie had said, "It's enough to have your jet plus a couple of jet helicopters from Haven buzzing around out west. This will be a common and uninteresting business trip made by a corporate jet that makes the occasional, semi-regular run from Charleston to Chicago. And," he added thoughtfully, "if I know him, he'll offer us a penthouse apartment in some swanky riverfront high-rise once we get there where we can stay for the duration."

Brodie used one of the *very* secure phones in their base to place the call, and wasn't at all surprised when Josh Long announced the jet would be ready and waiting in Charleston within two hours, offered more than one jet if needed, and indeed a large, full-service penthouse apartment overlooking Lake Michigan, at their disposal for as long as necessary.

Brodie accepted one jet and the apartment, rather amused.

On impulse, and since he knew his friend had long wanted to do something more active than "merely" supply transportation, equipment, and other necessities, Brodie said, "You and the others all like kids, right? Have quite a few between you?"

"Not enough," Josh answered promptly. "Zach and Teddy have been talking about adopting, and so have most of the rest of us. Plenty to offer, you know, and plenty of kids who need good, loving homes."

"Happy to hear that."

Josh had learned not to ask too many questions, but one amused question did emerge. "You're looking to adopt out kids now?"

"I'll let you know. They'd likely be . . . special kids, Josh."

Without hesitation, Josh Long replied, "We all learned to appreciate special kids a long time ago. Put us on your list, John. And just say when."

Brodie started to thank him, but ended up listening, unsurprised, to the dial tone.

"So," Murphy said, having listened unabashedly, "you're thinking ahead to placing possibly psychic babies into good homes."

"You said it yourself. The very best use we could have for some of our deep-cover assets is to take care of those women and babies. And kids, for all we know, maybe old enough to be in school, and *maybe* not living in places anywhere close to the sort of homes and lives they deserve."

"I'm not disagreeing. Start your list. Between all of us, I'm thinking we'll have enough assets to provide good homes for a lot of those kids. Quite a few in some of our cells have also expressed interest now that word's spreading."

"Maybe Duran should run an adoption agency," Brodie said dryly. "Serve him right."

Murphy looked . . . thoughtful.

# TWENTY

Robin Brook and David Grant were recent newcomers to the Chicago cell, they confessed while meeting Tasha and Brodie. *Very* recent. They had been bonded for more than a year, both telepaths, aware of what had been going on for longer than that, and had elected to be among those psychics living in plain sight but not necessarily calling attention to themselves.

"Until the babies," Robin told them starkly. "We both heard them, and when we did . . . We couldn't just stand by and do nothing. Because they were reaching out for help." She shook her head, delicate face clearly showing sorrow. "We couldn't help them. But if there are other babies we can help—"

"There are," Tasha told her. "A lot of them, in fact. And if we can do what we're supposed to here, we can help them all." She looked at Brodie, suddenly frowning. "So far, no instincts kicking in," she said.

"Yeah, I know." He looked at the other couple. "How

about you two? Any idea of just what we're supposed to actually *do* here, or has Murphy been stretching the truth again?"

They were sitting across from each other in a small but nicely bustling café just down the block from the high-rise whose address they'd all been given.

"We weren't told much about the mechanics of what we need to do," David said frankly. "Just the basics. Where to meet you two, which building and even which floor and which boardroom we're supposed to be . . . concentrating on . . . pretty damned early tomorrow morning, especially for an office building and on a Sunday to boot."

Tasha nodded wryly. "We checked out the building before dark, and it sure isn't the kind where people work on the weekends. But there are apartments on several of the upper floors."

"Their people, I'm guessing," David said matter-of-factly. "Some of them, anyway. But not the suits we're after. Those're more likely to live in penthouse condos or some of those places in Lincoln Park or, even more likely, the Gold Coast."

"Or on one of those estates outside the city in the suburbs," Robin added. "There's some insane wealth out there."

Brodie frowned thoughtfully. "I wouldn't expect the suits to be living too grandly, at least not from the outside looking in. They wouldn't want to draw attention either way, by living too plainly or too . . . plushly."

"Plushly?" Tasha looked at him, one eyebrow lifting.

"Don't give me a hard time, my head's still spinning from yesterday."

"Ours too," David said, and when Brodie looked at

him added, "Not many secrets about our visitors left on our side, I'm afraid. At least among the bonded psychics. And nobody seems all that surprised, so apparently some of us had considered the possibility before now." His voice was low, but casual. "We seem to be linking up somehow, sharing knowledge, even the ones who aren't telepaths. Ever since what happened Monday, Robin and I have been more and more aware of what we've been mostly trying not to think about for the last year and more."

"It's not that we didn't want to help," Robin began, but Tasha waved away the explanation.

"Listen, lots made the same choice, and we've all had our reasons for whatever choices we've made. No judgment from anybody on that." She was frowning now as she looked at Brodie, and added, "What? We already know most of it, so why would you expect more?"

"It's the linked-up business that bothers me," he said readily. "Because I don't think we are. And I think that could be my fault."

"It's nobody's fault. We're new at this."

"We can't afford to be new at this, not with what's supposed to happen in just a few hours."

"Hate to echo Murphy, but I really do think we'll both know when the time comes. I think we'll know what to do, and I think your ability will be triggered—and will enhance or even supersede mine."

It was Brodie's turn to frown.

Robin laughed a little, saying, "Don't take this the wrong way, but it's sort of nice to see another couple struggling with this. We've been amazingly close—and have from time to time gotten on each other's nerves in an amazingly irritating way."

David nodded a solemn agreement. "Takes a lot of adjusting to, this stuff, even when you're nuts about each other and have no question about your commitment. We do tend to self-censor when talking out loud, but not so much with the thinking. For instance," he added to Brodie, "you might want to watch those random sexist-pig moments, no matter how fleeting."

Tasha lifted an eyebrow at Brodie again. "Do you have those?"

"Probably," he said a little dryly. "It's pretty much stamped into the Y chromosome."

"I consider myself warned," Tasha murmured, then said to the other couple, "Still, when it comes to what we're supposed to do, I don't at all understand how it's possible."

"No way to know for sure until we do the thing," David said, "but if you ask me, something critical was triggered in a whole lot of us when those women and babies were murdered. I don't know what Duran—that's his name, right?—was trying to do, what traits he believed would build a better psychic, but he may have done a hell of a lot more than he ever intended."

---

There were only four people in the cell tagged to move on the shadow breeding house on this side of Richmond, in part because there were two of them in the city, and others in the cell had been needed to move against the other one.

Elijah, the calm, steady-eyed former military leader of the Richmond cell, wasn't happy that his team had been forced to split up, even though he trusted Leo, another former military officer Elijah had named as leader of the other part of the cell. But splitting up had been necessary; both were soldiers, and both knew the importance of surprise.

Both these shadow breeding houses had to be taken at the same time, the same time as *all* those in the rescue operation they were running before dawn today. Not only were the lives of Elijah's people at risk, but the lives of women and unborn children—and any civilians who would need to be treated as noncombatants yet also rendered nonthreatening.

Zara slipped up beside him, silent in the darkness of this moonless night, her exotic beauty oddly at home in the operation, and whispered, "I did a complete circuit around the property. Clear. No sign of any guards."

"So far, so good," Elijah whispered in return, the clock in his head ticking off the seconds. "Where's Patrick?"

"Just finishing his check. The intel we were given made it easy for him to put all the cameras on a loop so they see what we want them to see. Virginia says the same goes for the rest of the security system; she's got all the relevant lines cut or rerouted so there won't be an alarm. Not here and not at their base. Until Duran is alerted and runs a security check, nobody on their side will know that anything out of the ordinary has happened."

"But he'll know as soon as he runs the check?"

"Yeah, as planned. A couple of deliberately triggered alarms will alert him, and his own system will inform him that his entire network was hacked. All the dominoes will fall exactly the way we want them to, in perfect timing."

She had barely finished the report when a slender, dark young man joined them, reaching for the backpack on the ground beside Elijah and slipping into it the laptop he carried. "We're good to go," he whispered. "Cameras are on a loop, and other security's been defanged."

"We own the joint," Virginia confirmed, her whisper as calm as the others as she handed another laptop to Patrick so it could be secured in the backpack. She was a stocky woman in her early forties, her pale hair gleaming even in what little light was present. "And the hackers took care of any neighborhood cameras that might have caught us. We're clear, Elijah."

"Okay. Everybody remember what we're here for. The women should remain asleep for the duration, but keep an eye out just in case. No infants or children on-site, according to our intel. The staff here should be noncombatants, but we put them out or help them sleep a little deeper with the tranquilizers. We split up, two going in the front and two in the back. We take care of this fast, quiet, and by the numbers. Got it?"

His three team members nodded, automatically adjusting the tranquilizer pistols on their belts, the other more lethal handguns that would only be used in case of dire necessity, and double-checked pockets to make sure they had the loaded hypodermics they would use if they found the caretakers sleeping peacefully—which was the preference.

"Let's move," Elijah whispered, and his team moved out through the predawn darkness of the quiet, peaceful neighborhood.

---

Leo made a last pass through the comfortable house in Richmond, checking every room even though his team had cleared it. The caretakers slept in their beds, the male administrator snoring rather loudly, and Leo couldn't help but smile a bit grimly as he closed that bedroom door.

They were getting off lightly in his opinion, these "caretakers" of damaged women carrying babies whose very DNA or something even more basic had been manipulated to produce what the other side viewed as weapons. Leo trusted that decisions made far higher up the chain of command than the space he occupied were correct, that the caretakers likely didn't know the part they had played in evil, but he didn't have to like it.

But he did his job and did it well, knowing for certain that they were both helping these poor women and their innocent offspring *and* throwing a sizable wrench into the plans of the other side.

He could live with that.

He made his way silently through the house, pleased that his team had done their jobs without doing anything to rouse the neighborhood. And when he reached the garage end of the house, he was pleased again that this part of the operation was proceeding just as silently. Even the normally noisy garage doors had been raised in near-silence, their tracks carefully oiled for the purpose.

The only light came from inside the ambulance.

The four pregnant women in this house, still sleeping peacefully, had been loaded gently onto stretchers and placed into the waiting specially-modified ambulance, its engine idling with a quiet that was unusual, and the medic was checking them over while the driver and the other three members of Leo's team waited.

Leo reached the open doors of the ambulance and waited until the medic looked at him. "All good?" He didn't whisper, but his voice was low.

"Yeah, they're all fine. Good vitals. They should sleep through most if not all the trip."

"Okay, then. Let's get moving."

He closed the ambulance doors quietly and stood with his team at the open mouth of the garage until the ambulance had pulled quietly out of the driveway and gone on its way, carrying the women and their unborn children to a place where they would be safe and cared for in every sense of the term.

He wondered if any of them would ever be normal again, and could only hope that they would be.

The sky was lightening in the east when Leo and his team slipped from the neighborhood as silently as they had come barely more than an hour earlier.

---

"Okay, Jace." Bella, her pleasant face and mild eyes hiding the brilliant mind of a security expert and former cop, looked less happy than she might have been, which was explained by her next words. "The ambulance holding the moms is clear, well on its way to the safe house. The rest of the team made it to their car and are out of here. We're clear too, with no sign anybody in this neighborhood noticed a damned thing. So do we *have* to trip the alarms now?"

A little amused, the leader of this Nashville cell said to

his lieutenant, "Part of the plan, Bella, you know that. This whole thing falls apart unless Duran is alerted so *he* can check the rest of his network and alert his bosses. Our part in this is done, at least for now. We trip the alarms and get the hell out of here."

"But the other teams—"

"We're the last out." Jace glanced toward the eastern sky, where spectacular colors announced that dawn was well under way. "I heard from base about two minutes before you got back to me; every other cell on the rescue operation has reported in, jobs done. Part of our job is to trip the alarm, so that's what we do." He grinned faintly, looking as so many genius IT guys looked, far younger than he should have, and added, "Hey, I hate it as much as you do, but at least everybody knows or will know it was deliberate and not a fuck-up."

Bella rolled her eyes, but looked a bit more cheerful. "Okay, okay. Give me two minutes and it's done."

Jace checked his watch. "Perfect."

---

Murphy opened her eyes reluctantly, trying to ignore the pounding in her head long enough to focus on a small hand being held out to her. In the hand were several capsules.

"For your headache," Annabel said gravely.

"Thanks, kid." Murphy accepted the capsules and washed them down with a sip of cold latte. "Sarah—"

"I know, I know. Sorry, Murphy. But it's the quickest, most efficient way to keep track of all the cells and teams, and you know it. There's at least one psychic on every team, and all of us are linked up now, so I didn't even need bread crumbs. Everything hinged on this first part going as planned, so I had to make sure."

"Yeah, no argument." Murphy frowned at the other woman, bringing her into focus. "But am I wrong in thinking you sort of . . . darted into the crossroads there at the end?"

Sarah smiled. "It's not really a place."

"You know what I mean."

"I just . . . needed to confirm in one more way that what your astrophysicist friend discovered is accurate. And try to get some kind of timeframe. Knowing a far more powerful and ruthless enemy is likely heading your way is bad enough without knowing how long you have to prepare for that."

Murphy nodded, unsurprised. "And the answer you got: generations. If we're lucky. But even with time to prepare, we'll need help. Need all that knowledge and tech stored at the labs. Need Duran and his people thinking about that enemy and what they're capable of. And feeling the need to defend their homeworld—*this* homeworld now—from that enemy."

It was Sarah's turn to nod, soberly. "We'll need them and their knowledge. And our best minds working on it. Too many of our world leaders never bother to turn their eyes toward the stars."

"Well," Murphy said, "we'll just have to change that, won't we?"

---

It was a closely guarded secret among Sebring's most trusted lieutenants that she never took an active role in a field mission. She planned it down to the last detail, and she was always close enough to see what unfolded—virtually always just as she'd planned—and to take the credit for success.

She did not like failure.

So when members of the "resistance" moved against one of her teams unexpectedly not far outside Chicago as they were about to take a rather gifted telepath, she was near enough to see.

But not to intervene.

She hadn't actually been paying much attention, her mind on the psychic she'd sent to Charleston, the one who had failed to report in as he should have done by now. But all thoughts of him vanished as she heard gunfire and watched two of her lieutenants go down.

It was an unwelcome shock, even worse a *surprise* that the resistance team was very deliberately shooting to kill in a clear escalation of their . . . conflict. She could tell from the way they moved that these people were former military, well trained and grimly determined to complete their mission, and she had to believe that this was a deliberate escalation.

For the first time in her memory, those trying to keep them from taking psychics were on the offense.

Something had changed.

Sebring remained where she was long enough to watch as those grim people checked out her fallen lieutenants, probably verifying their targets. Watched as they communicated with each other using a bare minimum of words, and then melted away into the predawn darkness.

She activated the headset she wore, angrily aware that her routine mission had been upended in less than four minutes. "Sark?"

"What the hell happened?" His voice was tight but controlled.

"I don't know. Get a clean-up crew here. We leave nothing to interest the local police. Got it?"

"Yeah, got it."

"Then report to base." Without waiting for him to copy the transmission, she deactivated her headset, already on the move.

*Goddammit. Goddammit.*

---

*What do you see, beloved?*

*The schedules and diagrams were all accurate. Only one guard in that pretty, disguised gatepost, and only the two entrances.*

Miranda lifted her binoculars and studied the deceptively innocent building that looked like a small, innocuous company or merely a suite of offices, even if in a very remote location. Not very many parking spots, and nice landscaping that didn't encourage people to get too close to the seemingly innocent building unless it was to clearly approach an entrance.

*They know all the tricks. The electronic security the place is practically bristling with isn't visible. The exterior and landscaping look . . . ordinary. Just like a place where some blameless business is conducted. It isn't even obvious this building has a second floor, far less an extensive underground space a lot larger than a simple basement.*

*Easier for us.* Bishop's mind-voice sounded as clear to her as if he stood beside her and spoke quietly aloud, not like he was fifty-odd miles away at an almost identical innocuous building.

*You guys see anything unexpected?* Sarah's mind-voice, as distinctly soft and serene as her speaking voice.

Miranda did a last thorough check with her binoculars, knowing her partner and husband was doing the same.

*Nothing unexpected,* Bishop reported. *But we need to reach out with an extra sense or two before we go in there. Four minutes. Do we have them?*

There was a brief pause, and then: *You have them. Go.*

Neither Bishop nor Miranda actually moved, but both went utterly still, no binoculars shielding their gazes as each reached out and into their respective targets.

With each of them as well, strategically placed around each building, were the other members of their teams. They had not been granted much time to get to know each other, but every person on each team recognized a pro in every other person. They were trained, armed, and utterly dedicated to their mission.

And to these two remarkable leaders.

Miranda caught her breath suddenly. *Henry. Henry McCord. He's here. In the underground structure.*

*I've got Emma. And Katie Swan,* Bishop responded. *Underground as well. Can you reach Henry?*

*Wait. Let me . . . Today, everyone seems to be a telepath. He's waking up. He thought it was a dream, but . . . Okay. Okay, I'm pretty sure I got through to him. He'll be ready. What about Katie?*

*The same. She's shaky, but . . . determined. They didn't break her. She's mad. She's good and mad.*

*And Emma?*

*Scared. But relieved to hear from me.*

*I'll bet.*

Miranda could feel herself smile even as her spider senses probed a bit more, still searching. *I think there's another captive psychic, but can't get a fix. Should be able to once I'm inside. Only a couple more psychics here. Theirs. All sleeping, but . . . Murphy may be right. These are damaged people. Not sure we'll ever get them back. Not sure we ever had them.*

*We'll get them out anyway. Have to be sure.*

*Of course. Those psychics are on the upper level. In their bedrooms. Can't tell if they're sleeping or meditating, but I'm certain they aren't aware of any danger. There are healers here too. Four . . . no, five of them. Duran told the truth. Their sleep is almost like a kind of hibernation. They are really out.*

*Maybe how they're able to extend their life spans.*

*Maybe. And those shadows they're able to project may come straight from their unconscious minds, whether they're awake or out, because I can feel them too. Cold, slimy, shifting away when I try to see them clearly. No wonder so many psychics find them terrifying. I know it's only an illusion, and still they send chills through me. All five are on the lower level, same as Henry. We bring the building down on them, and this place will be their grave.*

*Same here. Counting . . . six healers. All out, all in the lower level, same as Emma and Katie. And . . . four of their psychics. Two are awake for certain. Some kind of routine mental exercises they're supposed to be doing. Bored, though.*

*Six healers and four of their psychics in your building. Be careful, Noah.*

*You know I will. You too, beloved.*

*Four minutes.* Sarah's calm mind-voice. *All the teams on*

*the rescue operation have completed their missions and cleared the areas. The alarms deliberately raised have alerted Duran, and he's alerted the suits. He also made sure the other faction's suits were alerted when several of their field operations went south. As per their protocol, they'll do a routine security check of the labs, and will discover all is well. All attention should remain fixed on the shadow house raids and the unsuccessful field operations.*

*Copy,* they sent in unison.

*Miranda?* Pendragon.

*Yes?*

*You have the lab belonging to Sebring's superiors. It is a very, very dark place. Bad place. Sad place.*

*Copy.* On a part of her consciousness, Miranda had already begun building a tough inner barrier to protect herself as much as possible from the cold despair she could feel in this place. They knew some of the abducted psychics had been tortured and killed, and had been fairly certain this was the lab where the worst of those terrible acts had taken place.

Still, Miranda appreciated the heads-up.

*Take great care, beloved.*

*Yes. I will. You too.*

Miranda stirred, closed her eyes briefly, then looked at her waiting team. The sky was just beginning to, faintly, lighten in the east, but she wouldn't have needed the extra light to see them all. Calm faces, trained and athletic bodies relaxed in that deceptive way only people of action ever were.

"Let's move," she said softly.

# TWENTY-ONE

Tasha knew she shouldn't be so tense. The others weren't, she knew. Robin and David. Very alert, yes, but not tense. She could feel that through the increasingly strong link between all of them—and others, distant and yet coming nearer, following the link they all shared. Everyone intent, focused. And what she sensed through her connection with Brodie was the same, his concentration, his focus.

What she should have been feeling, thinking.

And they had, after all, gained entry to the building with almost ridiculous ease on this Sunday morning. The door codes Tucker had provided—and the tiny metallic "biometrics" Murphy had somehow persuaded Duran to supply, each secured to their forearms with an organic tape that would read as their own skin—had made getting in through doors and past scanners they knew were there but never saw a fast and simple process.

So what was bugging her?

She had been aware, on some level of her mind, of Sarah's quiet voice checking off the boxes of today's operations as each was completed. The shadow houses and clinics raided, the Stepford moms and their unborn babies safely away. A dozen field operations halted in quick succession, a number of the soldiers of Sebring's faction and three of Duran's—very carefully selected—taken out.

All smoothly, as planned.

Tucker or one of their other technical geniuses had hacked into the supposedly unhackable building's security to make sure that the scanners would record only residents going up to their apartments after, perhaps, a morning run, since they were all casually dressed as though they had done just that. No scanner would note that the elevator stopped briefly on a certain floor, or that the "residents" got out there.

No camera would see them, their blank electronic stares on a peaceful loop monitored by a technical genius perhaps far away who would return the cameras to good working order as soon as the right people began arriving.

Which was, they had been told, less than an hour away.

The big boardroom, still empty, was where it was supposed to be, no receptionist or executive assistant in the foyer space outside it, the doors to executive offices lining the long hallway closed and locked.

They checked everything. Double-checked that all was as it was supposed to be so early on a seemingly peaceful Sunday morning.

As Brodie and David were checking the stairwells for a final time, Robin slid up beside Tasha, frowning.

"What is it?" Her voice was low.

Tasha bit her lip, then shook her head. "I don't know. Everything is just the way it's supposed to be. Right?"

"Yeah." Robin's frown deepened. "But you're feeling something else. Deeper than thought. Maybe instinct. You've never been here before?"

"No, never."

Robin glanced at the watch on her wrist, then grimaced when she realized it had stopped, and shifted her gaze to a clock behind the receptionist's desk, where decorative indoor "trees" were intended to soften the very sterile look of the area. "I know you've been getting the verifications, same as me. The rescue operations down south have been completed successfully. The suits should be getting the word from Duran. Once they learn more than fifty shadow houses have been raided, the women and kids gone, caretakers left sedated, *and* that a dozen field operations this morning have been stopped, the bosses will want to meet here ASAP."

"Here in less than an hour, I know."

"We have people from the Chicago cell all around us," Robin reminded her. "They know who should be here and who shouldn't, know the schedules, the cleaning crews, which security guards patrol, and where, and when. They know this place as well as they know their own homes. And they're busy, constantly monitoring the security, watching from nearby buildings, just in case something goes wrong, just in case they're needed."

"I know. I know." Tasha wanted to relax, but something was tapping away inside her, deep inside her, a weird, dark fear she couldn't shake.

Robin gripped her arm. "Tasha, we have to be on the same page here. We all have to be concentrating on the same thing. We're going to be *rewiring* these guys, reprogramming their brains, and it'll take all the concentration we've got *plus* all the concentration of those we're linked with to pull it off. You get that, right?"

"Of course I do. Of course." Tasha straightened her shoulders, only then realizing they had been slumped, almost as if her instinct was to hide herself.

No wonder Robin was concerned.

"Okay," the other woman was saying, her voice calm again. "The guys are heading back our way, and when they get here we all just follow the plan. We take up our positions outside on that pretty, very expensive terrace wasted on a boardroom, where more of these nice potted trees will give us shade *and* cover."

"But allow us to see in. To see the suits. Yeah, I remember." Tasha turned along with Robin, both of them watching their men returning to them, briskly but without making a sound on the carpeted hallway.

Tasha stepped forward to meet Brodie, about to say something casual or reassuring to ease the sudden attention and concern she could feel. But even as she opened her mouth, she realized abruptly that one of the trees behind the receptionist's desk was casting a shadow, the wrong *kind* of shadow.

Faster than thought she turned her head, everything in her mind reaching out to probe, instantly aware of coldness and darkness and something slimy, something to fear. And as quickly as that, she saw the other woman, stepping out of the shadow that had hidden her, her lovely, exotic face twisted in hate, her arm extending, the wicked black gun with its deadly long silencer pointed straight at Tasha's head.

And Tasha knew.

*Sebring. Nobody reported in that they got Sebring!*

---

Miranda's team breached the "way past pretty damned good" security of the lab with barely a pause, thanks to a solid plan, seamless teamwork—and Tucker's genius.

The guard at the gate never saw them coming, never saw the gun in Miranda's hand that sneezed softly and sent him on his way to hell. Another of her team acted almost in the same instant to push the guard back into his innocuous little post and closed the door so that the post looked empty. As if the guard had, perhaps, merely stepped away to answer the call of nature.

Knowing that the cameras were looped and showing nothing interesting to the guards inside the building who were watching their monitors, Miranda used the door code Tucker had promised would not betray them in any way, and found him as usual as good as his word. The door code and the "biometrics" implants they wore taped to the inside of their forearms beneath the long sleeves of their black jumpsuits allowed them to slip in quickly and without making a sound to betray them.

She knew another part of her team was entering the rear of the building, knew they too had entered in silence, unseen.

The guards in the security room managed to get to their feet, but not one weapon cleared their belts—and not one finger reached the alarm button.

The team moved swiftly then, clearing the main floor without haste but quickly nevertheless, making certain no threat lurked in any room or any corner. The other psychic on their team was sent up to the second floor, along with two other team members, with orders to locate and tranquilize the two psychics and take them out of the building once the rest of that floor was cleared of any threat.

Some of the computer storage they expected to find was just where the floor plans showed, though the computers, as Duran had warned, did not resemble any computers Miranda or her team had ever seen. But the four people assigned the task knew what to look for *and* how to transfer all files into the storage devices they carried in backpacks.

"Good to go?" Miranda paused in the doorway just long enough to check with one of her information retrieval team. She kept her voice low, the clock in her head ticking off the seconds.

"Yeah, we're good." She was staring fixedly at a screen that had appeared like a hologram to hover in the air before her, on which lines and lines of information appeared, first in a strange, symbolic language like hieroglyphs and then wavering and transforming into English and mathematical equations. "Our Rosetta stone's working like a charm. Ten minutes, Miranda, maybe less."

"Good. The data storage on the lower level is supposed to dwarf this one, so be prepared to move downstairs as soon as you're finished here."

"Copy."

Miranda left the two information retrieval specialists doing their work on this floor, with two more of her team standing guard to make sure their work was not in any way hindered. The upstairs had been cleared quickly and easily, two unconscious female psychics carried out to a waiting van, and those team members had rejoined

Miranda. Other team members had already locked off the elevator on this main floor and located the stairwell.

They fully expected to encounter both more resistance and quite likely signs or results of stomach-twisting "experiments" in the lower level, which would make it the most difficult level to clear. And the most important, since the demolition charges three of her team carried needed to be placed both quickly and in precisely the right locations to bring the entire building down in the most quiet and controlled manner possible once they had completed the rest of their mission and cleared out.

They had to locate and rescue any imprisoned psychics; they had to make certain that the "healers" either awake or in whatever state of hibernation they were found were destroyed; and they had to make very, very sure that only themselves and the psychics they intended to rescue came out of the lab alive.

The skills and dedication of her team being vital to the successful completion of her mission had caused Miranda to choose very carefully the people who would go down into the bowels of this place with her.

She and Bishop had been given necessary information on the team members awaiting them, and the time to study that intel on the jet, so Miranda knew the four men and two women on her team whose job was to help her clear the lower level of its evil, even if that evil looked human and wore nice white lab coats, were entirely up to the job.

She led the way.

---

*"Tasha!"* As quick as Sebring was, Brodie was quicker. But he was one step too far away from Tasha and, as he

would say later, it never even occurred to him to reach for his gun because Sebring's was already aimed at Tasha's head, her finger tightening on the trigger.

He acted purely on instinct, stretching out one hand toward Sebring, everything in him driven to protect the woman he loved from a deadly threat.

The gun in Sebring's hand literally flew down the hallway, narrowly missing David, and the woman herself was lifted two feet off the floor and slammed with incredible force backward into the wall between the two potted trees.

The wall was formed of concrete reinforced with rebar, but they all heard it groan and both heard and saw it crumple behind the woman, almost enfolding her in a cold, unloving embrace. For an instant, everything was still and silent, and then she dropped to the floor.

"Wow," David said. "Cool ability." He wasted no time in moving around the reception desk to check the pulse of the fallen enemy. He looked down at her rather pitilessly, then at the damaged wall, and said without emotion, "Broken neck. Hell, maybe broken back." He bent and hoisted her easily over his shoulder in a fireman's carry, straightening to add, "I'll dump her in the stairwell. Pity she fell. Really shouldn't have been climbing all those stairs in heels."

"That's sexist," Robin called after him, clearly no more disturbed by what had happened than David was.

"Practical," he called back to her.

Brodie was the one who was disturbed, but only because Tasha had come so close to being shot.

"Jesus," he muttered, lifting her off her feet in a powerful hug that didn't hurt her a bit.

Tasha returned the hug, then leaned her head back far enough to see his face, saying, "Told you it'd be triggered. And—wow. *Very* cool ability."

"Yeah," Robin said, watching them with interest. "When he says he doesn't know his own strength, he'll *mean* it."

Brodie set Tasha on her feet and looked over at the damaged wall. "I did that?"

"Yes, and thank you," Tasha said seriously, adding, "I wonder if she would have tried for all of us if I hadn't realized that shadow wasn't natural."

"Probably," Robin said. "So she was Sebring? That's the name that was in your mind."

"Yeah. And that's what was bugging me. We were told the suits here were her bosses, not Duran's, but she was supposed to be targeted and removed out in the field. I suddenly realized somebody should have told us if she *had* been removed. Specifically her, since she posed the greatest threat to us. That was when it struck me that the shadow beside that tree on the left was all wrong."

"Your ability to see them even with one of their shadows trying to hide them saved your life," Brodie said.

"No, you did that. Did I thank you?"

"Yes, you did." He was still rather subdued, for Brodie, but obviously not because a rather astonishingly powerful—and rare—telekinetic ability had been triggered in him. "Are you sure you're all right?"

"I'm fine." Tasha considered, then nodded. "No tension or anxiety at all. But why did she even *have* a shadow? Weren't the healers supposed to be dead and gone by now?"

Brodie looked at the clock now barely hanging on to

the damaged wall. "The operations at the labs are under way by now, but that doesn't mean all the healers are dead yet. They couldn't even start to move until the rescue operation had been completed and had drawn all the right attention."

"Speaking of," David said politely as he rejoined them, "I believe we're expecting suits anytime now. So maybe we'd better get outside on the terrace and get set."

Brodie took Tasha's hand. "Definitely."

Robin said, "Somebody better push those two trees together to hide the dimple in the wall."

"Dimple?" David shook his head at her as he went to push the trees together.

---

The fairly vast lower level of the lab was a maze of corridors, tiny cells, and larger rooms filled with stark, unidentifiable but nevertheless threatening tools, equipment, and machines. Everything was whitewashed concrete, smooth, featureless metal, and glass observation windows.

Miranda left one of her team stationed at the bottom of the stairwell to prevent the egress of anyone they didn't want to leave, and took her remaining people with her to clear this lower level. They were faced with three corridors leading off in different directions, an immediate indication that this level was far larger than anyone would have expected if they'd had only the size of the building above to offer a guesstimate.

A quick, silent gesture was enough to split her team up, with at least two people taking each corridor. Miranda chose the main corridor for herself and two of her team members, in part because according to their intel it was likely prisoners would be kept there. And because Miranda could feel a stronger sense of the cold despair and echoes of old pain.

It was very quiet; clearly, no one upstairs had managed to raise the alarm.

The first door she came to gave no indication she could see of its contents or purpose, and Miranda was wary as she eased the door open. She stood there in the doorway for a long moment, then stepped back and closed the door with the same care and silence.

"Miranda?" It was only the breath of a question.

She shook off as much as she could of a lingering chill, then whispered, "If either of you have any doubts about this place being evil, just look in there."

"I got no doubts," Winters said, his level gray eyes calm and infinitely old. "We rescue prisoners, take out or otherwise immobilize healers and everybody else, and then we send the whole fucking horror show straight to hell."

"No questions here, either," Sanders said, her voice also low and calm.

"Good," Miranda said, and continued on, reflecting, not for the first time, that they were lucky to have so many utterly dedicated people on their side.

They cleared two more rooms, both empty, and then Winters opened a door on the other side of the hallway, paused only an instant, and then put two bullets into the head of the creature who had greeted the intrusion with very large blinking eyes.

"Clear," Winters said softly as he eased the door shut. "A healer, Miranda. Intel was right. They look human except for the size and metallic look of the eyes."

"Copy."

Miranda found two more healers behind the next door she opened, both of them stirring only as the door opened. They occupied a featureless room that boasted only two palletlike cushions on which they sat, apparently meditating or hibernating until they were disturbed. Both looked completely inoffensive.

She killed them both without hesitating.

"That's three of the five healers," she breathed as she eased the door closed.

*H-hello?*

Miranda stopped her team with a quick gesture, and sent out a probing telepathic touch.

*Who are you?*

*I'm . . . Juno. Juno Hicks.*

It was a name Miranda recognized, though she had to dig in her memory for an instant. A telepath Bishop had found early on in his efforts to recruit psychics for the SCU, she had not been interested in becoming any kind of cop. That had been years ago.

*Juno. Miranda Bishop. We're going to get you out of here.*

*Oh. Oh, God. Are you real? Are you really here?*

*Yes, I promise you we are. Just hang on, okay?*

*Yeah. Yeah . . . Oh—there's another psychic—*

*Henry McCord. Don't worry, we're going to get both of you out of here.*

Miranda would have tried to pinpoint Juno's location right then, but another door farther down the hallway opened, and a man in a white lab coat stepped out. He was quick, seeing them and beginning to cry out only seconds before bullets from Miranda and Sanders reached him.

It wasn't much of a warning, but other doors began to open, and Miranda's team did all they could do to pick off "scientists" in white coats and two more healers before anyone could get off a shot at them. But they managed, their efforts even more grimly determined when they located Juno Hicks and saw her mangled left hand.

After that, nobody hesitated even an instant.

---

"You know," Tasha said absently as she studied the gathering of a dozen executives in the large boardroom, "it only just occurred to me that Robin's description of what we have to do here is a good one. We *are* rewiring these guys, assuming we can."

She had kept her voice low, but since they could see and yet not hear the people clearly having an animated discussion on the other side of the thick glass, it was a safe bet that no one in there could hear them.

Politely, Brodie said, "It only just occurred to you?"

"Well, like that."

*Are you all ready?*

Tasha blinked and turned slightly so she could look up at Brodie. "Was that Pendragon?"

*Yes, it's me.*

*Why?* Brodie tried, experimentally.

*Because Annabel was right. They made me. I understand how their minds work. And how we can fix that.*

"I'm glad he's on our side," Tasha murmured.

*Don't waste any sympathy on them,* Pendragon advised. *They may look like businesspeople, but they are far more dangerous and ruthless than anyone you've ever heard of.*

"Okay, got it. Didn't really doubt that, you know. Just

tell us what to do." Tasha looked across the terrace to the other end, where Robin and David waited, knowing both had heard Pendragon.

*You're going to be surprised how easy it is. All the links are opening . . . focus on that room . . . We'll start with the man at the head of the table . . . He doesn't know anything about shadow breeding houses . . . or about psychics . . . or about aliens . . . He's only concerned with the takeover move by another giant corporation, and how his company can weather it . . .*

They were surprised.

Because, in the end, it wasn't hard at all.

---

"Emma?"

She turned a tense, expectant face toward the open door, her delicate features easing, almost crumpling, looking very much a lost and frightened child. "Bishop! Oh, God, I'm so glad to see you!"

"Same here, Emma. Are you okay?"

"I am now. Can we leave? Can we leave right now?"

He kept his gun down at his side and reached with his free hand to squeeze her shoulder reassuringly. "I want you to go with Andie; she'll take you upstairs and out to our van. The rest of us have a bit more cleanup to do down here."

"Oh! Katie—"

"We'll get Katie. It's all right, Emma."

"Come on, Emma," Andie said cheerfully, her open expression and warm brown eyes so friendly it was easy to miss the businesslike gun she carried in one hand. "Let's get you out of here."

Emma went willingly.

A trim, middle-aged man with blond hair and sharp blue eyes eased up beside Bishop. "We only have the last half dozen rooms on this corridor to clear, Bishop. All their psychics have been located and taken out to the van, sedated. We've counted five healers down." He kept his voice low, but didn't whisper.

"Good. Conners, you come with me. The rest of you help set the charges and do a last sweep. Once we leave here, nobody's coming back. Copy?"

"Copy." The others nodded and headed off to obey, still alert and wary, and Bishop went on with Conners to clear the final rooms. It was quick work, since the first three rooms were empty, and Bishop gestured for Conners to go help the others as he approached the final doorway.

He opened the door and peered inside the very small cell, hastily jerking his head back as a wicked-looking scalpel rocketed past him and stuck—deeply—into the wall on the other side of this narrow hallway.

"Damn you! I told you to keep your hands off me, you slimy son of a bitch!"

"Katie?"

"Bishop? God, is that you? I'm so sorry!"

He peered around the doorway a bit more warily, then smiled as she came toward him, several scalpels in one hand. She looked a bit bruised, but he'd never seen her stand so straight—or felt more genuine, healthy *mad* coming off her in waves.

"Don't be sorry. You were defending yourself." He glanced down to one side where a healer lay with a shocked look on his face and a scalpel buried for most of its length between his slightly unusual metallic eyes, and added judiciously, "And very well, from the look of things."

Katie Swan stopped about a step away from Bishop and eyed him carefully. "You *are* real, right? I mean, they kept trying to show me stuff that wasn't real so I'd get mad and throw things."

"I'm very real," he assured her. "And since that was the last healer I was looking for, we're ready to get out of here and blow up this joint. Ready to leave?"

"Am I ever." She stepped out into the hall to join him, her eyes widening as she saw a woman in a black jumpsuit such as the one Bishop wore kneeling not far away as she molded what looked like modeling clay at the base of a concrete pillar. "You really do mean blow up the joint, don't you?"

"By the time we're finished," he assured her, "the only thing left here will be a lot of rubble in a deep crater. Within a week, we'll have bulldozers out here shoving more natural-looking rubble into the crater. This place is about to disappear from the world completely."

"Good." She took a step, then hesitated. "Bishop—there was a girl, a kid—"

"Emma Garrick. We've got her, Katie. She's scared, but they hadn't started on her yet."

Katie was visibly relieved. "I heard her voice in my head, and she sounded so scared. That's what finally made me mad, really. Did anybody else make it?"

His face never changed expression, but the scar twisting down his left cheek seemed to pale, a sure barometer of his emotions. "No one else from this lab survived," he told her quietly, not about to describe some of the failed "experiments" both he and Miranda had found in their respective labs. "But two more of our missing psychics, Henry McCord and Juno Hicks, made it out of another lab. They're with Miranda. We'll meet up with them at a nearby airstrip and get the hell out of here."

"I can't tell you how glad I am to hear that." Katie suddenly noticed the scalpels in her grip. She frowned, then flicked her hand back over one shoulder—and six scalpels stuck, quivering, to their hilts in the concrete wall.

He watched them quiver.

"Bishop? I changed my mind. I want to join the SCU."

Bishop took her arm and began leading her down that narrow hallway toward a distant stairwell. "You know, I believe that's something I can arrange," he told her seriously.

# EPILOGUE

The July day was already sunny and growing hot, even here in the high elevation of this remote location in Wyoming. Duran liked the heat, so he was comfortable. He stood just inside the tree line, looking down into the small valley at the remains of the lab he could see more than a mile away.

And only because he knew it had been there.

Beneath the trees and boulders and dirt many people with bulldozers had very efficiently used weeks before, there was, in fact, nothing more than a crater in the earth. Possibly a salted crater, though Duran wasn't at all certain Murphy hadn't intended that to be something of a joke.

Either way, it had been a very thorough destruction.

"Couldn't be helped," Murphy said, joining him.

"Reading me?" he asked, almost idly.

"Bread crumbs," she said. "Even through shields. Once that path is there, it does seem to linger. For some of us."

"A path you mean to . . . maintain?" He turned his head in time to see her fleeting smile.

"Well. It's a way of keeping an eye on you, so to speak. I did tell you we would. This next part could be really tricky for you, after all. We both know there are some holdouts. And it probably won't be at all easy convincing what was once a warrior race to lay down their arms for good. Or at least for peace."

She reached into her ever-present leather bag and produced a flash drive. "The favor you wanted. Those questions answered, I think. And the answers to a few other questions I imagine you might have. The intel could help you with your people. Help you make them understand the truth. It's all in English, by the way. Probably best that ancient language of yours vanishes for good. None of you need it here, after all."

He accepted the drive from her and slipped it into a pocket. "Thank you. I notice there's not nearly enough storage on this drive to contain even a fraction of the information your people were able to recover from the labs."

"Did you expect me to just hand that over?"

He felt a faint smile curve his own lips, the expression still a somewhat unfamiliar one. "No. You were always one to hedge your bets, Murphy."

"It's partly that," she agreed. "But your people didn't land in just this country. Our organization was never confined to just this country. And I have counterparts all over the world who will put this intel and more we have to share to good use. To disarm and integrate their own . . . warriors."

"By force?" His tone was neutral.

"You should know better than that by now. Force

should always be a last resort, and I don't expect we'll need it. Besides, despite some questionable periods in our history, and quite a few questionable leaders along the way, we aren't a conquering species. We'd far rather unite than divide. It's what most of us are always striving to do, despite all our differences."

She turned her head and looked out over the spectacular scenery, her gaze directed far above the destroyed lab, and she said almost absently, "It's a nice little world. Beautiful in so many ways. And the people are . . . promising, by and large. Quite a long way to go yet, but definitely promising."

"Yes," he said.

Murphy looked at him, a smile playing around her lips and making her look almost beautiful herself. "That's something worth being part of, I think. That journey. To leave the world better than you found it. To be far more than just a worker bee, a cog in a wheel. To live a life that really matters, a life that accomplishes positive things. A life that leaves footprints behind you. On the world where you belong."

Duran nodded slowly. "On a world where we belong."

"A world you might help to defend someday. When all those long-ago messages to your homeworld inevitably draw that old enemy . . . here. To Earth."

"You can't know that will happen."

"No, I'm not a precog. But I am logical enough to see the possibility. To help my people plan for it. Even to believe that when it *does* happen, your people will join mine in fighting them. Because the enemy of your enemy is your friend. And the enemy of my enemy is my friend."

After a moment, he nodded.

"It was a success, you know. Coming here. Saving your race, or at the very least the best aspects of your race."

"Was it?"

"Sure."

"We failed," he said, disagreeing. "The first ones are gone, and were never able to breed a viable hybrid generation. Those like me were never intended to pass on the valued traits of our race. And the breeding programs ultimately produced nothing of value."

"Well, see, that's the thing. Our human biology is stubborn. Doesn't like to be forced. But things can and do happen . . . naturally. They always have, and a lot more often than you might think. A woman hundreds of years in the past meets an unusual man on a moonlit night . . . and nine months later a child is born. A girl child, who grows up to meet and marry a man with psychic ability. And so a new bloodline is begun, naturally mixing the best traits of your people . . . and mine. Without any medical intervention at all."

"You know this for a fact?"

"Couldn't know it for sure until we mapped the human genome. Until we dug even deeper and learned to sequence our DNA, and could see the blueprint for building an organism. Until we acquired the knowledge and tech to understand what we were looking at. And even then, there had to be questions, the right ones. There had to be the awareness to perform comparisons over generations, to know what we were looking *for*."

"Murphy—"

"Quite a few branches on the human family tree by now, begun on moonlit nights a long, long time ago, and in all the generations since. Matings your first ones never noticed happening under their very noses. Viable matings that produced viable offspring. Only girls for a long time, for whatever reason. Probably something to do with the human Y chromosome. So only girls, born with traits they were able to pass on to the next generation. But sooner or later, that stubborn Y chromosome had to adapt, so there have been a few males born with those valuable traits your people wanted to pass on. A very few—so far."

She reached into her bag again, and this time handed him a thick envelope, unsealed. "Nothing for you and yours to manipulate here if you're ever tempted, but I thought you might like to know that the bloodline of your people is flourishing. This report tracks only one branch, only one direct line, almost exclusively through females, but as you can see the generations continue to this very day."

Duran was studying the report, noting there were no names, only subject identification numbers and dates, beginning in the late 1700s and ending with a single female child born thirty-odd years before. And even though he was not a scientist, he could see, in the genetic sequencing, the very markers their scientists had worked in vain to produce and replicate.

"It's not an original saying, but life finds a way," Murphy told him. "The best of your people survive. Which is what evolution is all about."

Duran frowned at the topmost page of the report, then looked at Murphy. "How do I trust this? There's no name, no identity."

Murphy reached into a pocket and produced a small switchblade knife, opening it as smoothly as she had produced it. She calmly used the razor-sharp point to make a small cut on her index finger, then reached over to smear bright red blood across the upper left corner of the report.

"Now you have a name," she said.

He was surprised. And, yet . . . somehow not shocked. There had always, after all, been something *about* Murphy.

She closed and pocketed the knife and began moving away, the smile lingering. "Be seeing you, Duran."

"Will you?"

"Oh, yeah," Murphy said. "We have a lot in common, after all. A lot. Probably want to talk about that someday. And there's that thing about you being a telepath. Most of us need a little help adjusting. You have my number, Duran."

He watched her until she disappeared from view into the forest, then returned his own gaze to the scenery, this time looking, as she had, beyond destruction to beauty.

The beauty of a nice little world.

Where he belonged.

Keep reading for an excerpt from the newest Bishop/Special Crimes Unit Novel by Kay Hooper

## HOLD BACK THE DARK

Available now from Berkley.

TUESDAY, OCTOBER 7

Olivia Castle had experienced some monster headaches in her time, but this one, she felt sure, was about to make her head quite literally explode. It had come out of nowhere, as if something had just yanked her head into an invisible, tightening vise without warning. A vise with teeth. In pain, queasy, and shaking, she managed to lever herself up from the couch, holding one hand against the head she was sure was about to fall off, and hardly spared a moment to wonder why she'd been on the couch.

Work. She should have been at work.

Shouldn't she be at work?

Had she come home for lunch? She didn't remember.

Her head hurt too much to keep thinking about that.

She made it to the kitchen by holding on to various pieces of furniture as she passed, fighting nausea and accidentally grabbing Rex's tail when she gripped the edge of the sink.

*"Waaaurr!"*

"Sorry, sorry," she muttered, the headache so bad by then that her cat's cry sounded like a dozen angry crows, her own quiet voice sounded like booming thunder in her head, and even her vision was affected in some way she didn't understand; she couldn't see the pleasant Vermont view normally visible from this window. She couldn't see any real view at all.

She was seeing colors she was reasonably sure didn't exist in nature. Or anywhere else, for that matter. Moving, swirling, like colorful smoke driven by a capricious breeze, opaque and translucent by turn. And everything was so damned *bright.* "Shouldn't sit on the counter. How many times have I told you? Didn't see you, pal. Oh, *damn*, what is going on?"

There was a large economy-sized bottle of an OTC painkiller near the sink (just as there was one in almost every room of her small house, and in her purse, with a box of extra bottles in the storage closet, in case the zombie apocalypse came without warning and all the pharmacies got looted before she could get to them). Olivia closed her eyes against the unnatural brightness, fumbling the bottle open while bitterly cursing childproof caps foisted upon people who had no children, fumbled just as blindly for a glass and the faucet, and managed, finally, to swallow about eight pills, hoping she could keep them down long enough to do some good.

*"Prrupp,"* Rex said.

"I know it's too many, you don't have to tell me that." She stood there, eyes still closed, still hanging on to the edge of the sink with one hand and her head with the other, trying to breathe normally despite the pain keeping all her muscles rigid and snatching at her ability to breathe at all, her stomach churning, the weird colors still swirling even though her eyes were closed, wishing pain meds took effect faster. Like immediately. It would have been nice, she thought, to just take a shot of morphine and become unconscious for the duration. But she'd discovered the hard way that both the law and doctors frowned on patients self-medicating, far less walking out the door of any hospital, clinic, or pharmacy with their own supply of morphine or any other industrial-strength painkiller. And besides, they said it was only migraines.

Only migraines. *Only migraines. Jesus.* Even though no migraine remedy known to medical science and quite a few exotic possibilities Olivia had experimented with herself had so much as touched her periodic killer headaches.

She fumbled blindly for the bottle again.

*"Waauurr!"*

"All right, all right. I know there hasn't been enough time. But if the pain doesn't stop soon, I'm gonna take more. *Shit.*"

A moment later, Rex hissed.

Olivia managed to pry her eyes open no matter how much the ungodly brightness all around her hurt, and squinted at her cat in surprise. Because Rex didn't hiss, or at least never had. But as she focused on her rather odd-looking cat, his brindle-tortie coat at odds with the brilliant blue eyes of a Siamese, she realized even through the bright, swirling colors she was still seeing that Rex was scared.

Really scared.

And Rex didn't scare easily. Or . . . at all.

He was staring past her into the space behind her, the kitchen and den, and his pupils were so narrow that his eyes looked incredibly creepy, like the unnaturally blue eyes of a snake. The fur along his back was standing straight up, and his tail was about three times its natural size.

At the same time, Olivia began hearing a strange rustling sound. At first it sounded like dry leaves skittering along pavement, which was weird enough to hear inside her house with no pavement around. But then she realized it was . . . whispering. Lots of voices. Lots and lots of voices. Whispering.

It was coming from behind her.

Olivia did *not* want to turn around. Her mouth was dry despite the nausea, her skin was crawling unpleasantly, the pain in her head was getting impossibly worse rather than better, and she was afraid if she turned to confront an axe murderer, she'd beg him to just cut off her head and be quick about it.

*Axe murderer. Idiot.*

Not an axe murderer, of course. Not anyone.

Not any one . . . thing. Because she heard more than one whisper, many whispers, countless whispers. And she didn't know what they were saying, but she had the eerie feeling they were all whispering the same thing. The same words.

Still holding the edge of the sink with one hand, Olivia turned slowly to see what so frightened her cat and was making her own skin crawl in a sensation she'd never felt before.

"Oh, shit," she whispered.

The headache that was still hellishly painful didn't seem such a big deal now. Because despite all the swirling colors nearly blinding her, she could see, very clearly, why Rex was afraid. Every sharp object in her kitchen and den—every single one from every kitchen knife and fork she owned to three letter openers, two pairs of scissors, two box cutters with razor blades visible, the iron fireplace poker, and half a dozen pens and twice that many sharpened pencils—floated in midair. Different levels, some low, some as high as eye level.

With their pointy ends aimed right at her.

And they were all whispering.

*"Waaurr,"* Rex muttered, his voice unusually quiet, questioning.

"I'm not doing it. I'd know if I were doing it, right? I always know. I have to concentrate to do it. I mean, unless I'm mad. Angry, not crazy. Though maybe crazy too. Because this has never . . . And, anyway, even if I'm mad, I don't . . . know how . . . to make anything . . . whisper."

Or how to stop it when she instinctively tried, an effort that was definitely not rewarded.

Unconsciously, both her hands lifted to her head, pressing as if to hold something in, because the headache suddenly grew horribly worse, impossibly worse, dragging a guttural groan from somewhere deep inside her, and through the bright swirl of colors that was beginning to truly blind her, she could still see all the scary-sharp weapons floating inexorably toward her.

Whispering.

What was whispering? Inanimate objects couldn't communicate, right? Not like this, at least.

The pain edged into agony, but even so she heard as if from a great distance her own shaking, pleading question.

"What? What are you saying? What do you want of me?"

And from the same great distance, she heard the whispered demand that made no sense to her.

*Prosperity. Go to Prosperity.*

They were still floating eerily toward her, all the pointy things that promised even more pain if they came much closer, and hard as she tried, Olivia couldn't do anything about it, couldn't stop it, couldn't see anything but them or hear anything except for that whispered demand.

*Go to Prosperity.*

*Go to Prosperity.*

Olivia heard one last thing: A moan of agony escaped her, and then everything went black.

*NEW YORK TIMES* BESTSELLING AUTHOR

# KAY HOOPER

"Kay Hooper...provide[s] a welcome chill on a hot summer's day."

—*Orlando Sentinel*

## PRAISE FOR KAY HOOPER'S BISHOP / SPECIAL CRIMES UNIT NOVELS

"Seethes and sizzles. A fast-paced, atmospheric tale that vibrates with tension, passion, and mystery. Readers will devour it."

—*New York Times* bestselling author Jayne Ann Krentz

"Kay Hooper . . . provide[s] a welcome chill on a hot summer's day."

—*Orlando Sentinel*

"A stirring and evocative thriller." —*Palo Alto Daily News*

"Filled with page-turning suspense."

—*The Sunday Oklahoman*

"A well-told, scary story." —*Toronto Sun*

"It passed the 'stay up late to finish it in one night' test."

—*The Denver Post*

"Harrowing good fun . . . [Readers] will shiver and shudder."

—*Publishers Weekly*

"Fans will be captivated—at every turn . . . [Hooper's] creative blend of the paranormal and suspense are truly distinctive."

—*Suspense Magazine*

"You won't want to turn the lights out after reading this book!" —RT Book Reviews

"Hooper's unerring story sense and ability to keep the pages flying can't be denied." —*Ellery Queen Mystery Magazine*

"Enjoyable . . . thought-provoking entertainment."

—*Calgary Herald*

"A full-force, page-turning, suspense-driven read . . . It had this reader anxiously gripping the pages."

—*The Mystery Reader*